# Perceived Threat

Enjoy the mysteries of life, Craig!

All My Best,
Elisa

# Perceived Threat

**a novel**

*Elisa Koopmans*

Two Harbors Press, Minneapolis

Two Harbors Press
322 First Avenue N, 5th floor
Minneapolis, MN 55401
612.455.2293
www.TwoHarborsPress.com



ISBN-13: 978-1-63413-364-7
LCCN: 2015902098

Distributed by Itasca Books

Front Cover Design by Jared Schwartz
Back Cover Design by Alan Pranke
Typeset by Colleen Rollins

*Printed in the United States of America*

*The strictest justice is sometimes the greatest injustice.*

—Terence (Publius Terentius Afer)

For my children,

who have grown into incredibly wonderful adults.

## Acknowledgments

Thank you to my father, Kenneth W. Koopmans, for his editorial expertise in completing the first edit. Dad, I love you and am particularly grateful to you for your willingness to read my fictional "whodunit," given your primary interest is nonfiction.

Thank you to my friends Debra Crane, Tami Salisbury, Carolyn Oshry and Lyssie Lakatos, who at every opportunity supported my writing and publishing this book. Thanks also to Debra Crane's mom, Marylynn Crane, who emphatically declared that this book absolutely, no question about it, had to be published. Ladies, your encouragement and enthusiasm were a constant source of strength to me and I really appreciate it!

Thank you to Acadia Cutschall, a talented New York City painter, who educated me on the very real challenges facing foster children when they reach the age of legal majority and leave the foster care system. I am so happy, Acadia, that you overcame the obstacles most foster children face and successfully graduated from college.

Thank you to my Two Harbors Press editors, Kate Ankofski, a fellow native Michigander/Michiganian (depending upon which demonym is preferred), and Tricia Parker, formerly from Washington, DC, where most of this story takes place. I so appreciate your kindness, strong knowledge of effective commercial editing and expertise regarding the *Chicago Manual of Style*, which were all invaluable in finalizing the text of this book.

Thank you to my son, Jared Schwartz, a brilliant artist and 3D computer animator for film who exhibited yet another skillful and artistic endeavor in designing and creating the front cover of this book. Jared, your artistic talents and computer skills never cease to amaze me and it was so kind of you to take time away from your latest film to create the front cover for me. I love you so much!

# *Chapter One*

THE AUDIENCE'S EYES WERE RIVETED to Annalisa Vermeer, as if a palpable magnetism radiated from her. Was it her dynamic speaking ability that elicited such focus or the provocative nature of her message? Probably both. A highly acclaimed speaker and author, Annalisa spoke with confidence and passion, owning her message despite being only thirty-seven years old and having a five-foot-three stature, which barely made her visible above the podium.

For as long as Annalisa and her parents could remember, Annalisa had an intense interest in history and government. Her parents were intrigued that their child brought home books from her elementary school library about the United States' founding fathers and the history of its early years. Annalisa never lost her passion for these subjects and graduated from the University of Michigan with undergraduate degrees in history and political science and a PhD in political science.

After years of working as a congressional aide, and then at a think tank specializing in political science, Annalisa solidified her ideas on the flaws inherent in the legislative branch of the US government. She wrote a book, *A Paradigm for Legislating*, and began traveling the country, giving speeches to advocate for her ideas. It was not long before she was noticed by both the public, which she argued deserved better treatment from its government, and the government itself, which she argued needed to dramatically change.

"Ladies and gentlemen," Annalisa said, "the United States has taken an aspect of civilized society and moved it to the level of absurdity. That aspect is the continued striving to create endless new laws. While laws are a necessary and desirable part of a working society, we now have far too many of them in this country. They control virtually every facet of our lives, and I'm certain none of us go a week without violating some law, whether on purpose or in total ignorance that our actions were civilly or criminally illegal.

"How is it we have come to enact more laws in this country than anyone could ever count? We cannot assume it is because of necessity, or for the benefit of our overall society. Many laws are brought to life for the sole benefit of special interests, paid for in a myriad of ways. Nor can we assume the laws passed under the auspices of being for the general good are actually beneficial to the people or entities within our society. What I do know is we have a host of new laws brought onto the books each year because we employ people full time to primarily do just that."

The audience, which was composed of a substantial cross section of politicians, public figures and private citizens was silent. No one whispered or took out cell phones to check for incoming text messages. Annalisa maintained constant eye contact with the crowd and spoke with a fierce intensity. Some in the audience restlessly shifted in their seats, possibly uncomfortable with her words. After all, this was Washington, DC, and the audience was peppered with political figures, some of whom had to feel personally attacked by Annalisa.

"Currently, the legislative body known as the US Congress has 541 members when there are no vacancies – 100 senators, 435 voting members of the House of Representatives and 6 nonvoting delegates of the House of Representatives. These senators and representatives are referred to routinely as 'lawmakers.' While these individual men and women have some functions in their roles that are unrelated to lawmaking, their main purpose is to enact new laws, amend existing laws, and, when repealing a law, to generally replace it with a new law. They are paid to create new laws for society whether we need them or not. In fact, the American public is so misled in expecting that responsibility to be met that one could surmise if Congress failed to enact any new legislation the citizens might conclude the senators and representatives weren't doing their jobs. Do we really want an expectation met when there's no benefit in doing so?"

Though the question was rhetorical, four middle-aged men in the second row simultaneously rose to their feet and shouted, "No!" As they sat back in their seats, many in the audience clapped as they stared at the men while others scowled at what they either viewed as an inappropriate interruption of the speech or unwarranted support for Annalisa's words. Unflinchingly, Annalisa gave the men a swift smile and continued speaking.

"Unfortunately, the problem is worse than this. What I've described to this point is only what's occurring at the federal level. In addition, 7,383 state legislators are layering laws on top of the already-existing federal and state laws. After all, it's their primary job responsibility to do so. Can we blame them for doing what they're paid to do? To top this off, as icing on the cake, countless local legislators—in cities, towns, villages, townships and hamlets—are enacting ordinances for the governance of their local domains. Some of these ordinances duplicate the language of a state statute, which could be applied by the municipality, but the local level of government wants its own laws as well. Finally, the sprinkles on the icing are the legally enforceable rules established and enacted by subdivision associations, cooperative boards, condominium associations, architectural control committees and the like to control life in the immediate domain of your home.

"There is no escape, ladies and gentlemen, from the power and control of our elected legislators. We have empowered them to layer law after law upon us, and we pay most of them a hefty salary for doing so. Let me be clear: I do not advocate for an anarchical society. I do not espouse for one second that the answer is a society without laws or government. What I do advocate is revamping the job description of legislators at all levels. There should be no implicit expectation or requirement that new laws be continually enacted. It should be acceptable and encouraged that legislators refrain from enacting new laws unless there is an absolute need for it. Legislators need not wield the power they possess just because they can."

A large segment of the 300 or so people could no longer contain their enthusiasm and clapped while yelling out, "Oh, yeah!" or loudly whistling. Bursts of excitement pierced the decorum that had been present as Annalisa spoke. She smiled broadly as her eyes moved from side to side observing the audible reaction to her words. There were still those in the audience who remained silent or whispered among themselves with serious looks. Annalisa observed them as well, or at least those she could see in the first few rows. She understood far more people either hated or loved her message than remained lukewarm about her words. Annalisa waited for silence before concluding her speech.

"Further, they do not need to be in the public eye constantly, displaying partisan animosity and advocating partisan politics instead of the best interests of society. Not only should we have legislators who agree to enact legislation with commonsense restraint, but we should eliminate partisan politics altogether. There is no need for political parties, no reason for Democrats, Republicans or Libertarians. Each senator and representative at any level of government should act as would the majority of his or her constituents. Each time a legislator needs to take a stand on an issue, whether or not relative to enacting a law, the legislator should understand the thinking of his or her constituency and advocate as a true representative of the constituents. To do other than this is to not comply with the position of our founding fathers—that a legislator is to represent the position and interest of the voters who elected him or her."

Loud applause erupted from many in the audience. No organization sponsored the speech, as Annalisa scheduled her own events at hotels and other conference centers. She earned her living from sales of her recently published book, as well as from the paid admissions to her speaking engagements. She knew she was not beholden to any organization or other special interest. Her opinions were her own, and nobody else would ever control, influence or take credit for them. Just as she despised lobbyists and their hold over legislators, she despised sponsorship, as it always came at a price.

Amid the applause, two men sitting together near the back of the room silently slipped through the back doors to the adjacent atrium area. Mark Hampton was a senator from Idaho and his friend and colleague Harrison Gibbs was a representative from the district in Idaho where Senator Hampton grew up. Senator Hampton was distinguished looking with salt-and-pepper hair, which deceptively made him appear older than he was. At just over six feet tall, he carried himself with confidence. Representative Gibbs radiated a similar confidence, but he had a round, boyish face, was barely five foot seven and 130 pounds and was a good ten years younger than Senator Hampton.

Once they reached a corner of the atrium, Senator Hampton looked squarely at Representative Gibbs. "She is one gutsy dynamo, especially when she knows her audience here inside the Beltway includes political figures and lobbyists."

"Frankly, I'm numb," said Representative Gibbs. "She may not be an anarchist, but her opinions are the most radical I've heard in my time here on the Hill. She wants us to stop enacting laws and give up our allegiance to our political parties. She's a nutcase."

"Well," said Senator Hampton, "whether she's a nutcase or not seems to be irrelevant. Hundreds of people in the audience were willing to pay to hear her thoughts, and she elicited plenty of applause at the end. She's not standing alone in her advocacy. She's surrounded by like-minded people who've just not yet chosen to speak."

"Mark, do you really think she's starting a movement toward action?" asked Representative Gibbs. "How can any group of people instigate the changes she's proposing? Making laws and membership in political parties have been mainstays of our society for more than 200 years."

Just then, the doors of the auditorium flew open and droves of people filled the atrium. It was an eclectic group. Men and women, old and young alike, appeared to equally fill the ranks of listeners. Some were in expensive designer suits, and others, including some college students, were in jeans and casual wear. Large groups that may have ridden together on a bus also converged in the atrium. Annalisa's words had caught the interest and attention of a large cross section of American society, and a representative group of that cross section had congregated for her latest speech.

Standing at the railing of the atrium and looking down to the first floor of the hotel were Senator Scott Wagner and his assistant, Kendra Miles. Senator Wagner was barely in his late forties, but had been in the US Congress for almost twenty years. He was elected at age thirty to replace his father, who had held the office until his death. Senator Wagner was from New York, a powerful state, and not much happened in Congress without his involvement, directly or behind closed doors. He was an imposing figure: tall, masculine and handsome. It was a running joke among his friends that had he not entered politics, he would be on the silver screen. He caught the eye of all who saw him and was a master of diplomacy, accomplishing his goals with a smile, a handshake, and, if necessary, a promise or a thinly veiled threat. He was the epitome of a veteran politician, and his self-confidence was viewed by many as blatant arrogance.

Kendra Miles had advised and assisted Senator Wagner in his political efforts for ten years. She was bright, analytical and intuitive—all skills that worked synergistically with Senator Wagner's political agenda. There was a side to her that was absent in Senator

Wagner. Her kind and compassionate heart always played a role in analyzing an issue. She saw past politics and understood there were individuals affected by each and every decision made on Capitol Hill. She strove daily to remind Senator Wagner of the human side of every issue. At times, her message pierced his tough skin, and other times it just rolled off his back with no effect.

"Kendra," Senator Wagner said, "why did you insist on wasting our time here listening to the ranting and raving of that harebrained lunatic? There were important matters we could have attended to instead."

"Senator," Kendra said firmly, "Ms. Vermeer isn't a lunatic. She bases her arguments on a solid foundation. I know this may appall you, but I agree with many of her statements. You know we often pass laws just because we can—because a special interest convinces us to or because we're expected to do so. I'm amazed most of our citizens haven't been arrested at least once because it's nearly impossible for them to not violate some criminal law due to the sheer number of them."

"Kendra, please stop," Senator Wagner cut in. "You sound as irrational as she did. You fail to make a distinction between people breaking laws and getting caught, and those who break laws and go undetected. There would be no arrest if the violation went unnoticed by the authorities. Anyway, back to my main point. We only enact legislation that's needed to make our society work. Just because a special interest receives benefits or is the impetus for a particular law doesn't mean the rest of society won't benefit as well."

"I believe you've been working within the system of the status quo so long you don't even realize a change may be appropriate, that it may actually improve our system," said Kendra.

Two reporters from the *Washington, DC Press*, Miranda Lewis and Spencer Van Otter, walked up to Senator Wagner and Kendra and identified themselves. Miranda was tall and blond, with intense gray eyes, and Spencer was young and assertive. "Senator Wagner," asked Miranda, "do you have any formal statement regarding your opinion of Ms. Vermeer's speech?"

"Ms. Lewis, I believe everyone is entitled to his or her own opinion. Ms. Vermeer has her opinion regarding how our government should operate and I happen to feel her premises and conclusions are misguided. If she were better informed about what goes on in Congress, then I believe she would modify her opinions." The reporters could not help but hear the authoritative tone in Senator Wagner's voice.

"I would like to add to that, *if I may*," interjected Representative Sylvia Rossman, a highly experienced legislator in her sixties who joined the group while Senator Wagner was speaking. "Political parties provide the yin and yang needed to balance the efforts made by the congressional legislators. There are some basic political differences in play in each legislative discussion, and these political differences follow Republican or Democratic party lines. It is efficient to define each of us by our political party in that these basic political differences are identified merely by reference to our party affiliation. If we were just senators or representatives, then how would anyone know what our basic beliefs were without having to talk to us individually?"

"Representative Rossman, *if I may*," said Spencer, "it seems to me in this day and age any given issue has too many complexities for a legislator to take a stance based primarily on being in a political party. Each aspect of an issue must be analyzed and evaluated based on its own merits. The legislator then needs to inform his or her constituents and give them the opportunity to provide their input to guide the legislator in the final decision. Doesn't that seem to be the reasonable course, Representative Rossman?"

"No, Mr. Van Otter, I don't believe that to be the reasonable course," said Representative Rossman. "We are elected because our constituents trust us to make decisions based upon our own opinions on a matter. Our constituents made their decision to elect us with their votes, and I don't believe they want or expect us to consult them each time an issue arises that requires a vote. I vote based upon my own opinion, which is first based on my beliefs as a member of my political party. With that said, I must leave now for an appointment." Representative Rossman disappeared as quickly as she had first appeared.

"I'd enjoy continuing this banter, Mr. Van Otter and Ms. Lewis," Senator Wagner said, "but Ms. Miles and I must also leave to get back to our office." He turned and walked away, with Kendra trailing after him.

Spencer's attention turned to a group gathering around Annalisa as she exited the auditorium. Looking up at an imposing figure, her deep brown eyes were fixed intently on the man's face as her medium brown hair rested loosely on her shoulders. Miranda suggested they join the group. As they approached, they heard a harsh, raised voice chastising Annalisa.

"What are you trying to do, Ms. Vermeer, start a riot?" demanded Senator Sid Dobbins, an elder statesman whose lifelong career had been serving as a senator from Pennsylvania. He stared at Annalisa over the top of his reading glasses while his slightly gnarled forefinger pointed at her face.

"No, sir, I'm not trying to start a riot," said Annalisa. "I'm trying to start a reasoned dialogue that may foster a reasoned change in a legislative process that has gotten out of hand. I'm asking people to open their minds to acknowledging we have too many laws, that lawmakers spend their days striving to create more laws and that political parties interfere with reasoned governance. I also suggest they dedicate themselves to changing the system so it makes more sense in a world that demands effectiveness."

"Look, Ms. Vermeer, you are entirely off base in your arguments and your continued efforts will lead to no good. Mark my words—you would be smart to stop advocating such nonsense!" Cutting off further dialogue, Senator Dobbins stormed off down the stairs in a huff. At that point, Miranda spoke up.

"Ms. Vermeer, I'm Miranda Lewis of the *Washington, DC Press*. I suggest you write off Senator Dobbins, as he's lived most of his adult life entrenched in the current system and, therefore, can't imagine the system operating any differently. I found your speech quite intriguing and wonder if you could speak further to the issue of too many laws."

"Certainly," said Annalisa. "Every year legislators at each level of government assume they're obligated to pass new laws, so they do. Yes, some laws are necessary, but we are to the point where the founding fathers' concept of freedom barely exists any longer. Virtually every aspect of a person's life is regulated in some way outside the personal control of a free citizenry. Yes, we can generally come and go as we please, but we can't, for example, say the word 'bomb' at an airport without the risk of getting arrested. We can't contradict an airline employee without the risk of being arrested, despite behaving in a reasonable fashion. We can't urinate in the woods of a park with no bathroom without the threat of ending up on a sex offender registry, if arrested."

"Do you think there's some motive for laws beyond the safe and orderly regulation of society?" asked Spencer.

"Yes, I do," said Annalisa. "A number of reasons are unrelated to the health and welfare of citizens. First, an entire branch of government is dedicated to the full-time service of enacting laws, which you already heard about in my speech. Beyond that is the issue of money. When a law is broken and the violation is discovered, there are substantial financial penalties in the form of costs, fines and fees. Even complying with a law can be costly, such as the building code laws requiring permit fees and a myriad of other fees, often outrageously and unjustifiably expensive. Legislators and the jurisdictions they represent have come to count on these deposits to the coffers of governmental entities. Without laws, there would be no violations and no prosecution and, consequently, no additional funds in the applicable bank account. Governments don't want to lose these funds, so they seek to create as many opportunities as possible to make more money. In addition, there is also the control factor, as humans relish the ability to control others. Legislators, law enforcement officials and regulators can control the general public with countless laws, rules and regulations."

"Wow, that's even more provocative than what you said in your speech," exclaimed Spencer.

"Provocative, yes, but unfortunately also true," Annalisa stated with sadness in her voice. "If the financial records of, say, a municipality were analyzed, it would become clear that along with the often very costly property tax, a significant amount of its revenue is from mandated-by-law dog licenses, tickets for civil traffic infractions, fines and costs for misdemeanor convictions and fees for required building permits. It just goes on and on, all under the auspices of necessary statutes and ordinances, but a primary reason for much of it is to bring in money for the governmental entity."

Annalisa's cell phone rang and she answered it. She paused. It was her husband, Brad, whom she had met while working as a congressional aide. "Yes, honey, I'm done here and I'll be home soon. Love you." She hung up, thanked the group for coming, told them she had to leave and headed for the stairs. As she exited the hotel, she took a deep breath of cold, fresh air, pleased to feel free of the oppressive attacks that always followed her speeches, yet grateful for the open minds that thoughtfully considered her ideas.

At the intersection in front of the hotel, the do-not-walk light had just started blinking, but no traffic was coming, so Annalisa decided to cross the street. Just as she took her first step, a car came seemingly from out of nowhere and sped around the corner, nearly striking her. She fell back onto the sidewalk, brushed by the cold February air that rushed between her and the speeding car. It took her breath away and she sat on the curb gathering her wits before she stood up and walked home.

# *Chapter Two*

Forty minutes later, Annalisa walked up the steps onto the expansive front porch of her Glover Park Federal-style home. She took one last deep breath and stepped through the doorway. Brad looked up from working on his laptop at a desk in the living room. Brad was a good-looking, but not handsome, thirtysomething man with sandy brown hair and distinctive high Dutch cheekbones. He was a feature writer for a national news magazine headquartered in Washington, DC. As Annalisa stood under the archway entrance into the room, he noticed a fatigue in her face he had never seen before.

"Annie, what's wrong?" he asked with concern in his voice.

"Nothing, really. I was just hoping that walking home would release the stress of the evening, but I feel as tense as I did when I left the Omni."

"You walked home from the Omni? Goodness, that's almost two miles from here. No wonder you look so fatigued. Sit down and I'll get you a drink. Want some freshly brewed mint green tea? I made it myself especially for you."

"You're a dear. Yes, iced tea sounds perfect right now."

Brad left the room and returned shortly with a tall glass of tea brimming with ice. At first, Annalisa did not acknowledge Brad's presence, but gazed out a window with a pensive look. Brad sat down in silence, not wanting to intrude on her moment, and waited for her to speak. Without interrupting her gaze, she spoke.

"Brad, this town is disturbingly closed minded. I know every time I speak here in DC I'm going to be rebuffed, ridiculed and rebuked, but tonight it was worse. Don't get me wrong—plenty of people there supported my position, but the naysayers were particularly dark. Perhaps that's good because it means they take me seriously and fear I might actually make a difference and bring about change."

"Annie, you have to expect serious resistance to virtually every position you advocate since your arrow of change is piercing the heart of this entire city."

"I get that, but these senators and representatives won't look past their own personal interests to see the big picture of how our society could benefit from a new approach. They just want to retain their personal power and to hell with the rest of us. It's so exasperating!"

"Yes, but also perfectly human, and to be expected in a venue where personal power is coveted and rewarded. I guess it's good you'll be out of town for the next three days to speak in Omaha, Kansas City and Tulsa. Midwesterners are well grounded, practical and will thoughtfully consider an idea before accepting or rejecting it. They'll be more receptive to your ideas than the people here, whose source of power you seek to upend."

"Midwest drivers are also more cautious than our DC drivers. I remember when I was a teenage driver in Madison, Wisconsin, and I would complain to my mom that other drivers would seldom pass slower cars, resulting in it taking me forever to get anywhere. Mom just smiled and said I would eventually get used to it. She knew that was how adults drove in Madison. Now when we go visit my parents, I really appreciate the careful drivers."

"I do too. Tell me, did you have some type of interaction tonight with a driver?"

"Yes, although there's not much to tell. I still had the light to cross the street, but it was flashing, which must have made the driver feel entitled to turn the corner. The real problem was that the driver was traveling at high speed. I didn't even see the car until it was practically at my feet, which is why I fell back on the curb as it nearly grazed me."

"Are you sure, Annie, that the driver wasn't trying to run you down?"

"Not at all sure. Actually, I'm concerned—no, worried—that the driver intended to hit me. At that speed, I could have easily been killed. I think it would be naïve of me to conclude this was just a careless driver moving at a high speed."

"I agree. After all, you're broadcasting to national audiences your message of revamping this country's entire legislative system at the national, state and local levels. As if that weren't enough, you're further advocating the abolishment of political parties and lobbying. Consequently, there are people out there who see you as an imminent threat."

"I wish those people would see my ideas can be initiated without ruining anyone's life," Annalisa said. "I'm a proponent of major changes, yes, but these legislators can keep their jobs, even if they don't continually enact new laws and aren't affiliated with a political party. Political parties just get in the way; they prevent legislators from thinking from the bottom up. Instead, they start thinking halfway up because they're forced to adopt the thinking of their political party."

"Annie, don't discount neuroscience, as the human brain is designed to overreact to a perceived threat."

Annalisa waved her hand away from her body, as if to brush away the thought of anyone attempting to harm her. "Enough about me," she said. "What about you? What were you working on when I walked in?"

"I'm writing an article on municipalities' efforts to conserve income during the economic downturn. There's a bit of controversy involved, however, because I'm asking why the municipalities only initiate these efforts in a flailing economy and not when the economy is thriving. I assert in the article that municipalities would have amassed huge savings if they'd taken these same cost-cutting measures over the last twenty or more years. They should be looking for the best deals for products and services whether they're cash strapped or rolling in the dough."

"We make quite a team, don't we, Brad?" Annalisa asked. "We'll have every governmental official despising both of us." Annalisa gave Brad a loving kiss and headed up the stairs as she said, "I'm going to take a bath." Brad returned to writing his article, but in his mind he could not help but wonder what dangers lurked ahead for Annalisa.

# *Chapter Three*

"LADIES AND GENTLEMEN OF OKLAHOMA, thank you for coming today," Annalisa said. "I'd like to start by talking about the damage political parties cause to the workings of national and state legislatures. An issue of concern is presented to one or more legislators, along with a request to enact a law to resolve the issue. Ideally legislators should work cooperatively to research, analyze, brainstorm and problem solve to determine the appropriate response to the issue. Instead legislators generally team up solely among their fellow party members and take a party stance in responding to the issue. If Democratic legislators take a stand that conflicts with Republican legislators' party stand, then the focus moves from resolving the issue to determining which party position can win on the issue. With constant debate and delay, there may never be an appropriate resolution, or the *compromise* may be so unsatisfactory as to make the resolution pointless. This is standard operating procedure much of the time, and it is a travesty."

Sitting alone in a far back corner of the auditorium was a man in his early forties with blond hair. He was dressed in a black suit, pale mint-green shirt and dark green tie. He hung on Annalisa's every word and held a digital communication device of some type, which he continually typed on as she spoke. Electronic recording of the speech was not permitted, so the man appeared to be serving as the recording device. Annalisa did not notice him among the 200 or so listeners. During the applause at the end of the speech, the man pocketed his device and exited the auditorium.

Annalisa returned home in an upbeat mood, free of the wanness that overcame her after her appearance in DC. As she expected, her Midwestern audiences were generally receptive and supportive of her positions and advocacy for change. They invigorated her, breathing new energy and excitement into her spirit, which had been deflated and defused by the Washington political class. After being gone for a few days, she missed Brad and threw her newfound energy into preparing a sizzling platter of steak and chicken fajitas surrounded by homemade guacamole, black beans, cheese and other delectable side dishes. When Brad walked through the door after work, he appeared happy to be greeted by both his loving wife and a succulent Mexican feast.

Brad smiled as he entered the kitchen, where Annalisa stood facing the refrigerator as she rummaged for sour cream and salsa. When she closed the door, she caught sight of him in her peripheral vision and was slightly startled.

"I didn't hear you come in, Brad. The kitchen is spotless. Did you even use it while I was gone?" Annalisa asked with a playful twinkle in her eye.

"You were only gone for three days—not a lot of time for me to do much damage." Brad chuckled as he walked over to Annalisa. He gave her a loving and lingering hug, followed by a heartfelt kiss. "Sure smells good in here. I can't think of a better way to start the weekend than over a home-cooked meal with my wife."

Annalisa smiled at Brad. "Will you set the table while I warm up the tortillas?"

"Happy to help, Annie." Brad moved about the kitchen setting the table and putting the food into serving bowls. As he sat down, Annalisa opened the refrigerator. She turned around with a large glass pitcher filled with margaritas swirling in copious cubes of ice. She poured them each a drink and joined Brad at the table.

"How did the Tulsa event go yesterday?" he asked.

"Well, very well. I was received with openness and agreement for the most part, and it wasn't just in Tulsa. I encountered the same support in Kansas City and Omaha. In fact, there was a group of a dozen or so in Omaha who told me they've formed their own advocacy organization to present my points to their local citizens and legislators. This is the first grassroots organization I'm aware of that's been created to continue the dialogue after I leave."

"That's fantastic! Your hammering has finally made a permanent dent. My only concern is whether this group has a sufficient grasp of your analysis, arguments and advocacy to accurately be your mouthpiece in Omaha. How many times have they even heard you speak?"

"That's the special aspect of this group," Annalisa said. "At least six of them have heard me speak multiple times, as they travel together to as many venues as they can. In talking with them, I believe they do grasp my message and can convey it with accuracy. In addition, they have my book to look to should they have questions. To have my message continue on in Omaha when I'm not there is monumental and can be highly effective."

Looking up from his plate, Brad beamed. "This is delicious. Congratulations on your message for change taking root. I suspect it will continue to grow as this group searches for fertile ground upon which it can spread your thoughts."

"I like the metaphor," Annalisa said. "I'm excited to see what this group can accomplish. Changing the subject, don't we have the fundraiser dinner hosted by the local journalists tomorrow night?"

"Yes, Annie, we're raising money to buy new computers for two local DC high schools that are teaching classes on antique equipment. I understand the tickets are all sold out. That's huge because the ballroom we're using holds 600 people."

"That's a strong turnout among the journalist community, Brad. It's good to see that type of philanthropic commitment."

"Oh, it's not just journalists who will be attending. There's been a massive outreach into the political world, educational institutions, museums, nonprofits and local businesses."

"It should be a fun evening with such an interesting mix of people," said Annalisa.

"Yes, I'm really looking forward to it. I'm seldom in a position to socialize with my journalism colleagues, so this will be a special opportunity to catch up with them. Networking with the other attendees will be valuable too."

"Brad, it sounds like you're taking your work with us to the party. Try to leave the notepad at home and just relax into social conversations, OK?"

"Fine, Annie, I'll forget the story and focus on the fun. Let's go watch a movie. We can clean this up later."

"The dishes can wait, but the leftovers must be put away," Annalisa said. "I don't want our lunch for tomorrow to spoil. I'll meet you in the living room in a couple of minutes. Feel free to select the movie. I'm flexible. Choose whatever you want."

As Annalisa wrapped up the leftovers, save for the guacamole, which she surrounded with fresh chips on a platter for her and Brad to enjoy while watching their movie, she was unaware that someone was gazing intently at her through a window on the side of her home. The figure stood motionless, draped in darkness and a hooded sweatshirt, making it impossible to identify the gender. When Annalisa left the room to join Brad, the figure slowly turned away from the window and disappeared into the night.

* * *

Early the next evening, Annalisa and Brad dressed for the fundraiser. Brad put on a sharply tailored Armani suit and Annalisa slipped into an ivory satin tea-length evening dress sparsely splattered with hand-sewn ivory beads. It was a dress of muted sophistication and elegant sparkle. As they readied themselves, Brad turned to Annalisa.

"My friends Spencer Van Otter and Miranda Lewis will be there tonight and I want you to meet them. We've crossed paths many times over the years, especially Spence and I, and I think you'll find them interesting, enthusiastic and open to your ideas, although I hope you'll take your own advice and leave your soapbox at home so you can just enjoy yourself tonight."

"That's my intention," Annalisa said. "I've given enough speeches this week. All I want to do is hear other people talk about anything. Relaxation is my mantra for the night. By the way, I believe I met your friend Miranda Lewis at the Omni the other day. She was friendly and supportive."

"That's Miranda," declared Brad.

Later that night, when Brad and Annalisa entered the ballroom at the hotel where the fundraising event was being held, they stepped into a magical world. Their first step was onto a red velvet carpet that ran across the long expanse of the ballroom, ending at the top of the stairs to the stage. The walls were draped with layers of taffeta in a color one variant shade away from the trademarked Tiffany blue. The taffeta shimmered in the light and elicited a feeling of glamour and elegance. Hundreds of one-foot-wide silver stars hung across the entire twelve feet high ceiling, outlined in miniature LED white lights. Each star featured the name of an attendee in glittery red sequins that matched the red carpet. It was 1950s Hollywood at its best, and electricity was in the air as people mingled while enjoying the big band sound of a twenty-piece orchestra.

The same taffeta that covered the walls also covered the tables, and the silk fabric reflected the lights from the hanging stars. Megaphone vases brimming with colorful blossoms served as centerpieces. The blossoms' color varied from table to table, and as a group they spanned the entire color spectrum. The ambiance made each guest feel as if he or she were a star walking into the Academy Awards. The shimmers, sparkles and sounds, as well as the singing from the orchestra's lead vocalist, transported the room to another time and place. As each guest entered the ballroom, a photographer snapped a photo, just as the paparazzi capture images of a Hollywood star.

As Brad and Annalisa circulated among the other guests, they encountered Spencer. Brad and Spencer simultaneously shook hands and hugged, then turned to introduce their wives to each other.

"Spence, I'd like you to meet my wife, Annalisa."

"Actually," interjected Spencer, "I've already had the pleasure of meeting your wife several days ago."

"I thought you looked familiar," said Annalisa. "Didn't we talk after my speech at the Omni? You were with Miranda Lewis from the *DC Press*, I believe."

"Great memory, Ms. Vermeer, considering the number of people you meet each week," complimented Spencer.

"Oh, please set aside formalities and call me Annalisa." Annalisa turned to Spencer's wife, who had been patiently and silently observing the other three speak, and introduced herself. Spencer's wife smiled. "I'm Nicole, and I'm happy to meet you. Spence talked with me some about the comments you made last week in your speech. I found it most intriguing, but don't you ruffle a lot of feathers along the way?"

"Most definitely, and that's the downside to my life. So many politicians view my ideas as a threat to their livelihoods, lifestyles and power that they don't stop to consider that it may just be possible to integrate my ideas into the political system without destroying their way of life in the process. Change can be good, even better than the status quo, but the thought of living through the change can be overwhelmingly daunting."

"I agree," said Nicole. "Change isn't a process most of us look forward to or seek in our lives, even when our lives may be lacking in some respect."

"We get comfortable with our lives," said Spencer. "We get worn into them, just as our feet mold themselves into a pair of shoes we've worn for a long time. We're more comfortable wearing the worn-in shoes than buying a new and shiny pair because the new shoes will hurt, at least until we wear them in."

"Some people have melded so firmly into their lives that any sort of change is simply too much for them," said Annalisa. "Take Senator Dobbins, for example. He won't consider for a second that any of my thoughts have merit. He's entrenched in the political system, having lived in it for most of his adult life, and it's a part of him. He has no intention of wearing in a new path in his life when the worn trail he's made for himself suits him just fine."

"I think change will come with the younger men and women in power at all levels of government," asserted Spencer. "They've lived through change upon change during their lifetimes and are not entirely opposed to considering new ways to accomplish current and future goals."

"I tell Annie the same thing," said Brad. "She'll make headway with her initiatives, but it will come slowly from within segments of open-minded people, most of whom are probably not currently part of the political machine. It will come from supporters who run businesses, practice medicine, farm the land and so on because they are removed enough to not be invested in maintaining the status quo, yet close enough to know our system isn't entirely working for the overall benefit of the country."

"Well said, Brad," said Miranda as she joined the couples. After greeting everyone, she continued, "I was just talking to Jake Mendelson, who is a professor in the history department at Georgetown, and he contends history supports many of your ideas. He asserts the founding fathers and their contemporaries viewed the role of legislators as one of making laws *as needed* for the proper governance of society. Their intention wasn't to have legislators erect statute upon statute, year after year, just because they *can*."

"Annie," said Brad, "Professor Mendelson sounds an awful lot like you. Has he heard Annie speak, Miranda?"

"Yes, he told me he's heard her speak several times, but has never actually met her."

"Maybe I'll have the opportunity to meet him tonight," said Annalisa. "I meet so many opponents that it would be refreshing to meet a proponent for a change."

"Enough shoptalk, everyone," demanded Brad. "Annie, may I have this dance?"

Annalisa playfully curtsied to Brad. She smiled at Spencer, Nicole and Miranda, and turned toward the dance floor as she slipped her hand under Brad's bent arm. At six feet tall, Brad towered over Annalisa as they danced through "Earth Angel," "I Only Have Eyes for You" and "Lucille" before strolling to one of the many bars in the room for tall glasses of ice water. Standing at the bar was Senator Dobbins, one of the last people Annalisa wanted to run into that evening. They exchanged glances, nodded at each other and with a scowl Senator Dobbins strutted away. Annalisa shook her head in exasperation. At that moment, Senator Wagner approached her. In stark contrast to Senator Dobbins, Senator Wagner beamed a smile and offered his hand to her.

"Good evening, Ms. Vermeer. Are you enjoying yourself?" he asked.

"As a matter of fact, I am," answered Annalisa while firmly shaking his hand. "Have we met before?"

"Not directly, but I heard you speak the other day at the Omni," declared Senator Wagner. "I'm Scott Wagner and I'm the senior senator from New York."

A woman appearing about thirty-five years old approached, a brunette beauty with pin-straight hair poking into her shoulders. She was thin enough and tall enough to be a model, but her walk and perfectly proportioned face shouted "movie star." Possibly she was a prop for the party, a decoration of sorts to breathe more life into the theme that evening. When she reached them, she latched onto Senator Wagner's arm and arched her high-heeled feet so she could reach his face, firmly planting a kiss on his unready lips. Annalisa expected a camera flash to immediately follow, as if the kiss had been staged on the woman's part.

"Scott, where have you been? I've been looking for you for ten minutes," the woman stated with frustration in her voice.

Senator Wagner appeared unconcerned and calm. He turned to Annalisa. "Ms. Vermeer, I'd like you to meet my wife, Daphne. Daphne, this is Annalisa, the advocate for revamping this country's entire legislative system of government. Kendra and I heard her speak the other day. I believe I mentioned it to you."

"Hello, Ms. Wagner," Annalisa said. "It's a pleasure to meet you. Your gown is exquisite."

"Thank you. It's Valentino, from the latest collection. The baby-blue satin has the most sensuous feel, don't you think?" Ms. Wagner inquired as she held the fabric away from her body for Annalisa to touch.

Though taken a bit aback, Annalisa reached out and gently ran her fingers across the cloth. "Yes, Ms. Wagner, it is textured perfectly. Excuse me, but I must go join my husband. It was a pleasure to meet you." She looked toward Senator Wagner. "It was a pleasure to meet you as well, and thank you for attending my presentation at the Omni." With that she walked over to the other end of the bar where Brad was talking with an older woman who seemed serious and concerned.

"Annie, this is Sylvia Rossman, a representative from Illinois," said Brad. "Representative Rossman, this is my wife, Annalisa."

Representative Rossman's skin went ashen as she recognized Annalisa as the brash speaker who offended her with talk of party disintegration. Her sustained stare moved Annalisa to speak first.

"How do you do, Representative Rossman? I'm pleased to meet you," Annalisa politely stated.

Representative Rossman recovered her tongue and her diplomacy. "I'm pleased to meet you as well. I had no idea you were Brad's wife, although I should have surmised some sort of relationship since you have the same uncommon last name." Representative Rossman forced a smile. "Your husband and I have coordinated our efforts through the years on articles he has written. I have contributed my political expertise on many of his topics. He has been a delight to engage with, my dear."

"Yes, Annie," Brad said. "Sylvia has been most helpful in providing me with the politician's take on issues I've written about, especially since she's been in the House for thirty-five years. That, of course, gives her a wealth of personal experience in tackling many of these issues."

Representative Rossman genuinely beamed. "Brad, I'm happy to assist you in any way I can," she said, demurely. "After all, a representative's duty and honor is to serve."

"Thank you, Sylvia," Brad said. "I have been most fortunate in having you as my personal mentor over the years. You have selflessly been there for me and, as always, I appreciate having your point of view and thoughtful analysis to keep me grounded."

The back scratching was becoming so thick that Annalisa was having difficulty breathing. She readied her escape by turning to Representative Rossman to excuse herself. Just as Annalisa opened her mouth to speak, Representative Rossman looked her squarely in the eye, her false smile melting away as she spoke at Annalisa.

"Ms. Vermeer, your husband is a gem, and frankly I cannot imagine the two of you being married to each other given your diametrically opposed personalities and viewpoints. Brad is reasonable and, while he wishes at times to effect change, he doesn't propose the demise of our entire political and legislative systems, as do you." Representative Rossman's eyes remained firmly planted on Annalisa's eyes.

Brad, in shock, immediately came to Annalisa's defense.

"Sylvia . . ."

"Representative Rossman," Annalisa interrupted, returning the laser-like glare, "it seems you're familiar with my work. While you are most certainly entitled to your opinion, I believe your statement is only half correct. Yes, Brad is reasonable and he doesn't seek the demise you described in proposing different approaches to dealing with issues. However, you misunderstand my arguments if you look at them as advocating the death of our political and legislative systems."

Now it was Representative Rossman's turn to feel shock. She could not believe Annalisa's hubris. She readied herself to speak, but Annalisa's momentum was not to be stopped.

"You do not need to be a Democrat or a Republican to serve in your position as representative of your constituents," Annalisa continued. "Your constituents have their viewpoints and can convey them, as well as their reasoning, to you, if you make the effort to communicate with them. You are an intelligent woman or Brad wouldn't consult you, so you are perfectly capable of reaching your own conclusions on an issue by utilizing independent analysis and reliance on the voice of your constituency. You do not need a political party to muddy the waters and cloud your thinking."

Annalisa continued her focused look at the representative. By now, Representative Rossman was fully composed and, appearing unfazed, immediately responded.

"Well, Ms. Vermeer, while you do have a way with words, spinning them to support your advocacy, that is all they really are: a spin on the truth. You cannot simply eliminate political parties and expect our legislative system to continue on without chaos. In addition, my constituents, though intelligent people, do not have the inclination, time or expertise to competently analyze and form an opinion on the resolution of any particular issue. That is why constituents vote for their representatives and senators—because they expect we will do the thinking, the legwork and the analysis in addressing issues that arise."

Annalisa fired back, "Legislators too often forget their constituents are the cogs in the wheel that make this country run. You would have little, if anything, to legislate if there were no constituents. Constituents don't live in a vacuum. They are engineers, educators, artists, garbage collectors, lawyers, accountants, doctors, business leaders and so on and so on. They possess expertise in areas that legislators do not, and they can contribute both practical and reasonable opinions to their representatives in government."

"That is why we representatives are in constant dialogue with PACs," retorted Representative Rossman. "Political action committees represent the special interests and expertise of our constituents and keep us well abreast of the facts we need to consider in the legislative process."

"I do not equate political action committees with constituents," Annalisa responded. "Constituents include the vast spectrum of society and thereby bring all sides of an issue to the table. The lobbyists from PACs are one-dimensional, as they only bring to the table the side of an issue that benefits the special interest funding the PAC. Lobbyists undermine the concept of majority rule and the approach of taking into consideration the opinions and best interests of all. Those who must live with decisions must be part of the decision-making process."

At that moment, a man on the stage announced dinner was to be served and all guests should proceed to their tables. Annalisa told Representative Rossman that she would be interested in continuing their conversation at another time. Representative Rossman nodded, but the fierce look in her eyes indicated any further conversation would be no more amicable than this one had been. Brad, who had been silently watching the ladies trade volleys, took Annalisa by the hand. He politely told Sylvia he would see her later and whisked Annalisa to the table where their seating placards were located.

After locating their table, they joined their tablemates—Senator Wagner, Senator Hampton, Professor Mendelson and their wives. After the customary introductions, they were each served Caesar salad, freshly baked warm bread and award-winning wine from local Virginia wineries. For a time, conversations diminished as the famished tablemates imbibed their wine and enjoyed the delectable culinary productions.

To Brad's delight, most of the table conversation was light. The other couples all had children, and that provided fodder for great stories and laughter, even the stories about the teenagers, which were not always so funny to the affected parents. The various entrees were delicious, particularly the sautéed salmon drizzled with a teriyaki glaze and topped with finely chopped fresh pineapple and mango. Eventually, as parents exhausted their "children" anecdotes, the conversations gravitated to professional matters. Senator Hampton was the first to broach the subject of Annalisa's speech at the Omni.

"Ms. Vermeer, I had the pleasure of attending your speech last week at the Omni. You certainly do seem to have a significant following despite the controversial nature of your message."

"Well, Senator Hampton," said Annalisa, "it doesn't seem so significant here in the DC area, but in some other areas, such as the Midwest and Oklahoma, although some consider Oklahoma to be in the Midwest, there is some related activism coming alive. It seems I'm not alone any longer in advocating for change."

"Seriously, Ms. Vermeer?" Senator Wagner asked. "Are there actually grassroots organizations developing to support you?"

"Not just to support me, but to actually advocate to elicit real change—first at their local level, and who knows where it will go from there," answered Annalisa.

"She's correct, Scott," said Senator Wagner's wife, Daphne, who then addressed Annalisa, but spoke to the entire table. "About a month ago I was visiting my sister in Prairie du Rocher, Illinois, which is near St. Louis. I read an extensive article in a St. Louis newspaper about how many people in the Midwest are latching onto your ideas and attempting to institute them at the municipality level in their communities. While politicians here in DC may disregard your notions, growing numbers in this country are listening to and learning from you, which is leading them to action."

"Interesting, Daphne," said Senator Wagner. "No offense to you, Ms. Vermeer, but I had no idea you were garnering notice from outside of your speaking sites."

"None taken, Senator," assured Annalisa. "I guess with enough determination one person can actually make a difference and effect positive change."

Professor Mendelson chimed in, "Throughout history we have seen one person's voice become a contagion, in a good sense, spreading a message to numerous other voices until it becomes loud enough to cause a lasting effect. Take our founding fathers, for example. As you know, they were originally content English colonists who over time advocated civil disobedience and eventually independence from England. The voice of a few eventually became the voice of the majority."

"That was the tenor of the article I read, Professor," said Daphne. "The article's author is convinced these grassroots organizations will make great strides in dismantling and remolding our legislative system as long as the leader, Ms. Vermeer, continues to preach her sermons to these enthusiastic audiences."

"I'm flattered, Ms. Wagner," Annalisa said quietly while blushing, "but I believe the author is using media hype to inflate the actual effect I'm having. Yes, my ideas do have outside support, but I suspect it will take years for any substantive changes to occur."

"You are too modest, Ms. Vermeer," asserted Daphne. "I believe you are underestimating the results of your efforts. At the rate you're going, change within the short term is imminent."

Professor Mendelson's wife, Ariel, a slim, middle-aged woman with short brown hair and soft facial features, broke in. "Ms. Vermeer, I am a professor of sociology at Georgetown and find your movement of great sociological interest. The ramifications to government behavior and the effects on society as a whole could be monumental."

"I appreciate your positive thoughts, but enough about me. There are seven other people at this table, each talented and accomplished. Let's talk about somebody else," suggested Annalisa.

The host appeared onstage and invited the guests to dance and mingle for thirty minutes while the tables were cleared and dessert served. The guests welcomed the opportunity to move about and the dance floor soon became packed. As Annalisa moved toward the dance floor, she did not notice the man standing at the opposite end of the ballroom—the same man who had been hurriedly typing her speech in Tulsa. This time he was not alone. Standing next to him was Senator Dobbins. The men were engaged in what appeared to be a deeply serious conversation.

"Senator, I assume you've thoroughly reviewed the Tulsa document I sent you?" asked Edward Hawthorne, a private political consultant who was often hired by Senator Dobbins to consult on confidential matters requiring extreme discretion.

"Yes, Edward, I have, and it's most disturbing," Senator Dobbins said. "The problem is as bad as, if not worse than, I imagined a year ago when I first put my focus on it. You keep listening to her, but I've determined the time for merely observing has ended. It's time to take action." The senator's clenched fist was moving at his side.

"Do you have any instructions for me, sir?" asked Edward.

"Not at this time. I have matters under control. You can either leave now or stay and enjoy yourself because your work for the evening is complete." Edward bowed slightly and walked away. The senator dialed a number on his cell phone and spoke for no more than a minute. Since the orchestra was in full swing, no one heard his words. After he finished his call, he joined a group of men sitting at a table near one of the bars.

The host announced that dessert was served and the crowd paraded like ants toward a mound of spilled sugar as they returned to their tables where large slices of creamy cheesecake topped with cherries covered with sauce awaited them. Steaming cups of coffee and tea complemented the cheesecake, and the guests reveled in light conversation and laughter as the orchestra accompanied them with lively jazz music in the background.

An hour or so later, as Ms. Mendelson discussed the despondency and ostracism newly released prisoners tended to feel, Annalisa noticed a burning sensation on her tongue and felt nauseous. She silently passed it off as an overconsumption of rich food and spicy flavorings. As time passed, the intensity of the nausea increased and stomach pains developed. Annalisa could no longer feign health and whispered in Brad's ear that she felt ill and needed to go home. They politely excused themselves and headed toward the door.

As they were driving home, Annalisa started to moan in pain and they had to stop the car for her to vomit. "Could I have food poisoning?" she asked in agony. "I feel so awful, and my stomach is turning somersaults inside itself."

"Unless you were given a piece of undercooked or spoiled salmon, I doubt it's food poisoning because nobody else showed signs of illness."

"Brad, we don't know if anyone else is ill because no one at our table knows I'm sick." Annalisa continued moaning and squirming in her seat. "I'm scared. I really feel awful."

"Let's get you home and into bed and we'll see how you are in a couple of hours. Maybe you can sleep through the night and you'll feel better in the morning."

Fortunately, it was a short drive home. Once there, Brad lovingly readied Annalisa for bed and tucked her in. She attempted to sleep, but fitfully tossed around as she tried to minimize her stomach distress. She continued to vomit and developed an excruciating headache. By 4:00 a.m., Annalisa was too weak to even crawl to the bathroom and she started shivering.

"Annie, you must have a bad stomach flu bug. If you show signs of dehydration, then we'll have to go to the hospital," Brad said with concern in his voice.

Annalisa did not respond, but lay in bed in the fetal position trying to alleviate the stomach and intestinal pain. Brad encouraged her to drink a bit of water and suck on ice cubes to stay hydrated, but she found it difficult to even swallow and her tongue still burned. At 5:00 a.m., Brad wrapped Annalisa in a blanket and carried her to the car. She was pale and limp, shivering despite the thick blanket encasing her. She spoke no words during the drive, but periodically moaned in pain. A few minutes later, she was wheeled into the emergency room, barely able to speak.

# *Chapter Four*

THE EMERGENCY ROOM PHYSICIAN ASSIGNED to Annalisa, Dr. William Mathis, inundated Brad with questions in order to best assess her medical history, symptoms and condition. He examined her, initially suspecting appendicitis. He had blood drawn, requested a urine sample and obtained vomit specimens to confirm his suspicions. A nurse started an intravenous flow of saline solution infused with electrolytes to hydrate her.

"Mr. Vermeer," said Dr. Mathis, "other than the IV drip, I'm not starting any other treatment until I definitively determine what's wrong. While I believe she has appendicitis, I need to confirm that before going into surgery. I'm testing all her fluids to see if they explain the cause of her sudden and intense symptoms."

"I understand, Dr. Mathis," Brad said. "Will it take you long to get back the test results?"

"No. Given the hydration issue your wife is exhibiting, I put a rush on the tests. I should have the results within thirty minutes. I suggest you sit and give her whatever comfort you can while we wait. I'll be back as soon as I have the lab report."

Brad nodded and turned to enter Annalisa's room as Dr. Mathis went the opposite direction down the hallway. Annalisa was curled up and clearly still in agony, but her moans had grown more muffled given her weakened state. Brad did not speak, but gently brushed the wet hair away from her face and held both her hands. He kissed her forehead and waited for Dr. Mathis to return. In his mind, Brad retraced the events of the prior evening, hoping to rekindle a memory that would expose the cause of Annalisa's illness. He could not help but believe someone did this to her.

As he looked down at Annalisa, Brad began to speak, not knowing whether she could even hear him. His words were more for him than for her.

"Has someone hurt the love of my life? How could I let this happen? Could I not have protected you from this? Maybe it's time for your work to stop, for you to switch directions and focus on non-controversial topics and goals."

The door to Annalisa's room opened and Brad looked up, assuming Dr. Mathis had returned. Instead, a nurse entered and informed Brad she was there to take Annalisa's vital signs. As she checked Annalisa's temperature, she asked Brad if there was anything she could do to make him more comfortable. Her soft smile and gentle voice brought Brad out of his questioning mood. He smiled back at her.

"Thank you, but I'm fine, or as fine as I can be given my wife's condition," he said.

"Dr. Mathis is a fine doctor. If anyone can help your wife, it's him. You must have faith in his medical expertise and compassion," explained the nurse.  At that moment, Brad's cell phone rang and he excused himself from the room.

"Hello," answered Brad.

"Hi, Brad. This is Jeremiah from the magazine. Sorry to bother you so early on a Sunday morning, but I wanted you to know the fact checker for your last article ran into some issues and took care of the problems last night. So, it's now clear sailing for you."

"Thanks for letting me know, Jeremiah. I need to go now and I don't expect to be in the office tomorrow. My wife is ill and I need to be by her side."

"I completely understand. We have everything under control here, so you should just concentrate on your wife," encouraged Jeremiah.

Without giving Brad an opportunity to respond, Jeremiah hung up. Brad quickly returned to Annalisa's room. The nurse was gone and Annalisa was silent. He returned to her side and breathed a deep sigh.

What seemed like an eternity passed before Dr. Mathis entered the room with a gurney and an orderly. Dr. Mathis looked concerned, and Brad assumed Annalisa was about to be taken into surgery—for what he did not know.

"Mr. Vermeer," said Dr. Mathis, "could I have a word with you outside, please?"

"Certainly," said Brad, who now had similar concern in his eyes. They went out into the hallway and Dr. Mathis walked about thirty feet to be well beyond earshot of Annalisa.

"Mr. Vermeer, your wife doesn't have appendicitis after all," Dr. Mathis explained. "I'm sorry to tell you this, but your wife has apparently been poisoned, and we're going to have to perform gastric lavage—we have to pump her stomach—to ensure any remaining poison in her stomach is extracted. It's impossible to determine how much poison she's consumed given she vomited extensively at home before she arrived here. We can talk details later, as I'm sure you have a multitude of questions, but for now I need to return to your wife and have her readied for the procedure, once you give your consent."

Brad stared at Dr. Mathis without speaking a word. Dr. Mathis requested Brad sit down in the waiting room until Annalisa was given a regular room after the procedure was completed.

"I promise, Mr. Vermeer, I will discuss this matter further with you later, but right now I must get ready for the gastric lavage."

Brad finally spoke, but with hesitation. "I understand, Doctor."

Dr. Mathis quickly moved off down the hallway, stopping momentarily at Annalisa's room where he instructed the orderly to obtain Mr. Vermeer's signature on the consent form, then move and prepare Annalisa for the procedure. Brad watched the physician disappear around the corner and then he returned to Annalisa's room to sign the form. He kissed Annalisa again on her forehead and told her she was going to be just fine. He stumbled down the hallway to the waiting room where he tried to grasp that his suspicions about Annalisa being poisoned were true.

Sometime later, as Brad stared at nothing, Dr. Mathis entered the waiting room and sat down. "Mr. Vermeer," Dr. Mathis called to divert Brad's attention away from the white wall across from them. As Brad turned to face Dr. Mathis, the physician explained, "Your wife is resting in her room. We've sedated her so she can sleep for a few hours and be free from the pain of the poison and of the gastric lavage. The lavage was successful in that we extracted several poisonous berries. While it will take a few days for her to recover, your wife will be just fine."

Brad sighed, but the concern on his face remained as intense as before the lavage. "Thank you, Doctor, for saving my wife's life, which is what I believe you did, right?"

"Well, possibly. This poison doesn't necessarily kill a person, despite wreaking havoc on their digestive system. It depends upon the amount of poison ingested. Obviously, the more given, the higher the potential for death. If given enough poison, her condition would have continued to deteriorate until she became comatose and died."

"Doctor, you mentioned you extracted several poisonous berries. What poison did my wife ingest?"

"She ingested berries from a deciduous ornamental shrub commonly known as mezereon. Many people have them growing in their yards because of the pink flowers that bloom very early in the spring. I have a couple growing in my own yard. Birds love the bright red berries, but don't get sick ingesting them. People, on the other hand, are a completely different story. The more berries they ingest, the more symptoms they show and the greater the risk of death."

"Apparently my wife ingested a number of berries to have reacted to the extent she did," said Brad.

"Yes, we extracted pieces from at least ten berries, and I'm certain there were more in the vomit from earlier. What I don't understand is how she ingested them, considering they were ingested whole and don't have a good flavor, at least to humans."

"My guess would be they were mixed in with the cherries and sauce that covered the cheesecake dessert we had last evening," Brad said. "The cherries and sauce were very sweet, so it's possible the poisonous berries were disguised by the cherries."

"That seems logical, but we'll leave it to the police to make a final determination. There were also cherries present in your wife's stomach contents, so she clearly ingested both cherries and berries. I saved the entire lavage extraction for the police, which, by the way, we contacted upon our diagnosis of attempted murder by poisoning."

"Thank you for saving my wife's life and for contacting the police," Brad said. "My wife has plenty of enemies, powerful enemies, so she'll need protection and a vigorous police investigation if there's to be no second attempt on her life."

A nurse approached Dr. Mathis about another patient. While they spoke, Brad retraced his steps with Annalisa just before dessert was served, hoping he would trigger his memory and recall unusual activity around their table. Hard as he tried, nothing came to mind. The nurse left and Dr. Mathis again spoke to Brad.

"A policeman is stationed outside of her room right now, which is room 477, and someone will continue to be there until she's discharged. I know there's at least one other police officer here reviewing her chart to assess all the facts we have. I'm sure you'll soon be questioned to fill in the gaps."

"Can I see Annie now?"

"Yes, you're free to stay with her from here on out, but understand she'll be sleeping for the next few hours. Maybe it would be best if you went home for a few hours of rest yourself after you speak with the police officer. Then, when your wife wakes up, you'll be back here refreshed and ready to support her in her recovery and throughout the course of the investigation."

"I agree that logically and medically it makes sense for me to sleep," Brad said, "but I'll have to do so in Annie's room in a chair because I don't want to leave her, especially if her life is still in danger."

"I understand. I'll ask a nurse to have a reclining chair brought into the room so you can be as comfortable as possible. I'll be in to check on your wife in a few hours, but for now I must leave you to see other patients. Do you have any other questions before I leave?"

"Probably a hundred, but I'm unable to focus on them for now. All I can think about is being with Annie and keeping her safe from the maniac who's trying to kill her. Thank you again for your invaluable assistance. I'll see you later."

Before going to Annalisa's room, Brad called her worried parents and informed them she would fully recover and now just needed sleep. They had planned to start their drive to the hospital from Wisconsin that day, but Brad assured them it was not necessary, as the danger of Annalisa dying had passed. They trusted him, so they agreed to remain in Wisconsin as long as Brad put her on the phone with them just as soon as she was able to speak. He assured them they would hear from Annalisa once she regained enough strength. In the meantime, he would keep them apprised of any changes to her condition. Once they felt as comfortable as they could with the situation, Brad hung up so he could be with Annalisa.

As he approached room 477, he saw the uniformed officer Dr. Mathis had mentioned. Brad found it comforting that the officer required his driver's license to prove his identity as Annalisa's husband. Inside the room he found Annalisa sleeping peacefully, free of the agonizing pain caused by the toxin that ravaged her body. He slid a chair next to her bed, sat and gently wrapped his fingers around her right hand as he watched the repetitive dripping of her IV fluids from the bag into the tube. It was a mindless focus, but appropriate for a mind racing and wondering who tried to murder his wife.

A few minutes later, a woman entered the room. Instead of medical attire, she wore a tailored suit dress feminized by a ruffled lapel and pleated hemline. She appeared to be in her early forties. She was pretty with shoulder-length brown hair and serious blue eyes. She gazed momentarily at Annalisa, then walked over to Brad.

"Mr. Vermeer, my name is Quinn Thomas and I'm the lead detective from the Metropolitan Police Department assigned to investigate the attempted murder of your wife."

Brad extended his arm and firmly shook her hand. "Thank you for coming so quickly."

Detective Thomas smiled at Brad. "You're welcome. Part of my job is to start my investigation immediately, before witnesses, evidence and suspects disappear, and before memories fade. I understand you're upset right now, but I need to ask you some questions. Would you mind stepping outside so we can freely talk?"

"I'll do whatever I can to help you find the monster who did this to Annie. We can go into the hallway to talk so Annie won't hear us speaking in case she wakes up. I don't know how much the doctor wants her to know at this point," explained Brad.

They walked down the hallway to a grouping of chairs. Hanging across from them was a painting of a serene landscape with a babbling brook cutting through a forest floor. Brad wished he could whisk Annalisa there so they could feel safe and be at peace. Cognizant of the presence of Detective Thomas, he knew it could not be so. He turned from the painting and looked at the detective. She launched into her litany of questions while being sensitive to Brad's emotional state.

"Mr. Vermeer, before we discuss the specifics of last evening, do you know who may want to murder your wife?"

"Unfortunately, there are probably too many people to count," lamented Brad.

"I don't know your wife, but why would a young woman who's not a part of the criminal element of society acquire so many enemies, especially ones willing to kill?"

"Annie advocates provocative thoughts. She fights for dramatic change to both our political system and our entire system of lawmaking. She hasn't kept these thoughts to herself. Instead, she travels the country giving speeches, spreading her message to anyone who will listen. Fortunately, or unfortunately, depending on who you are and how you view the issues, she's garnered quite a following. Grassroots organizations are forming in an effort to implement Annie's changes at various local levels. Many politicians are angered and threatened by her actions."

Detective Thomas and Brad spoke at great length about Annalisa's work and the people whom Brad specifically knew had expressed disdain or more for her. Their discussion shifted to the party the previous evening.

"Detective, there were hundreds of people at the fundraiser and a significant number of those people are politicians," Brad said. "In addition to the guests, many hotel employees were working the event. It will take you forever just to talk to each person who was there."

Brad's frustration was evident. He sighed and buried his face in his hands as he stared at the floor. Detective Thomas remained silent, allowing Brad to regroup and compose himself. She then shifted to the positive in the hopes she would lift his spirits.

"Yes, it will take some time to question each person," she said, "but please know that members of my team are already at the hotel gathering forensic evidence. While the staff removed the food and cleaned the table settings last night, the tables, chairs and bars haven't yet been moved because there's a function scheduled for tonight that uses the same setup. Of course, given that the ballroom is now a crime scene, that function has been moved to another room.

We even stopped the staff from cleaning the floor this morning. So, the attempted murderer will be disappointed to learn that the crime scene is still largely intact."

"That's good to hear. With the food all gone, how will you find any trace of the tainted cherry cheesecake Annie ate?" asked Brad.

"It's likely we won't, but thanks to Dr. Mathis, we have your wife's stomach contents, which is sufficient to prove the source of the poisoning. The only food your wife ate that could have disguised the presence and taste of mezereon berries was the cherries in the sauce. Now my job is to determine who with motive and opportunity acted on them."

A woman with a quick gait approached. She seemed to be about the same age as Detective Thomas, but had darker hair and eyes and a Mediterranean appearance. Her attire was nonmedical and more casual than Detective Thomas's in that she wore dress pants, a matching jacket and a light purple shirt. She looked first to Brad. "Mr. Vermeer, my name is Catalonia Garza. I'm a detective on Detective Thomas's team. I've been heading up efforts at the hotel and I want to assure you every effort is being made to apprehend the person who poisoned your wife."

"Thank you, Detective Garza. I appreciate your efforts."

Detective Garza turned to Detective Thomas. "We retrieved all the garbage from the Dumpsters, so all we've lost is the food that went down the garbage disposals. We're also collecting all the fingerprints in the room, although there's limited utility in that since we already know who attended the party. Plus, people who were in the room for prior events likely left their fingerprints. We're hoping if we find prints for a person who wasn't a guest at the fundraiser—an employee or someone who attended a prior function—we can identify his or her fingerprints using one of our databases."

"Cat," Detective Thomas asked, "have you been able to obtain a list of the guests and has the hotel furnished the names and contact information for all the employees who worked the function and all the outside companies that provided services or products to the function?"

"Yes, the journalist organization that hosted the event provided us with the guest list and contact information. The hotel did the same with its employees and outside contractors. We're conducting interviews now, but it being a Sunday, it will be difficult to contact most of the businesses. We'll contact them starting tomorrow," responded Detective Garza.

"Good," said Detective Thomas. "How is the hotel dealing with the ballroom and its related kitchen being cordoned off today? Are you finding resistance or cooperation?"

"Full cooperation. The hotel has other ballrooms and another kitchen, so it's been able to juggle the location of its functions. It also helps that it's a Sunday, a day with fewer events. Not all rooms were being used anyway, so there's been no problem. In fact, since an attempted murder is bad publicity for the venue, the hotel will do just about anything to help us find the perpetrator."

"Again, good," said Detective Thomas. "Were there surveillance cameras in the room and at all ingress and egress areas?"

"Yes, and the hotel has produced all the recordings and they're being viewed at the lab as we speak. The problem is that many people were milling about the room, and Ms. Vermeer's table was likely blocked from the cameras' views. However, there's a chance the poisoner acted when there was a lull in traffic so that the scene was captured by a camera."

As Brad listened to the detectives, he thought about how crowded it was during the party. People were everywhere and he remembered saying "Excuse me" countless times as he tried to maneuver around other guests. He did not hold out much hope for there ever being any lull in traffic around their table.

"Cat, it's also possible that the toxin was applied to the cheesecake in the kitchen. Are there any cameras in the kitchen?" asked Detective Thomas.

"Yes, several, which speaks to the concerns management has about the areas where food is prepared and employees congregate. Hopefully, with less traffic there, we'll be able to discover the culprit's actions if he—or she—acted in the kitchen. However, given that a person not part of the hotel staff or an outside vendor would be likely noticed in the kitchen, it's most probable that a party guest tainted the cherries while in the ballroom," stated Detective Garza.

"I agree. Please also have Gavin run criminal record checks on all guests, employees and contractors who serviced the event. We'll see if there's anyone with a previous record of violent conduct," explained Detective Thomas.

"Right, Quinn. I'll talk to Gavin. I'm headed back to the hotel now and I'll report back to you anything we find. Good-bye, Mr. Vermeer. I hope your wife fully recovers quickly," said Detective Garza.

Brad nodded and drifted back to his own thoughts. He replayed in his mind the conversation between Annalisa and Representative Rossman. Sylvia was furious with Annalisa and made no effort to hide her feelings. From experience, Brad knew Sylvia was used to getting her way. He could not help but wonder just how far Sylvia would go to get it.

"Mr. Vermeer," interrupted Detective Thomas, "do you know if anyone has made a direct verbal threat to your wife?"

"No, I don't. That doesn't mean a threat hasn't been made, just that I'm not aware of it. There have been times when Annie has felt concerned about comments made, but she hasn't conveyed to me if there were any actual threats. You'll have to talk to her about that once she wakes up. I do know recently she was almost hit by a car as she started to cross a street, but she couldn't definitively say it was an overt act."

"Once they're analyzed, even seemingly innocuous comments may be recognized as veiled threats," said Detective Thomas. "So, jogging your wife's memory may be enough to bring to her mind's forefront an actual threat that initially went unnoticed. She'll provide the facts and I'll view them through the eyes of an investigator. I look forward to your wife waking up so she can help direct my focus to those who may have verbally threatened her."

"I look forward to Annie waking up too," said Brad.

# *Chapter Five*

Since Annalisa was expected to sleep for several hours, Detective Thomas left the hospital for the hotel, knowing Annalisa was safe with Brad watching over her in the room and an officer stationed outside the doorway. Once at the ballroom, she watched as a multitude of crime scene technicians examined every nook and cranny. She entered the kitchen, where she found Detective Garza.

"Cat, have any traces of the poisonous berries been located in the food waste?"

"No, Quinn, and the team has tested all the cherries and sauce found in the trash bags. Initially I was concerned that much of the uneaten food would have been destroyed in the garbage disposals, but the kitchen staff told me that using the disposals is more work than dumping the waste in trash bags. So, food from the guest plates went in bags, which we were able to fully examine. It looks like there wasn't a mass poisoning or there would be some sign of a poisonous substance in the garbage. Not everyone would have eaten every last toxic berry. Also, no other guest reported becoming ill, so it appears to be a poisoning targeted solely at Ms. Vermeer."

"I'm glad no one else is sick," Detective Thomas said. "This poison debilitates people fairly quickly. Anyone who ate those berries would be sick by now. Once we've interviewed everyone who ate at the event, we can rule this poisoning as an attempt on only Ms. Vermeer's life. I assume the dishwashers were run or the dishes were otherwise cleaned prior to our arrival?"

"Yes, all utensils, cups, dishes and glasses were washed and put away before the staff was notified of Ms. Vermeer's poisoning," said Detective Garza.

"I'm headed back into the ballroom to talk with the technicians about the progress they've made out there," Detective Thomas said.

Detective Thomas left the kitchen and scanned the ballroom, looking for Greg Dallison, a crime scene technician with red hair, a slim build and a ruddy complexion. The ballroom was brightly lit and void of all the decorations and sparkle of the previous evening. The room had been stripped bare of its beauty and its magical quality had disappeared. The bare wooden dining tables had dents and gashes, and stains marred the carpet. At least twenty crime scene investigators scurried around. Some lifted fingerprints while others searched for physical evidence of poison. In a far corner near one of the bars, she spotted Greg, whom she quickly approached.

"Hi, Greg. Where are we at in this room?"

"Hi, Quinn. We're dusting every bit of the room for prints, including light switches, telephones, chairs and any other objects that were likely touched. We're checking the underside of the tables near the edges, but not the tabletops because they were covered by tablecloths, all of which have already been washed and dried. We'll run all prints against our available databases and determine if any attendee appears to be a suspect. Of course, our databases are limited, so much of the public doesn't appear on any of them. Do you know yet if we're looking for a person with only a vendetta against Ms. Vermeer or was this crime more expansive, meaning we have to look for a motive beyond Ms. Vermeer?"

"We're not completely sure yet, Greg, but we have no indication anyone else fell ill, so Ms. Vermeer was likely the only target," said Detective Thomas. "I can confirm that once we finish all the interviews with the guests. Considering there were 600 guests, plus staff, these interviews could take quite some time."

Another of the police department's crime scene technicians, a heavyset woman named Julia Markum, who stood nearly six feet tall with a lovely face and blond hair, approached Detective Thomas and Greg.

"It may not take as long as you might expect, Quinn," Julia said. "Sixty officers were called in today, each assigned to interview ten guests, plus a proportionate share of the staff. So, I expect they'll finish the interviews by tomorrow, except for people who are unavailable."

"Thanks, Julia, for the update. That's great news, but surprising. How did this case rank such a manpower commitment?" inquired Detective Thomas.

"My understanding is given the substantial number of high-profile dignitaries who attended the event, the higher-ups want the case solved quickly so nobody else gets hurt or worse," explained Julia.

"That's good for us. It makes our jobs easier, and the faster we move, the more likely we'll apprehend the culprit," asserted Detective Thomas.

"We've searched this room for any type of container used to hold the toxic berries, but have found none," said Julia. "It's amazing how many earrings were dropped that evening, and even two necklaces, but no items appearing to be related to the crime."

"It seems you two and your team have the hotel investigation well under control, so I'm going to the office to speak with Gavin and Jared. If you find any pertinent evidence, then either call me or talk to Cat, as she's in the kitchen dealing with the food waste," instructed Detective Thomas.

Detective Thomas walked into Jared Willoughby's office and found the computer technician watching television. When he saw her, he beamed a smile and invited her to sit down. The handsome, head- shaven young man in his mid-twenties explained to the detective what he was watching on the television screen.

"Quinn, the hotel sent me all the surveillance video from the ballroom and the kitchen. I've been watching the action from various views for hours. There are four cameras in the ballroom, one in each corner of the room, and ten cameras in the massive kitchen. The cameras are, interestingly enough, automatically activated by a sensor that detects movement. Therefore, filming only occurs when a person enters a room and continues to move. If there's no movement for five minutes, then the camera shuts off."

"It's interesting they use motion detectors to activate the cameras. It seems to be efficient," concluded Detective Thomas.

"It is, Quinn. Anyway, I've been watching about ten hours of coverage—the entire party, plus the preparation prior to the party and the subsequent cleanup. Given that I'm watching it from fourteen separate cameras, this viewing is going to take a while. Of course, where I can, I'm watching the footage in fast motion. I have good views in the kitchen, but limited views in the ballroom. The kitchen holds a relatively small amount of people and lots of cameras, while the ballroom was packed with people and monitored with only the four cameras. So far, I've found no suspicious activity."

"Please keep me apprised of any action you observe that seems suspicious in any way, Jared," said Detective Thomas.

"Certainly, Quinn—if I see anything, I'll call you immediately."

Detective Thomas walked down the hallway to Gavin Beckett's office. She found the crime lab's lead document examiner hunched over his desk, glancing back and forth between his computer monitor and a stack of papers. When he caught a glimpse of the detective, he looked up and removed his glasses.

"Hi, Quinn. I've been running the criminal record checks requested by Cat for all the guests and staff at the party. There's a long list of criminal charges, as well as some convictions in this group," said Gavin, with surprise in his voice.

"Well, it's a large group. Statistics tell us there has to be some criminal activity in such a large group of people, despite their stature in society," explained Detective Thomas.

"There are more arrests than convictions, which makes sense given the connections some of these people possess and the funds they can afford to spend on lawyers. The majority of the arrests are for drug possession, various charges related to alcohol coupled with driving and assaults. There have been some convictions for all these crimes. In addition, there are convictions for battery, reckless driving unrelated to alcohol use and various sexual offenses short of rape."

"Aside from the sexual offenses, were any of the assault and battery convictions violent enough to make us believe the perpetrator would attempt murder?" Detective Thomas asked.

"Not that I've seen, Quinn, but I haven't dug deep into any particular case yet. My first goal is to determine the crimes people were accused of, so I can assess the nature of those crimes. I'm planning on performing an initial check of each person who was in the ballroom or kitchen, and then I'll examine the specifics of arrests and convictions."

"That makes sense, Gavin. Please send me a written report of your conclusions when you're finished."

"It'll be on your desk the minute it's finalized."

A couple of hours later, Detective Thomas received a call from the hospital. Annalisa had awakened and was alert enough to speak with her. Within twenty minutes, the detective arrived at Annalisa's hospital room. She found Brad sitting next to Annalisa. He was using one hand to hold a glass of water and direct a straw into her mouth and the other to support the back of her neck. Annalisa was pale and gaunt. Her damp hair stuck to her face and neck, still wet with sweat. Without turning her head, Annalisa shifted her gaze toward the detective. Brad turned in order to see who had entered the room.

"Hello, Detective," he said. "Thanks for coming back so quickly."

"As you know, I want to speak with your wife just as soon as she's able," Detective Thomas said as she looked at Brad. She turned to Annalisa.

"Ms. Vermeer, my name is Quinn Thomas and I'm investigating your illness." She looked at Brad. Wanting to know if Annalisa was aware of the attempt on her life, she asked, "Mr. Vermeer, what conversation have you had with your wife regarding her medical condition?"

"Detective, I told Annie all I know, so you may speak freely. Annie, Detective Thomas is from the Metropolitan Police and she is the lead investigator of the team working to find out who tried to kill you," explained Brad.

Annalisa released her lips from around the straw, cleared her throat and attempted to speak through the hoarseness caused by repeated regurgitation and the gastric lavage.

"Thank you for your help, Detective," Annalisa quietly whispered.

"I know you're exhausted and talking is difficult, but if you could try to answer just a few questions it could be quite helpful in our investigation. Are you up to trying?" asked Detective Thomas.

"Yes, I want to help you, if I can," Annalisa said, struggling to get the words out.

"Do you have any idea who would want to kill you?" asked the detective.

"Kill me, no. Want to silence me, yes. I'm not sure if those turn out to be the same result."

"Can you elaborate on that thought?" asked Detective Thomas.

Annalisa coughed. The strain in her voice was evident, but she was determined to answer the detective's questions. Brad raised the glass toward Annalisa and offered her the straw. She slowly opened her mouth, pursed her lips around the straw and sipped the water. Again, she coughed. Detective Thomas glanced out the window, attempting to give Annalisa as much privacy as possible while she regained her voice. After one final sip, Annalisa spoke.

"Nobody has made a verbal death threat against me, at least not to my face. I did have a close call with an erratic driver a week or so ago at the Omni Hotel after one of my speeches, but I can't be certain the driver intended to hit me. I don't know. It was dark. I didn't see the driver and couldn't even identify the car."

"So, nobody threatened you at the fundraiser party?" asked the detective.

"No. Senator Dobbins scowled at me and Representative Rossman lectured me, chastising me for my alleged attack on our political system, but neither one of them verbally or physically threatened me in any way. A number of people don't like my ideas, and, therefore, me. Many of them I can't even identify, but I'm not aware of any actual voiced threats, although Senator Dobbins told me recently that my 'continued efforts will lead to no good.'"

"That may mean something, although it's definitely open to interpretation," said Detective Thomas. "I think that's all I need to ask you today. You rest and my team will continue our work while you heal. I'll let you and your husband know what we learn as the investigation progresses."

"Thank you, Detective. We appreciate the work of you and your team," Brad said. Annalisa closed her eyes as Detective Thomas left the room.

As Annalisa slept and Brad dozed next to her, a man dressed in a heavy dark coat and ski hat unlocked the back door to their home. He carried a small duffel bag over his right shoulder and easily entered the house without damaging the lock. He methodically moved from room to room, analyzing the décor and furniture layouts without touching any objects. Though anyone looking in from the outside might suspect the man was an interior designer planning an update to their home, he was not interested in redecorating the rooms.

After examining all rooms other than bathrooms, he returned to the living room and placed his bag on the couch. Opening it, he removed a tiny camera with a built-in microphone. He carefully placed it in the room to be hidden from view, yet capable of capturing all activity in the area of the couch. He appeared to have an endless supply of cameras as he moved throughout the house, placing a camera in each room so that no scene would go unfilmed. After outfitting every room where no one would try to dust, he quietly exited through the back door, locking it so no one would realize he had entered. He surreptitiously placed cameras in several areas of the yard and on the outside of the house. After he completed the installation, he threw his now-empty duffel bag over his shoulder and walked down the sidewalk away from the house.

Two days later, Annalisa was well enough to leave the hospital and return home, but Brad was terrified that without the protection of the policeman at their door that her life would continue to be in danger. He felt compelled not to leave her side, but he had to work and so did she. Annalisa had canceled her speaking engagements for the next week and Brad had taken a week's vacation, but then what? If he could not be there to protect her, then he would hire a bodyguard to travel with her and oversee the preparation of her meals when she stayed at hotels and ate out at local restaurants. If it was the last action he took, he would ensure no one would ever poison Annalisa again.

On her third day home, and after waking up from a now-routine afternoon nap, Annalisa sat down on the couch with a new novel to escape into for the rest of the afternoon. She was passionate about reading; it was her favorite pastime. There was always a partially read book lying on her nightstand. Brad joined her on the couch and gently lifted the book from her hands.

"Annie, soon you'll be fully recovered and we'll both return to work, which for you means significant travel. Whoever attempted to poison you is likely to make the attempt again. It may be by poison or it may be by some other fatal method. I can protect you when we're both home, particularly now that we're vigilant, but you're entirely vulnerable to attack when you're on the road. I want us to retain the services of a bodyguard who can travel with you to watch over you and especially guard over the preparation of your meals in public places."

"I don't know about that. I admit I'm afraid for my life, but am I really just letting the perpetrator win to an extent if I change my entire life? A bodyguard sounds expensive and I'm not certain I want someone trailing behind me all the time."

"I don't care how much it costs, if it means you'll be safe. The peace of mind it will bring me is worth whatever is the charge. As for him trailing behind you, he'll blend into the crowd with your speech attendees and he'll be in restaurant kitchens while you're in the dining rooms. He won't be following you around as if he were your five-year-old child," Brad assured her.

"If it can actually be arranged as you describe, then I believe the arrangement is tenable. How do you intend to find this bodyguard, Brad?"

"I'm looking for a former athlete who is strong, responsible and intelligent. I have some contacts that may be able to connect me with some viable prospects. Don't you worry about that—I'll take care of the hiring process. When I believe I've found the right candidate, I will introduce you to him and you can decide if he's right for you."

"Fine." Annalisa retrieved her book from Brad and leaned back on the couch. She opened the novel, signaling to Brad that the discussion was at its end. Brad moved to the desk where he flipped open his laptop and began typing. The continual rhythm of the movement of the keys was hypnotizing to Annalisa and she soon fell asleep. An hour later, Annalisa started screaming in her sleep. Brad rushed over to her and held her in his arms. She immediately woke up, visibly shaken, and spoke.

"A car just drove through the front of our house and ran me over. There was blood everywhere and I knew I was dying. I could barely breathe. When are these nightmares going to end?"

# *Chapter Six*

The next day, Detective Thomas called the Vermeers and asked to come to their home to update them on the investigation. They immediately invited her over and soon the three of them were sitting at the dining room table poring over documents in Detective Thomas's file.

"Prior to discussing specifics, I want you to know we don't know who put the poisonous berries on your cheesecake," said Detective Thomas.

"OK. What do you know?" asked Annalisa.

"We know you were the only person targeted by our assailant. None of the other guests or any of the hotel staff fell ill that evening with any of the symptoms you experienced. Now it's possible there were one or more other persons targeted who didn't eat their cheesecake, meaning they didn't ingest the poison, but there's such a slim likelihood of this that we've eliminated it as a reasonable possibility."

"So, someone specifically wants Annie dead," concluded Brad.

"Yes, we think that was the assailant's goal, as your wife ingested enough toxin to kill her. Had you not been there to intervene and seek treatment in the emergency room, she would have eventually died."

"Thank you, dear," said Annalisa gratefully as she turned to look at Brad. Brad smiled back.

"All fingerprints we found that we were able to match to one of our databases belonged to people who were supposed to be at the dinner. Granted, the majority of the fingerprints we isolated at the hotel weren't in any database, so we couldn't match them to any particular persons. However, at least those we did match resulted in us not finding anyone with a history of violent criminal offenses."

"It sounds as though the person who tried to kill Annie is either new at this or hasn't previously been caught," suggested Brad.

"Yes, that's correct," said Detective Thomas. "We don't suspect a hit man or woman, although we understand a hired gun would likely wear gloves and would leave no fingerprints, although a gloved person in the midst of a formal indoor party would stand out. Someone would have mentioned in their interview that they observed a person wearing gloves. We specifically asked each person if they noticed anyone at the party wearing any type of glove, formal or otherwise, and 'no' was the answer each time."

"While I have no proof to support my position, I believe the person who tried to kill me is personally threatened by my advocacy and is, therefore, a politician," said Annalisa.

"That's a reasonable assertion, Ms. Vermeer. "A significant number of politicians were at the dinner," agreed Detective Thomas.

"Did you interview each person who was there that night?" asked Annalisa.

"Yes, we did. There were approximately 600 guests, plus all the staff, so it took a few days to locate each person and conduct a thorough interview. While I'm convinced we interviewed the assailant, there was no interview that proved that."

"What about the surveillance cameras in the hotel? Did you see any suspicious activity?" asked Brad.

"Our department's lead computer technician watched about ten hours of recordings from fourteen cameras in the ballroom and kitchen, plus some of the cameras observing major ingress and egress areas of the hotel, but saw no activity connected to the poisoning. We don't believe the assailant added the berries to the cherries in the kitchen. We had a fairly clear view of the trays of cheesecake at all times, and no person even approached the trays until the servers carried them into the ballroom. We think the assailant added them once they were placed at your seat because it was the only surefire method for ensuring the berries were served to you. The lights in the ballroom were quite dim at the time the cheesecake was served because of the dancing. So, between the darkness and the constantly moving crowd, the cameras didn't capture the assailant lacing the cherries," explained Detective Thomas.

"You're telling us that despite hundreds of people being in the room and surveillance cameras being everywhere, someone was able to completely hide the act of adding berries to the cherries on Annie's cheesecake? That's unbelievable!" exclaimed Brad. He slammed his fist down on the table and stood up, expressing his anger and frustration at the dead end reached by the police department. He began pacing around the table. Annalisa was quick to respond.

"Brad, calm down. The detective and her team have been doing the best they can. You were there. The ballroom was teeming with people, and it was a challenge most of the time to move any distance without bumping into someone. It's not fair to expect the police to see what we probably wouldn't have seen if we were ten feet away from my plate."

"Mr. Vermeer, I understand your frustration. It's difficult to understand how, with so many people in the room, nobody saw the cheesecake being tampered with," said Detective Thomas.

"I apologize, Detective. I didn't mean to take my anger out on you. Annie is right—you're doing the best you can and I appreciate it," Brad stated contritely.

"Thank you, Mr. Vermeer," said Detective Thomas. "This investigation will remain open until it is solved, but unless new evidence comes forth, I don't expect a resolution. I don't wish to scare you, Ms. Vermeer, but it's possible that the person may attempt to harm you again. I ask that you be cautious and that you contact me immediately if you feel threatened in any way. Even if you believe a comment or action by someone doesn't rise to a level you feel merits notifying me, it may be just the clue that breaks this case wide open."

"I understand, and will contact you if I'm faced with any suspicious activity. I do believe the person will attack me again, so I take this matter very seriously and am, frankly, quite scared," Annalisa admitted.

"As for being cautious," said Brad, "we intend to hire a bodyguard who will oversee the preparation of Annie's food in restaurants. That way, there will be no further attempts at poisoning her."

"That should provide you with a sense of security," said Detective Thomas. "Well, I will be going now, but do call me if there are any new developments in your future contacts with others."

By the time Brad returned to work and Annalisa resumed her speaking engagements, they had hired Michael Savannah to act as Annalisa's bodyguard. Michael was a former college all-star wrestler who was solidly built with strong and flexible muscles. Michael had graduated from college the previous December, but, as with so many other recent college graduates, had not yet found employment in his chosen field. He was grateful for the part-time and temporary position of watching over Annalisa. Brad was confident the assailant would think twice about approaching Annalisa with Michael nearby.

A week later, Brad and Annalisa ventured out of their home for the first time to dine at a local restaurant. In general, Brad found it more difficult than he expected to arrange for Michael to oversee the preparation of Annalisa's food. Restaurant management was less than enamored with permitting Michael's intrusion into the kitchen, and his less than trustful eye watching the every move of the large staff that came in contact with Annalisa's meal. In contrast, it had been easy to arrange things when Annalisa was out of town, as she incorporated Michael into her speaking engagement contracts with the hotels.

That evening, they were dining at one of their favorite venues, where, over the years, they had come to know the owner quite well. The owner's familiarity with and fondness for Annalisa fostered his openness to Michael's duties, and, unlike most other restaurants Brad had contacted, he welcomed Michael into the kitchen. Brad and Annalisa had always felt relaxed there and found it the appropriate eatery for their first public meal since the poisoning. After the three of them approached the hostess podium, Michael was escorted into the kitchen by a waiter and the hostess seated Brad and Annalisa at their table. Almost immediately after sitting down, Annalisa heard her name being called out.

"Ms. Vermeer."

Annalisa and Brad turned toward the voice and spotted two familiar faces seated at the next table. Jennifer Hampton and Daphne Wagner, tablemates at the fundraiser dinner, were seated with three other women.

"Hello, Mr. and Ms. Vermeer," said Ms. Hampton.

"Hi, Ms. Hampton and Ms. Wagner," replied Annalisa. Brad nodded toward the women.

"It's so good to see you, Ms. Vermeer, and you look quite well," said Ms. Hampton. "I was horrified to hear that someone at the fundraiser poisoned you. What an unbelievable act that was, and I'm so sorry you both had to endure the experience."

"Thank you, Ms. Hampton. I appreciate your concern. It was certainly a life-changing experience," said Annalisa.

"Are you fully recovered now, Ms. Vermeer?" asked Ms. Wagner.

"Yes, I'm fine now and have regained both my energy and strength," said Annalisa.

"Let me introduce you to some women whom I believe you haven't met," said Ms. Wagner. "This is Dolores Williams, Genevieve Holmes and Marian Dobbins. Ladies, this is Annalisa Vermeer and her husband, Brad. Ms. Vermeer is the person you've heard about who is advocating major political change in this country."

"It's a pleasure to meet you both," said Ms. Holmes as she smiled at Annalisa and Brad.

"I'm pleased to meet you as well," added Ms. Williams.

Annalisa and Brad exchanged their pleasantries and noticed Ms. Dobbins remained silent. Feeling a bit uncomfortable with her silence, Annalisa addressed the women as a group.

"Are you ladies celebrating a special occasion tonight?"

"No, this is actually a working dinner. We are all wives of senators and so we belong to an organization called 'ASSIST.' Have you heard of it?" asked Ms. Hampton.

"No, I haven't. Please tell us about it," requested Annalisa.

"ASSIST is the acronym for 'Advocative Senators' Spouses Initiating Success Together.' Obviously, all the members are spouses of senators, although the tradition is that only wives, not husbands, of senators join the organization. We advocate for and initiate efforts that benefit persons who are essentially overlooked in society, such as the poor, the lonely, those with no support system in place in their lives and the homeless. We operate a number of different programs that assist various people and we have made great strides in some areas, but are stumbling in others," explained Ms. Hampton.

"So, where are you stumbling?" asked Annalisa with great interest.

"The main stumbling block we are trying to overcome is how to collect larger donations for our program that gives college scholarships to foster children. Most foster children have little, if any, adult support system once they age out of the foster care system. There are exceptions to this, as there are several state programs and various nonprofit organizations throughout this country sponsoring outstanding and comprehensive initiatives to assist foster children after they graduate from high school. Some are highly successful at providing not only scholarships for college, but also the adult mentoring that is so necessary to those young adults. On a much smaller scale, our group has been trying to emulate these larger and successful programs. We've sponsored a few fundraisers, but the needs are so great and the fundraisers have netted inadequate funds to make a substantial difference," explained Ms. Wagner.

Brad's interest immediately piqued and he chimed in, speaking for the first time since the women began their conversation. "I once wrote an article on the frustration felt by foster children once they reach the legal age of majority and are legally abandoned. Society believes these foster kids can stand on their own and be successful, but the reality is that parents of nonfoster children seldom stop exercising their parental responsibilities and giving their support when their children reach age eighteen or graduate from high school. Eighteen-year-olds still need adult guidance, emotional and financial support and ongoing attention. This is missing for most foster children, and the majority of them consequently feel lost. I agree there are some states and nonprofits sponsoring excellent initiatives that assist foster children, sometimes up to age twenty-one, in relation to college and other aspects of life, but the number of foster children needing the assistance is far greater than these existing initiatives can help."

Passion filled Brad's voice as he explained the dilemma. He clearly had empathy for the young adults' quandary in not knowing where to turn for guidance when they still needed it. They were lost and Brad had a complete grasp of their situation. The women found it quite touching. Annalisa's eyes were moist, but she sat silent.

"Well put, Mr. Vermeer. The problem is we continually need funds coming in for these scholarships. College is expensive and we want to support each child for his or her full four years, yet we want to support new children entering the program as well. There simply are not enough funds to meet our goals," said Ms. Holmes with frustration in her voice.

"I think I can help, if you're willing to accept assistance from a wife who isn't married to a senator," Annalisa said with a chuckle.

"What do you have in mind?" asked Ms. Williams.

"As some of you know, I speak throughout the country to audiences who purchase tickets. I could put a line item on the online ticket order form for an optional donation to your program for scholarships. When the purchaser pays for the speaking engagement, he or she can include an additional amount as a donation for the scholarships. This would be an ongoing donation program that would reach significant numbers of people all over the country. Would you be open to me trying this?" offered Annalisa.

Initially, the ASSIST women were silent, as they let the highly generous offer of assistance sink in. Ms. Wagner looked at the other women and turned to Annalisa as she spoke.

"Ms. Vermeer, we appreciate your kind offer, but we will need to discuss it more thoroughly among us board members before we can respond. Do you mind giving us a few minutes while we talk?"

"Not at all. Brad and I haven't even ordered yet, so we'll enjoy our meal and you can contact me at your convenience."

Brad and Annalisa slipped into their own conversation and relaxed as they ate. At that moment, Annalisa felt for the first time since her poisoning that her life was normal again, at least as normal as her life could be. She sensed an internal calm, despite knowing at any time another attempt could be made on her life. Somehow, those fears were pushed away, possibly because she and Brad were in a familiar and safe environment.

Periodically, Annalisa would glance in the women's direction and notice that at times the conversation appeared heated. She could not help feeling she was the cause of the conflict, given that Ms. Dobbins, who had a stern look on her face, appeared to be chastising the others, probably about them merely considering that Annalisa be associated with one of their programs.

As Brad and Annalisa rose from their seats to leave, Ms. Hampton asked them to come over to the women's table.

"Ms. Vermeer, we've given your very generous offer careful consideration and have decided to accept," Ms. Hampton said gratefully. "Thank you for your willingness to market our program and solicit funds through your ticket sales."

"You are welcome, ladies," said Annalisa. "I will need some written description of the scholarship program that I can add to my website so that readers understand the nature and purpose of the program. I may even set it up so that a donation can be made directly on the website without purchasing a ticket. That will increase the number of people making donations because not everyone who visits my website is in a position to attend one of my speaking engagements."

"Certainly, Ms. Vermeer. I will e-mail you a copy of the brochure we use for the program in our current solicitation campaigns," responded Ms. Wagner.

Brad and Annalisa left the women, who, with the exception of Ms. Dobbins, appeared pleased that they had more than accomplished the goals for their dinner meeting.

"Annie, it's a wonderful idea to garner financial support for the scholarships through your website and ticket sales," Brad said.

"Thanks, but I can't take full credit for suggesting the idea," Annalisa said. "I was motivated to help based upon your comment that eighteen-year-olds still need adult assistance both emotionally and financially. It made me think about just how much I still relied upon my parents after I was eighteen, and how they willingly continued to be the same parents for me that they were when I was a minor. There's no magical transformation that occurs on a person's eighteenth birthday or graduation from high school to cause them to become totally self-sufficient."

"I completely agree. The percentage of foster children who graduate from high school and immediately enter college is quite small. Two major causes are lack of finances and lack of adult support in all the aspects of researching colleges and completing the involved application process," said Brad.

"The more I think about this, the more enthusiastic I become," said Annalisa, with giddiness in her voice. "As soon as I receive the brochure from Ms. Wagner, I'll add the donation option to my website and ticket order form. I want to start collecting donations immediately."

"This will be good for you too," said Brad. "It will give you a positive outlet for your energies, along with your work. It'll also help get your thoughts off the attempt on your life."

"I do need that right now," conceded Annalisa, "but I also have to be vigilant and make note of any irregularity that appears in my routine. Detective Thomas is correct—the person who tried to kill me may attempt it again or may slip up and show his or her cards inadvertently."

As they walked toward their car, a few miles away a person intently stared at a computer monitor. Across the screen there were scenes of the activity of Annalisa and Brad in their home earlier that day. As the viewer pushed keys on a keyboard, the view shifted from room to room and the prerecorded words spoken by Brad and Annalisa accompanied their actions.

# *Chapter Seven*

On March 27, as the ASSIST members chatted in informal groups throughout the library room of a local literary club where Jennifer Hampton was a member, Ms. Hampton moved to the podium. "Ladies, please find a seat so we can begin our meeting." The women complied, quickly filing down the rows of chairs and silencing themselves as they faced Ms. Hampton.

"Welcome to tonight's ASSIST meeting, where the first order of business is to select the person who will be honored by our group at our Annual Honoree event in six weeks. I would like to make the first nomination in favor of Annalisa Vermeer, who has collected more than $15,000 in the last month for our foster children college scholarship program. This is the largest amount we have ever received for this program in any given year, and she has only been receiving donations for four weeks. This is monumental. In addition, she has agreed to continue to be the ambassador for foster kids who want to attend college, which means we will be able to assist more children for hopefully many years to come. Since Ms. Vermeer is single-handedly spearheading this effort, our group is free to devote time, energy and resources to other projects that are also near and dear to our hearts. Are there any other nominations?"

Ms. Dobbins rose from her chair and turned toward the group.

"Yes, I'd like to nominate Patty Witt, who's not only a member of our group, but has also worked tirelessly all year, single-handedly, to create large, gorgeous and thick quilts that are given to countless homeless people. Patty's quilts give them warmth and comfort whether they're sleeping in a shelter or out slumbering on a sidewalk. Her efforts have made the difference between life and death in some cases." As she glanced at the other women in search of support, she sat back down.

"Yes, Marian," Ms. Hampton stated, "Patty's outstanding quilting talents have made a significant difference in the lives of many. Are there any other nominations?" As she surveyed the room, everyone was silent. "In that case, I now open the floor to discussion on the two nominations. Does anyone wish to comment on either Ms. Vermeer or Patty?"

Ms. Wagner raised her hand.

"Yes, Daphne?" asked Ms. Hampton.

"I know Patty very well and she is a gem." Ms. Wagner extended her hand and arm toward Ms. Witt to direct the group's focus to Ms. Witt, who was sitting near the back of the room and smiling in appreciation at Ms. Wagner's comment. "Year in and year out she continues her mission under our auspices to bring warmth to those who, for various reasons, are unable to maintain a permanent residence of their own. Patty is very deserving of every honor, but I believe this year we should honor Ms. Vermeer. We honored Patty two years ago for her contributions, and it seems to me we should recognize Ms. Vermeer as a new contributor. She has brought in more money for the college scholarships than we could hope to do on our own in an entire year."

As Ms. Wagner sat down, Ms. Witt rose, maintaining her smile. She looked around at the other women. "You ladies are my friends and I appreciate the nomination you made on my behalf, Marian. I sew and gift quilts because it makes me feel I am contributing to improving society, one person at a time. It is very difficult for one person to change the world, but I believe I am making a change. As Daphne said, you honored my work two years ago, and I don't need to be honored again this year to know you all appreciate what I'm doing.

"Ms. Vermeer is making a bigger change in the world than I am. I help only those who receive one of my quilts, and my help lasts only as long as the quilt lasts, which will wear out over time. When a foster child graduates from college as the result of Ms. Vermeer's efforts, that child will become a contributing member of society. The domino effect will then kick in as that child, now an adult, affects the lives of others in a positive fashion. While I accept the nomination and am honored by it, I ask that you all vote in favor of Ms. Vermeer. I know I will." Ms. Witt smiled at those around her and sat down.

Ms. Dobbins again rose, tall and erect, but this time she walked to the podium where Ms. Hampton politely stepped aside. "Patty," stated Ms. Dobbins as she perused the audience, "you are too kind and self-effacing. You deserve this honor and I see no significance in the fact that you received our award two years ago. You have continued your mission, and this honor relates to what you have accomplished this year. What transpired two years ago is irrelevant to our actions this year.

"*In addition*, I request you withdraw your nomination of Ms. Vermeer, Jennifer, because she is a thorn in our sides and her ultimate goal is to destroy our way of life. The good she is bringing about from raising scholarship funds is far outweighed by the damage she is doing to our overall society. She is not deserving of our honor, correct ladies?"

As Ms. Dobbins walked away from the podium, the silent audience began to buzz. Rather than attempt to stymie the unstructured debate, Ms. Hampton instead announced there would be a fifteen-minute break, after which a vote would be taken to select the Honoree. Ms. Hampton walked over to Ms. Witt to thank her for her humility and graciousness.

As the women scattered to refill their cups with coffee or tea and their plates with appetizers, Ms. Dobbins mingled among them, lobbying for her position. Some were responsive in joining her bandwagon while others were in Ms. Hampton's camp. Those in support of Ms. Vermeer thought her opinions regarding the legislature and political parties were irrelevant to her fundraising efforts—efforts that unequivocally would benefit many foster children who were deserving of a college education. When Ms. Hampton recalled the meeting to order, she asked if there was anyone else who wanted to add to the discussion prior to the vote. One hand was raised and it belonged to Dolores Williams, who until then had remained silent. Ms. Hampton acknowledged her to take the floor.

"With all due respect to Ms. Vermeer's successful fundraising efforts, I completely agree with Marian in that Ms. Vermeer is advocating the destruction of our husbands' careers and our financial future. We are all part of a family of senators and Ms. Vermeer is an outside threat to our family. If we honor her for fundraising, then I believe we are also sending a message that we support her *in toto*. I, for one, will not do that to my husband."

Ms. Williams' comments sparked another buzz, only this time Ms. Hampton was quick to quell it. "Ladies," asserted Ms. Hampton, "it is now time to vote, as we have debated this issue long enough. Given the divisive nature of this matter, I am calling for a written vote by secret ballot, which I prepared during our brief recess. Daphne is handing out the ballots now, which are just blank one-half sheets of paper. Please write either Patty's name or Ms. Vermeer's name on your ballot, fold it in quarters and place it in the basket next to the podium. When all the votes are in, our treasurer, Genevieve Holmes, will count them and declare this year's Honoree."

Within a few minutes, all the votes were cast. After finishing her count, Ms. Holmes announced Annalisa was this year's Honoree by a margin of two to one, which she attributed to the encouragement by Ms. Witt to vote for the opponent. Noting the varying facial expressions in the room, Ms. Hampton concluded it was best to immediately move on to the next matter of business. "Let's now discuss the status of our canned food collections for the upcoming fall season since many of us will be away from DC in July and August."

# *Chapter Eight*

"Annie, Jennifer Hampton is on the phone for you," said Brad as he handed her the telephone.

"Hello, Ms. Hampton. How are you?"

"Please call me Jennifer. I'm fine, thanks for asking. I'm calling to inform you that ASSIST has voted you as our Annual Honoree for your outstanding efforts in raising funds at your events for scholarships."

For a moment, Annalisa was silent, unaware that there was an Annual Honoree. It was hard for her to imagine that a group of senators' spouses would consider her for any honor, given the disregard in which most of them held her.

"Well, Jennifer, thank you," Annalisa said. "I am most touched by the recognition your organization is bestowing upon me. I must admit I'm taken aback by the decision, however, given the pushback from many of the spouses about me and my thinking."

"I admit, Ms. Vermeer, there was some strife and debate after I nominated you," said Ms. Hampton. "However, ultimately many of the women who questioned the wisdom of the nomination came around. They understood that acknowledging and honoring you for raising scholarship money for foster children didn't mean we agreed with you on your other views. Even the other nominee for the award voted for you and encouraged the other members to honor you with their votes."

"Please call me Annalisa, Jennifer. It was certainly generous of the other nominee to support me as she did. I don't know what else to say, but I am most honored and I accept."

"Great!" said Ms. Hampton. "Now the only consideration is that the Annual Honoree event is in just six weeks. I know you travel a lot for your work, so I'm hoping your schedule will permit you to attend, as that is obviously a requirement of being the Annual Honoree. The event is on Saturday, May 10, at 6:30 p.m. in the Gathering Room at the DC Women's Literary Club. Your husband is also invited. Are you able to attend?"

"Let me just check my schedule. I generally don't travel on the weekends, so the date should work." Annalisa reviewed May's dates and found the tenth to be clear. "Jennifer, we are available that night and will be happy to attend. Do I need to prepare any type of an acceptance speech?"

"Yes, but nothing like you normally do. We're just looking for a two- or three-minute talk about your fundraising efforts and what it means to you to be helping these foster kids to attend college. Other than that, there will be a delicious dinner, interesting and fun conversation and a quartet that will perform after the dinner and presentation. I think you and your husband will enjoy yourselves very much."

"Thanks again, Jennifer. I look forward to attending and seeing you and the other members. Good-bye."

"You can expect a formal invitation in the mail shortly. Good-bye, Annalisa."

They hung up. Brad looked at Annalisa with a sly grin. "While I only heard your side of the conversation, I can tell you've received some type of an award from ASSIST. Quite amazing. I presume it's for your fundraising for college scholarships?"

"Yes, amazingly it is. I can't believe it. To think more than half the members of ASSIST actually voted for me over anyone else is most gratifying. They decided to look past their personal feelings about me as an advocate and focus instead on how my actions help benefit kids. I'm as surprised by their actions as they are by mine. We have mutually impressed the other."

"Congratulations, Annie. I wonder how some of their spouses reacted when they heard the news. Maybe they'll follow their mates' lead and come around to accepting you, if not for all your actions, then at least for those that are unrelated to your advocacy. After all, you are human and not the monster a few members have made you out to be."

Annalisa laughed heartily as she pictured herself as a monster on the prowl on Capitol Hill. "Yes, can you picture me stomping into offices, tearing them apart and chasing the legislators out into the hallways?" She kept laughing as she spoke, aware that her imaginary picture may not be that much different from what some legislators envisioned her to be, metaphorically speaking at least.

"Speaking of monsters," Brad said, shifting into a more somber mood, "I'll call Michael tomorrow to book his bodyguard services for that night in case any monster decides it's a good night to attack you."

"Fine, Brad. How long are we going to employ him to guard over my food at public functions? It's been weeks since I was poisoned and no further attempts have been made on my life. Plus, Michael may be able to safeguard my food, but there are other ways to kill someone, and Michael can't protect against all of them."

"You're arguing against yourself," Brad said. "You question whether I should stop calling Michael to monitor your food, yet your point that food may not be the only avenue to harm you makes me want to hire him to follow not just your food, but your every move as well. It's likely no one's poisoned your food because Michael is there. I love you and I want to keep you healthy and safe. Until the police have caught the person who poisoned you, please indulge me and permit Michael to observe your food being prepared and served."

"You're right, Brad. Michael can continue to watch over my food, but I hope that Detectives Thomas and Garza solve the mystery soon so I can move on with my life, free of death threats and Michael's observing eye."

The next day Annalisa spoke to a group of approximately 300 people at a local DC hotel. As discreetly as possible, Edward Hawthorne intently noted each word spoken from a rear corner of the auditorium. He effortlessly recorded each speech, as if he were a court reporter. Annalisa never noticed his presence, although the people sitting nearby often found his actions unusual, yet also intriguing as they imagined him to be a reporter for a publication spotlighting Annalisa.

Later that day, Edward walked through Senator Dobbins' open office door and sat down. "Senator, I attended Ms. Vermeer's speech this morning and forwarded you a copy of the content. Did you receive it?"

"Yes, Edward, I did, although I haven't yet had an opportunity to read it. Are there any particular statements she made of special importance?"

"No, Senator. In fact, she says basically the same thing in each of her speeches. Yes, she does vary the examples or the presentation of her points from speech to speech, but her points themselves don't change. She consistently advocates for eliminating political parties and changing the job description of legislative bodies at all levels of government.

"To be honest with you, I see no point in me attending any more of her speeches because I'm not going to learn anything new. She simply isn't going to advocate terrorism or violent anarchy, as you had anticipated. She doesn't even dabble in suggesting illegal activity of any sort and I'm convinced she never will. It's a waste of your time and mine to expect to discredit or arrest her based upon the content of her speeches."

"That is problematic, Edward," Senator Dobbins said. "Ms. Vermeer must be dealt with effectively and immediately if her mouth is to be shut permanently on these subjects of which she is so fond. Her quest to destroy time-honored traditions and expectations must be stopped."

"I understand, Senator, but I believe you'll have to use another approach to accomplish your goal. I will continue to attend her speeches if you want me to, but I think it's pointless."

"I agree, Edward," said Senator Dobbins. "You've been collecting content for weeks and you're correct that it's repetitive, reprehensible and consistently ridiculous, but not illegal. There's no reason for you to continue this particular approach. I'll let you know later what your next assignment will be in this regard. I need some time to think and to consult with my colleagues."

"Fine, sir, I will await your call." As Edward left the office, Senator Dobbins picked up his telephone and dialed. He spoke with great seriousness to the person on the other end.

"This isn't working. Ms. Vermeer is a threat, but not to the extent we can have her arrested. Edward has attended countless speeches and she's not advocating terrorism or anarchy, so her free speech allows her free reign in walking all over us."

"That is most disturbing, Sid, but it's as I expected." The voice was that of Sylvia Rossman. "I've taken another tack precisely because I never believed she could be destroyed by her words. She's too smart to publicly incriminate herself. I'm working to destroy her on a personal level where caution isn't foremost in her mind."

"What are you doing, Sylvia?" asked Senator Dobbins.

"Sid, for now, at least, I'd prefer to keep that to myself. It's best if no eyes or ears are privy to my plan, including yours."

"Fine, Sylvia, but you'd better work fast because my sources tell me her advocacy is gaining momentum in the Midwest and California. There may be little notice of what occurs in Omaha, but once the media latches onto the grassroots efforts in California, Ms.

Vermeer will quickly be thrust into the national spotlight. Even my considerable power isn't enough to quell the voices in California. The only way to resolve this situation is to abruptly silence Ms. Vermeer. Once she's silenced, her minions will fall by the wayside."

"Sid, my tack takes time, and implementing it is in part based on opportunity, but I'm doing what I can to accomplish my purposes sooner rather than later. I need to get to a meeting now, but I'll let you know if my plan works." Without waiting for a response, Representative Rossman hung up.

# *Chapter Nine*

Annalisa traveled the rest of the week, giving speeches in Phoenix, Los Angeles and San Jose. She also made a quick stop in Omaha to meet informally with the grassroots organization trying to implement her ideas at the local level. She felt her ideas were well received in the West and looked forward to her speaking engagements there. The only negative was that Michael traveled with her to observe the preparation and serving of her food. She appreciated Michael's efforts and his care, but his presence was still disconcerting and was wearing thin after all these weeks. Even though his watchful eye was for her benefit, the watching made her uncomfortable.

After her speech at The Fairmont in San Jose, Annalisa and Michael went to the main dining room for dinner. Michael waited until Annalisa ordered her meal and then retreated to the kitchen to observe. The staff at the hotel was most gracious in all respects and cooperated fully with Michael's viewing of the cooking and serving process. Annalisa ordered a roasted chicken breast, thereby making Michael's job easier, as there were no sauces involved. As Annalisa enjoyed her meal, a man with an affable smile approached. He apologized for interrupting her dinner, but explained he wanted to introduce himself, compliment her on her speechmaking skills and express his agreement with her message.

"My name is Glenn Sanders," he said, "and I've been a fan of yours for quite some time."

Annalisa smiled back and chuckled. "Please don't take offense at my laugh, but I've never had anyone say they were my fan. It brings to mind celebrity status, and I don't think of myself as a celebrity in any sense. However, I appreciate the compliment and your support of my message even more so."

"May I sit down with you while you finish your meal? I would very much like to give you some ideas I've come up with that fit in with your recommendations for political change," explained Mr. Sanders.

"Of course you may, Mr. Sanders. After all, I'd never want to push away a fan." Annalisa chuckled again and Mr. Sanders sat down in the chair directly across from her.

"Thanks," he said. "I'm particularly intrigued by the concept of eliminating lobbyists from the political system. In my opinion, PACs exist to enable legalized bribery. Why should a company or an organization have more access to the ear of politicians than an individual citizen?"

"If an individual citizen contacts his or her senator or representative, it's highly unlikely the citizen will ever have the ear of the legislator," said Annalisa. "A low-level staff member answers the telephone and the citizen is almost always told the legislator isn't there or available. Despite the citizen asking to leave a message for the legislator to personally return the call, generally the call is returned by another staff member, if at all. The reason usually given is that there's not enough time in the day for a legislator to talk to every constituent who calls, not if the legislator is expected to get any work done."

"Ms. Vermeer," said Mr. Sanders, "I'd argue that a substantial part of the legislator's work is listening to the constituents."

"Agreed, Mr. Sanders. Now shifting to the PACs and other lobbyists, it's routine for a legislator to meet directly with PAC representatives and individual lobbyists unaffiliated with a PAC. Often legislators give their ear to what benefits the sponsors of the PACs and lobbyists, which is often the antithesis of the best interests of the legislator's constituents."

Annalisa and Mr. Sanders then spoke at length about lobbyists and other aspects of her message until after she had finished her meal. Meanwhile, due to Annalisa's desire not to be watched constantly, Michael had, as usual, left the restaurant after her entire meal was served.

"Well, Mr. Sanders, I've enjoyed discussing these matters with you, and it was pleasant to have your company during dinner since I almost always eat alone when I'm on the road."

"It was entirely my pleasure, Ms. Vermeer, as I've watched you from afar without being in a position to share my opinions regarding your message. It was great to bounce these points around with you."

"It was my pleasure too, but I'm flying home early tomorrow morning, so I should go to my room now to get some sleep. Mr. Sanders, it was nice to meet you and I look forward to seeing you again another time."

"I'll walk with you to the elevator because I too need to get some sleep before I fly home to Sacramento at 7:00 a.m."

As they walked to the elevator, Mr. Sanders mentioned how many people in northern California, and in particular the Silicon Valley area, had embraced her concepts, analysis and solutions. This enthusiasm had brought people together into advocacy groups and caught the media's attention.

"I have copies of articles written by various northern California newspapers in my room," said Mr. Sanders as they got in the elevator and it climbed upward. "Would you like to see them before you go to your room?"

"I don't know," said Annalisa, with tiredness in her voice. "It's getting late and, as I said, I have an early day tomorrow."

"I understand, and I don't want to be construed as pushy, but I doubt you can see these articles online any longer. I've collected them over the last few months and some of the publications don't maintain all their articles online for more than a few weeks. It really won't take long."

"OK, fine, but I can only stay for a few minutes. What floor are you on?" asked Annalisa.

"The twentieth floor—all the way to the top. It has a great view of the city."

"I thought I had a great room when they put me on the twelfth floor, but your view has to be much nicer," said Annalisa.

"In a minute you'll see the difference, Ms. Vermeer."

The elevator opened and Annalisa followed Mr. Sanders down the hall toward his room. When he opened the door, Annalisa saw his room offered more than just a better view than her room. He had a large suite with an expansive living room and large windows revealing an exquisite view of the city. Once inside, she saw his bedroom was a separate room with a sprawling king bed—certainly more luxurious than her standard room with the queen-sized bed placed in the same room as the chair and television.

Annalisa moved toward the windows to admire the city's skyline. "Wow, this view is absolutely gorgeous, especially at night with all the buildings lit. It's just not the same on the twelfth floor."

Mr. Sanders laughed. "Some things are worth the extra money. Does the inside of your room look like this?" he asked, sweeping his right arm expansively to direct her eyes throughout the room.

She laughed as she explained her room did not compare to his. He offered a tour, which she accepted, thinking she was not likely to see a room like this in the near future. As they walked into the bedroom, she noticed a chair and coffee table in addition to the bed. She also saw a marble bathroom with a separate walk-in shower and bathtub.

"Please have a seat and I'll get the articles out of my suitcase."

As Annalisa sat in the chair, Mr. Sanders lifted a stack of papers out of his suitcase and began to lay them out on the coffee table in front of her. She leaned forward to read the one closest to her while Mr. Sanders laid the ones that did not fit on the table on the end of his bed. When he finished, he sat on the bed as she read. She was engrossed, as the journalists were enthused and embraced her advocacy. She was not used to seeing her vision so supported in newspaper articles. Mr. Sanders sat quietly as she read for about thirty minutes.

"May I get you something to drink from my room fridge?" he asked as she finished an article. She had not yet gotten through the stack sitting on the table.

Distracted, Annalisa nodded without saying a word. Mr. Sanders left the bedroom and soon returned with two wine glasses filled with what he described as a full-bodied Merlot from nearby Napa Valley. She made no response, as she was reading the next article, a story from an Omaha newspaper. She finally spoke.

"Mr. Sanders, this article isn't from a California publication. How is it that you have an article from an Omaha paper when you live in Sacramento?"

"I told you I was very interested in your ideas and the spread of them all over the Midwest and West. I simply searched online for current articles about you and either printed the article or ordered a hard copy of the newspaper from the publisher. That accounts for the monumental stack I've collected here."

"I thought you said it would only take a few minutes to show me the articles. I don't even dare look at my watch to see what time it is at this point."

"I guess I have more articles than even I realized," said Mr. Sanders. "I've collected them for a while, so I lost track of the extent of the collection. Sorry."

"No need to apologize, Mr. Sanders. I know you're simply sharing the good news with me and I appreciate it. May I use your bathroom?"

"Sure, Ms. Vermeer. Make sure you notice the extensive marble throughout." He smiled and followed her in, indicating he wanted to ensure it was clean enough for "company." After picking up a couple of shirts, he left the room, closing the door behind him. When Annalisa returned to the bedroom, she spotted a platter of cheese and crackers on the coffee table next to the stack of articles she had read.

"Where did that come from, Mr. Sanders?"

"It was delivered to me yesterday with the compliments of the hotel and I hadn't yet eaten it. I thought you might enjoy it with your wine as you read the rest of the articles." He pointed to an article lying on the bed. "Look at this one," he said. "It's from a large San Francisco paper with wide coverage and great respect from the public."

Annalisa walked over to him to look at the article, leaning against the edge of the bed as she read it. When she finished the article, she swiftly came out of the clouds and focused on her surroundings instead of on the articles. She was in the bedroom of a man she barely knew, who most definitely was not her husband, there was wine and food and they were alone. Instantly, she felt uncomfortable despite Mr. Sanders maintaining an appropriate distance from her at all times and making no verbal advances. He gave the impression that his only interest was in her reading the articles. She knew at that moment she had to leave immediately, but needed to do so with diplomatic poise.

"Mr. Sanders, I appreciate you making all these articles available to me, but it's gotten quite late and I really must leave now."

"But you haven't finished reading all the articles yet, Ms. Vermeer."

"I understand, but there are just so many of them. I simply can't take the time to read the remainder of them or I'll never be able to get up in the morning to catch my flight. Your flight is even earlier than mine and you need to get to sleep yourself. Even without reading all the articles I get the gist of it—there are journalists who are endorsing and marketing my ideas, and that pleases me immensely. Thanks again and good night," she said as she moved toward the door.

"You are welcome, Ms. Vermeer. I look forward to the next time we meet. Sweet dreams tonight." He smiled and she softly closed the door as she smiled back. She rushed to her room, not feeling able to breathe until her door was locked and she was safely inside.

When Annalisa returned home to DC, she immediately and sheepishly told Brad about her encounter with Mr. Sanders. She explained he was at all times appropriate, yet she understood she had allowed herself to be put in a compromising and potentially dangerous situation, all because she was consumed with reading journalistic public praises of her.

"Brad, I'm so embarrassed that I thought only of my vanity and my mission. How could I let common sense, discretion, propriety and safety completely escape my mind? How could it be replaced with giddy delight at being referred to as the 'one to be emulated as the fresh new voice in changing society for the better'? Forget poison—he could have killed me a dozen different ways."

"Or raped you," Brad said. "Any or all of the wine, cheese and crackers could have contained poison that you could have easily consumed without Michael's prior examination. Does Michael need to be with you every minute that you're not in your room to protect you from yourself?"

"Now I feel even worse. I'm so sorry, Brad, that I simply didn't think. No, I learned my lesson. Michael can stay in the kitchen and I'll be fine on my own. I won't go to anyone's room again—male or female—because I know I can't control the environment there."

"I'm going to count on that, Annie, so don't let us both down."

"I'll be good, I promise. I won't act foolishly and humiliate myself, or worse, put my life at risk. Let's go whip up something delicious for dinner and just relax. Clearly, it's been another taxing week and I need to eat a good meal and lounge on the couch all evening."

"Sounds good to me too," agreed Brad. "I've had a hectic week myself."

"Tell me all about it in the kitchen," Annalisa said as she strolled with Brad out of the living room. "Maybe we should go to the Newseum tomorrow and both forget about our work."

# *Chapter Ten*

It was a rare Tuesday when Annalisa did not schedule a speaking engagement, but given the events of the past week, she was happy to be home dusting furniture and vacuuming floors, sheltered from the world and from her own vulnerabilities. She was leaving the next day for a three-day jaunt to Detroit, Toledo and Cleveland where she would test the waters of the eastern portion of the Midwest. As she unloaded the dishwasher, she seriously considered reducing her speaking schedule to make this week's schedule the rule, rather than the exception. A four-day weekend may be just what she needed to pull her away from constant adversity and connect her more to home and Brad, the reality that most attracted her.

While Annalisa made their bed, the telephone rang. She saw that Brad was calling.

"Hi, Brad. How are you?"

"My article on illegal foreclosures by arrogant banks is going to be published in the next issue of our magazine, so I'm thrilled it made the cut," Brad said.

"That's fantastic news, Brad! I'm so happy for you. Haven't you had an article in each issue published this year?"

"Yes, I have. Listen, I didn't actually call to tell you about the article. I called to tell you that Spence just called me and relayed some disturbing news. One of his colleagues at the *Washington, DC Press* mentioned the paper just received an anonymous package of photos of you and a man in a hotel room at The Fairmont San Jose. There are about a dozen photos and a typed one-page explanation of who and where."

Annalisa was stunned and silent. Her time with Mr. Sanders went racing through her mind and her feelings of foolishness returned to the surface. She could not help but believe she somehow deserved this given her idiotic behavior. She had brought this disaster fully upon herself, so she willingly accepted primary blame. Finally, she responded to Brad.

"Oh, my. It was a setup. If they couldn't kill me, then they would instead kill my reputation. In fact, from their perspective, this may be a better approach. If they kill me, then I'm elevated to hero status and my words become more sacrosanct. On the other hand, if my reputation is destroyed, then my character and credibility are quashed."

"Yes, that makes sense, Annie, but despite the wine, the cheese, the bed and the man who wasn't your husband, you still weren't in the bed, you had all your clothes on and had a piece of paper in your hand with your eyes fixated on it at every moment, correct?"

"Yes, except for when he toured me around the room and when I needed to go to the bathroom, but I hope and pray there was no camera in the bathroom. I did have my clothes on, but no piece of paper in my hand. Unless the photos were doctored, it should just look like a business meeting in a bedroom. Boy, that doesn't sound good, does it?"

"No, but I understand what you mean. According to Spence, the editors are evaluating the photos and writing to determine their credibility and newsworthiness. Remember, you don't attract the media here like you do west of the Mississippi."

"I'll be so embarrassed if the *Press* publishes the photos, but I hope I'd be offered the opportunity to present my viewpoint."

"The editors at the *Press* are fair, and I'm sure you'll be contacted if they decide to publish an article with the photos. In fact, I may be contacted as the allegedly wronged husband."

"I can't believe how desperate and angry I've made someone. This setup took some real effort and money. Whoever did this to me has wealth and power. I'm going to call Detective Thomas to fill her in on this latest attempt. Even if the editors decide not to publish the photos, I was still set up, and maybe Detective Thomas can obtain fingerprints or DNA from the photos and the accompanying writing."

"Good idea. She'll appreciate the new evidence given the dead end she's reached on your poisoning case."

"OK, you try to get back to work and I'll call her now. Thanks for letting me know what might greet me when I open tomorrow's paper before I head to the airport. I'm beginning to wonder if my work is worth the danger and distress it attracts."

"Look, Annie, I want you to be safe, secure and satisfied with your work, but the goal of whoever is doing this to you is to silence you one way or the other. Stopping your work gives your detractor his or her victory and confirms that the end justifies the means. Is that what you really want?"

"No, of course not, but I don't want to die or have humiliating photos plastered in a nationally distributed newspaper either. Let me call Detective Thomas now and we can talk about this tonight. Bye."

"Bye, Annie."

Annalisa called Detective Thomas and briefly described the San Jose debacle and the fallout that was likely to occur that week. The detective agreed to immediately contact the appropriate editors at the *Press* to assess the situation and to collect what evidence she could.

* * *

Both Julia Markum and Greg Dallison accompanied Detective Thomas as she walked into the *Press*'s office. The two crime scene technicians hoped that not so many hands had touched the photos and writing as to make fingerprint and DNA analysis worthless.

A short and stocky man entered the lobby area and approached Detective Thomas. While scanning the three police officials in order to make eye contact, he smiled and introduced himself. "Good afternoon. My name is Brian Grindell and I'm the editor who received the package of photos you called about."

"Thank you for seeing us so quickly, Mr. Grindell. My name is Detective Quinn Thomas and I'm leading the investigation into the attempted murder of Annalisa Vermeer. This is Greg Dallison and Julia Markum, two of our crime scene technicians who will be collecting the photos, writing, packaging and anything else you received relative to this matter for analysis back at their lab." The group exchanged greetings, and Mr. Grindell spoke.

"Prior to you contacting me, Detective, we had already scanned the photos and writing into our computer system so we would have digital copies on hand. I have the originals in my office for you. Let's go there to discuss this matter more privately." The three police officials followed Mr. Grindell to his office where he offered each of them a seat and coffee. Accepting the seats and declining the coffee, they listened as Mr. Grindell continued.

"Let me ask you this, Detective. Do you believe there's some connection between the photos we received of Ms. Vermeer and her attempted murder? I ask this because there's no sign of any attempt to do harm to her in the photos."

"Mr. Grindell, until we examine and analyze the items you received, I can't say that there is or isn't a connection to the attempt on her life," said Detective Thomas. "What I can tell you is that according to Ms. Vermeer these photos were staged and she was encouraged to be in that hotel room based upon a false representation by the person occupying the room. These suspicious circumstances, along with them occurring only a few weeks after the attempt on her life, are sufficient to cause us to look into whether such a connection exists.

Without touching the items, can you please show us where they are?"

"Yes, certainly. They are on the table over there. No one has touched them since you called and asked us to treat them as police evidence. There are sixteen photos, all of Ms. Vermeer in the hotel room with the unidentified man. As you know, there was a one-page typed paper providing some explanation for the photos. They came in an envelope addressed to 'The Editor,' which was confusing for our mailroom staff given the large number of editors here. Given that I screen ideas for stories, the head of the mailroom delivered the package to me."

"Thank you for preserving the evidence once I called. "I'll need the names of all employees here who you're aware have touched the items so we can eliminate them as participants in this scheme. When did the *Press* receive the package?" inquired Detective Thomas.

"It came this morning. Beyond a few of us viewing it and copying it, no action had yet been taken before you called. It's only because Mr. Vermeer and Spencer Van Otter, a reporter here, are friends that the package became known to Spence. That started the ball rolling, bringing you to me."

Detective Thomas turned to Greg and Julia. "Would you please collect the evidence, packaging each item separately so I can take a look at them before we leave Mr. Grindell's office?"

"Sure, Quinn," Greg said while motioning to Julia to grab the evidence bags. As they packaged each item, Detective Thomas resumed questioning Mr. Grindell. "Was the package delivered by the US Postal Service, by another delivery service or hand-delivered by private courier?"

"Actually, I didn't pay attention to the envelope it came in other than the addressee name."

"Greg, Julia," Detective Thomas called, "would one of you please tell me how the package was delivered?"

Julia picked up the clear evidence bag that held the envelope and examined it. "There are US Postal Service stamps on it and a postmark from Forest Hills in Ward 3. The sender was smart enough to not use a postage meter or any other delivery service, as there'd be tracking information for the sender. Using the US Postal Service to send first-class mail using stamps is as anonymous as it gets. That is, unless the sender licked the stamps or the envelope, in which case we'll find DNA—and hopefully, that can be tracked," said Julia.

"Julia," Detective Thomas said, "please check the recordings from the surveillance cameras for all post offices in Forest Hills. Also see if any freestanding mailboxes in Forest Hills have cameras. We can see if anybody at the journalists' fundraiser matches up with anyone mailing a letter in Forest Hills, at least as to those for whom we have facial identification."

"Sure thing, Quinn. We'll also review the statements we took from the fundraiser attendees to see who lives in Forest Hills, although it's likely the sender was smart enough to leave his or her ward to mail the package."

"You're probably right, Julia," Detective Thomas said, "but checking for any and all connections is the prudent course of action. Greg, can I see the writing that accompanied the photos?"

Greg nodded and handed Detective Thomas the paper. She read it out loud:

> Enclosed please find photos of Annalisa Vermeer with a man who is not her husband in the man's hotel room at The Fairmont Hotel in San Jose, California, last week Thursday. Notice they are primarily in the bedroom and enjoying wine and cheese while they relax together. Possibly the speeches Ms. Vermeer gives around the country are not so much for their content as for a ruse to rendezvous with men other than her husband. How can anyone give credence to her thoughts when her actions betray her husband, showing her to be immoral, dishonest and unfaithful? The public should know who this woman

is, so please publish the photos ASAP.

"Would one of you please give me the photos now?" requested Detective Thomas.

Greg and Julia both handed clear evidence bags to Detective Thomas. The photos were innocuous enough, if one did not try to read any sinister conduct into them. Annalisa had her clothes on and so did the man, with even his tie remaining tight around his neck. There was a wine glass on the table in front of Annalisa set next to a plate of cheese and crackers, but in none of the photos was Annalisa drinking the wine or eating the food. Just as Annalisa had separately explained to Brad and to Detective Thomas, except for the short time when she was in the bathroom, she was at all times reading articles, barely paying any mind to Mr. Sanders. There was no physical contact between the two in any of the photos and most of the time they were several feet apart. Had the photos been taken anywhere other than in a hotel room, they would not gain a second glance.

"Looking at these convinces me Ms. Vermeer is being truthful when she tells me these are a setup," said Detective Thomas. "There isn't one iota of evidence to suggest these two people are intimate. It looks more like a work session in the comfort of a hotel room than a tryst."

Mr. Grindell spoke up. "My investigative skills as a journalist tell me this is an act of a desperate person determined to destroy the reputation of Ms. Vermeer, despite not having any basis for doing so. This person has waited for some skeleton to come out of her closet or for her to behave inappropriately in some fashion, but the waiting has resulted in nothing. So, with no intention of being thwarted, this person has attempted to create something from nothing, although the creation is no more than an illusion because there's no scandal in these photos."

"Does that mean, Mr. Grindell, that you'll not be printing them in your paper?" asked Detective Thomas.

"Yes, Detective, it does. I'll not enable a baseless attempt to ruin Ms. Vermeer's reputation or marriage, although it seems her husband believes her account of the facts."

"Thank you, Mr. Grindell," said Detective Thomas. "Ms. Vermeer and her husband will be most appreciative of your discretion and interest in promoting the truth, rather than sensationalizing a fictitious scandal."

"Detective, I'd be interested in knowing the outcome of your investigation," said Mr. Grindell. "If you discover the culprit who orchestrated this charade, then I'd entertain the idea of printing the story from the perspective of the setup—quite a different story than the sender desires."

Greg spoke before Detective Thomas had a chance to respond. "Quinn, I believe Julia and I have all we need here. We'll return to the lab to begin testing these items for organic and inorganic particulates, DNA and fingerprints. Mr. Grindell, when do you expect you can get us the information on the people here who have touched these items?"

"I expect you should have it within the next couple of hours. It will just take some time to figure out whose hands handled the package and its contents. Once I have that, gathering the contact information will be almost instant."

"Thank you, Mr. Grindell," Greg said. "Quinn, do you need us for anything else before we take off?"

"No, Greg, I can't think of a thing. I'll see you both later at the lab, but call me if you learn anything before I touch base with you." Greg nodded and he and Julia left.

"Mr. Grindell, the sender will be most distressed to learn you didn't publish the photos," Detective Thomas said. "You may receive a second communication, written or verbal, from the sender either eliciting a reason from you as to why there was no article or prodding you with additional fodder to entice you into reconsidering publication. Please let me know the minute you hear a word."

"Certainly, Detective. Let me walk you out."

They left his office and headed toward the elevator. Once back at the station, Detective Thomas contacted San Jose's police chief, Ken Sorenson, and explained her case to him. Chief Sorenson was agreeable to providing the manpower and authority to obtain all hotel surveillance recordings of Glenn Sanders, to search for fingerprints and DNA in the room he occupied and to copy any documents he signed at The Fairmont. She was most grateful for Chief Sorenson's graciousness, given that police investigations that cross jurisdictions, particularly state lines, can become political nightmares involving power plays. She was not interested in power, just in results.

# *Chapter Eleven*

Over the course of the remainder of the week, Detective Thomas's team reviewed the results of the forensics tests and finished watching the surveillance recordings. The team did not find any suspicious fingerprints or DNA on the photos, the writing or the envelope. The stamps were the typical self-stick ones, so there was no saliva to examine. The envelope, on the other hand, was a WAG, a water-activated gum envelope, but the water used was tap, not saliva. No particulates were present in or on the envelope or its contents, so no hairs, no fibers, no skin flakes, nothing. The package was essentially sterile, showing the sender knew to take all necessary precautions to protect his or her identity.

The stamps on the envelope were all "Forever" stamps. More postage was affixed than was required, making it appear the sender did not mail the package at a post office where either a clerk or the automated postal center would have affixed the correct postage. Instead, the sender guessed at the correct postage amount. Surveillance recordings from the Postal Service did not show anyone from the fundraising dinner. Most freestanding mailboxes had no cameras aimed at them, and plenty of people used them after dark.

As Detective Thomas sat at her desk mulling over the sender's cunning nature, Chief Sorenson called.

"Detective Thomas," he said, "using the photo you sent me of Mr. Sanders, as well as Ms. Vermeer's comment that he stated he was from Sacramento, we've done a search and found there is no Glenn Sanders living in Sacramento or its suburbs. So, he's either lied about his name, city of residence or both."

"That doesn't surprise me in the least, Chief, as he has to expect that a police officer would come knocking on his door as soon as the package was opened at the *Press*."

"He paid cash for every expense, so there's no check or credit card to track," said Chief Sorenson. "In addition, the room was clean. I don't mean clean because the housekeeping staff cleaned it numerous times over the last week. I mean practically sterilized clean, which means someone in addition to the maids was in that room purging it of everything but its furniture and flooring."

"Are you saying there were no fingerprints or DNA in the room at all?" asked Detective Thomas.

"Oh, there were fingerprints and DNA, but only for the staff and the one guest who set foot in that room since your Mr. Sanders checked out. There are no remaining fingerprints or DNA for Mr. Sanders, Ms. Vermeer or anyone who stayed in that room prior to Mr. Sanders. Fortunately, the one person who checked into that room after Mr. Sanders has been exceedingly cooperative in agreeing to change rooms and give us a DNA sample and fingerprints. Until you give me the OK, the hotel has willingly agreed to leave the room vacant. Not only is The Fairmont a luxury hotel, but its management has been first rate in cooperating with my people in our investigation."

"I have to agree with you," said Detective Thomas. "Someone else besides the regular housekeeping staff cleaned that room because even the maids at a luxury hotel don't routinely clean all surfaces between guests. Mr. Sanders had to have touched something in that room that didn't get dusted or otherwise regularly cleaned."

"Based on our interviews with staff, this is what we think happened," said Chief Sorenson. "Mr. Sanders checked out at 8:12 a.m. by calling the front desk from the room. We didn't find his key card in the room, so he likely took it with him. When the housekeeper passed by the room at approximately 9:30 a.m., the "Do Not Disturb" indicator was visible and so she did not enter. She believed that though her information indicated he had checked out, he must have still been in the room. Finally, at 1:00 p.m. she knocked on the door. When she heard no response, she gingerly went in and found the room empty. Finding the room clean, she was confused because she was the housekeeper assigned to clean the room that day. Assuming there was some mix-up, she left the room."

"So, Chief, it sounds like the cleaner came into the room soon after Mr. Sanders left and managed to work free of disruption or detection because the housekeeper thought Mr. Sanders was still there. Would you agree?" inquired Detective Thomas.

"Yes, that was my conclusion. During that time, the cleaner used a stronger bleach-to-water ratio for the cleaning solution than the hotel's housekeeping staff uses. We know that because we tested the residue in the room in comparison to the hotel's cleaning solution. He or she cleaned not only the expected surfaces, but also washed the walls and cleaned the carpet. Normally, we can detect fluids of various types on the carpet and bed comforter, fluids that housekeepers normally wouldn't even see to clean. In this case, both the carpet and comforter were completely cleaned. There's just nothing left to use to identify the man claiming to be Mr. Sanders. However, I expect any minute to receive the report on the surveillance camera recordings to determine if we have any further information on him."

"Chief, I really appreciate all you and your department have done to assist us in this investigation," said Detective Thomas. "It's almost impossible to believe Mr. Sanders or whomever he may be working for would take these extreme measures just to take a shot at ruining Ms. Vermeer's reputation."

"Yes, I agree. This attempt to discredit Ms. Vermeer has desperation written all over it." Someone knocked on Chief Sorenson's door, so he asked Detective Thomas to hold.

"Come in." A young blond woman dressed in a police uniform entered. Her hair was braided and pulled back. She handed Chief Sorenson a document.

"Chief, here's the report on the surveillance cameras. I was told you were anxious to see it as soon as it was done."

"Yes, Sarah, thank you." Seeing that he was on the telephone, Sarah smiled and immediately left.

"I just received the surveillance camera report," Chief Sorenson told Detective Thomas. "I'll just read it out loud so we can both get the results simultaneously." He began:

> Person of interest known as Glenn Sanders appears numerous times in the recordings and is at all times alone, with the exception of the time he was with Annalisa Vermeer on the evening of Thursday, April 3, 2014. There is no surveillance in his room. In all areas where he is recorded, he made no telephone calls nor is he viewed using a computer or text messaging services on a cellular telephone to communicate with anyone. He is viewed checking in at 7:44 p.m. on Wednesday, April 2, 2014, signing his name and paying cash for his two-night stay despite the front desk clerk telling him he need not pay until he checks out. He was told he only needed to leave a credit card number, but he indicated he did not have a credit card.
>
> He ate all his meals alone at the hotel, always paying in cash, and stayed inside the hotel until he checked out at 8:12 a.m. on Friday, April 4, 2014. He did attend the entire speech given by Ms. Vermeer on April 3, and when it concluded he went directly to the hotel restaurant where

he ate his dinner. Upon the completion of his meal, he approached Ms. Vermeer at her table and left the dining room with her, just as Ms. Vermeer indicated.

After Mr. Sanders checked out from his hotel room at 8:12 a.m. on April 4, he immediately went to the parking lot where he retrieved his car. The license plate number is identifiable as "California 9SNS721." This plate number is titled to Sierra Rental Car Agency. Contact with the agency indicates that the car was rented from its location at the San Jose International Airport from Wednesday, April 2 at 7:20 p.m. to Friday, April 4 at 8:40 a.m., showing he drove directly to and from the hotel/car rental agency.

Agency indicates lessee wanted to pay with cash, which was acceptable, but lessee complained when the agency demanded a credit card for security. Needing the car, he produced his driver's license and the credit card, which identified him as Agustin G. Sanders, living at 2805 Langdon Court, Washington, DC, which is in the Penn Quarter neighborhood. Agency indicates the car was returned undamaged.

"He finally made a mistake, forgetting or not knowing that cars can't be rented without a credit card securing the rental," said Detective Thomas. "A fake credit card would have completed the charade."

"That's right, Detective," said Chief Sorenson. "They almost always make at least one mistake. Orchestrating the perfect plan is nearly impossible, unless experience and expertise wean out all the errors. Something tells me this guy Sanders isn't a committed criminal, but rather an amateur caught up in a game where he knows the rules, but doesn't know how it ends when someone wins."

"I suspect you're correct, Chief," said Detective Thomas. "With a Washington, DC address, this case is now right back here in DC, and it seems there isn't a continuing California connection. I think this is all I need from you, but I'd like a copy of the report. Please let management at The Fairmont know I'm most appreciative of their cooperativeness, and they can release the room to occupants when they see fit. Thank you very much for your invaluable assistance."

"My pleasure, Detective. Good luck with solving this one and let me know if you need my services down the road. Good-bye."

"I will, Chief, good-bye." Detective Thomas immediately made another telephone call, this time to Detective Garza requesting Mr. Sanders be picked up and brought to the station for questioning.

# *Chapter Twelve*

Before she entered the interrogation room, Detective Thomas went to the adjacent room to observe Mr. Sanders through the one-way glass. He sat alone and had a forlorn look on his face. His head hung downward while he stared blankly at the table. His fingers were intertwined as his hands fidgeted on the tabletop. His nerves appeared frayed and his demeanor exhibited concern, maybe fear. Detective Thomas felt even more certain that Mr. Sanders had involved himself in a situation he probably did not fully understand. As she entered the room, Mr. Sanders raised his head and looked directly into her eyes.

"Mr. Sanders, thank you for cooperating with my officers today when they requested you accompany them here. My name is Detective Quinn Thomas and I'm the lead investigator into the attempted murder of Annalisa Vermeer." At that, Mr. Sanders' forlorn face transformed into an animated face signifying shock.

"Murder? I had nothing to do with any attempted murder. When she left me, she was just fine. May I go now?" His entire body was fidgeting, wiggling around like a three-year-old anxious to get to the bathroom.

"Please relax, Mr. Sanders," encouraged Detective Thomas. "I don't believe you tried to kill Ms. Vermeer. In fact, we have no evidence that places you at the site of the attempt. I've asked you here today to discuss your contact with Ms. Vermeer in San Jose."

"I assure you, I didn't hurt Ms. Vermeer. She is a very nice lady and I liked talking with her."

"Yes, Mr. Sanders, she is a nice lady and, from what we saw in the photos you took, it appears you two had a pleasant meeting."

"Photos? I didn't take any photos. Photos of what?" pleaded Mr. Sanders. Detective Thomas believed Mr. Sanders installed the hidden cameras in his room and removed them prior to leaving, but she felt she might learn more by drawing him out and following his lead.

"I'm talking about the photos that were taken with the cameras that were hidden in your room. Did you install the cameras?"

"No, Detective, not only did I not install the cameras, I didn't even know there were cameras there. What were the photos of?" Mr. Sanders' demeanor was changing; he was becoming proactive, obviously now interested in the mystery he had entangled himself in, the mystery he hoped to see unravel before him.

"They were photos of you and Ms. Vermeer in your hotel room as she was reading articles you showed her," answered Detective Thomas.

"Why would anyone want photos of that?" asked Mr. Sanders, becoming more intrigued by the minute and forgetting he was part and parcel of the mystery.

"Mr. Sanders, I believe we'll make more headway if I ask the questions and you tell me what you know in response. Now, you represented yourself to Ms. Vermeer as a fan of hers, correct?"

Mr. Sanders sank a bit in his chair and sheepishly looked down, remembering his involvement in the mystery before them. "Yes, I did."

"Are you a fan of Ms. Vermeer, following her work prior to April 3?"

"No, Detective, I'm not a fan of hers. However, don't get me wrong: I have nothing against Ms. Vermeer, as the only time I've ever seen her was that day, and she was very nice to me. It's true, however, that I only became aware of her existence a few days prior to meeting her."

"OK. I need you to help me understand why you were playing this charade with her, so please start at the beginning and tell me how it came to be that you went to see her in San Jose."

"No problem, I'll tell you anything you want to know. About two weeks ago, my neighbor, David Hawkins, approached me and asked if I'd like to do some independent contractor work in California to earn some big money quickly. Well, I jumped at the opportunity because I lost my job about six months ago and haven't been able to find a new position. I told David a couple of months ago that I'd lose my house later this year if I wasn't employed soon. So, I thought it was very neighborly of him to think of me for the job."

"Before you move forward, Mr. Sanders, please tell me what you know about David Hawkins, other than that he's your neighbor."

"David is an attorney and he works for a politician on Capitol Hill. He advises on the legal aspects of matters that come before his boss. I don't know her name; I only know he works for a woman who serves in Congress."

"Fine, thank you. That will give me a place to start in finding him. Do you know his home address?"

"Yes, since he lives two doors down from me, his address would be 2815 Langdon Court in Penn Quarter. Should I go on?" asked Mr. Sanders. Detective Thomas wrote the address on her pad of paper and nodded for him to continue.

"I'm an accountant, so I assumed the independent contract work involved accounting for a business in California, However, David said this was more of a personal job for him, rather than business work. He told me all I needed to do was attend a speech in San Jose and approach the speaker while she was eating dinner afterward in order to get her to read various articles that were written about her and her work. That sounded easy enough until he told me I had to pretend to be one of her followers. Given I'd never heard of her, I was concerned I wouldn't be able to convince her I was a supporter. David relieved my concerns by telling me all about her. In fact, we met at his house for about four hours one day in order for him to teach me all I needed to know."

"What reason did David give you for needing you to get her to read the articles?"

"Actually, no reason. I never asked him why I was doing this. There were only two concerns I had. The first was whether I could sell myself as a knowledgeable supporter of her cause, and the second was when I would get paid for my services."

"What was the pay for this service, Mr. Sanders?" inquired Detective Thomas.

"It was huge, at least to me. He paid me $5,000, plus another $3,000 for my expenses. He instructed me to pay for every expense in cash so there would be no trail back to me in case she ever figured out I wasn't an actual fan. He told me she lived in Washington, DC, so I was fearful if I wasn't convincing enough she might end up on my doorstep."

"So, you accepted this position, so to speak, without the slightest idea why you were getting her to read the articles?"

"Correct. There was nothing dangerous or illegal in asking her to read the articles, so it really didn't matter to me why David wanted her to read them so badly. I lived like a king for a couple of days, plus it was the easiest money I ever made, until your officers appeared on my doorstep."

"Mr. Sanders, before we continue, I'd like to give you some advice I'm sure you've heard countless times before, especially in relation to your accounting work. If a person is offered an inordinately large amount of cash to perform services, then at least some aspect of the services is probably illicit or illegal. Did you not think that

$5,000 in cash was quite a payout for two days of travel, one hour of listening to a speech and another hour or two of socializing with the speaker?"

"When you put it that way, yes, it does seem unreasonable, but when a person is desperate that person doesn't ask too many questions and doesn't look a gift horse in the mouth. I needed the money and so I took the job, knowing the only deception on my part was pretending to be a fan when I wasn't, and that isn't illegal."

"Mr. Sanders, you also lied about your first name. You told the hotel, the airline and Ms. Vermeer that your name was Glenn Sanders when your name is Agustin Sanders."

"No, I didn't lie about my name. My name is Agustin Glenn Sanders. I hate the name 'Agustin' and don't like 'Gus' any better, so I always go by 'Glenn.' David didn't ask me to use a fictitious name; he just asked me to lie about the city I was from so Ms. Vermeer couldn't track me down. He never gave me the slightest reason to believe the police would be after me."

"So, your only job was to get Ms. Vermeer into your hotel room and give her the articles to read?"

"Yes, that's correct. She needed to read the articles to see what people were saying about her. That's all there was to it."

"Actually, Mr. Sanders, we believe the sole purpose, at least from Mr. Hawkins' position, was to make it appear you and Ms. Vermeer were having an affair in your hotel room."

"Why would David want it to look like we were having an affair?" asked Mr. Sanders. "It makes no sense to me."

"Does it make any sense to you that you would need to get Ms. Vermeer to read articles she could read online on her own?"

"Detective, David said many of those articles either weren't online or were no longer online, so the only way she could see them was to be given the hard copies."

"Mr. Sanders, Ms. Vermeer is an adept and intelligent person. She could find hard copies of any articles she wanted. She didn't need you, as Mr. Hawkins' conduit, to provide the copies to her."

"Now that you explain it that way, you do make sense," said Mr. Sanders. "Clearly, my focus was on the money and not much else. I promise you, Detective, I never intended Ms. Vermeer any harm, and David never even hinted that I should."

"Speaking of the money, did David pay you the cash directly or did he directly deposit it in your account?"

"He came over the day after I agreed to go to San Jose and he paid me $8,000 in $100 bills. David said he gave me the money immediately because he wanted everything to go smoothly for me so I would be relaxed and able to do my job. How is it you found me anyway?"

"You used your credit card and driver's license at the car rental agency, which they copied in the event you stole the car," explained Detective Thomas.

"Right. I remember I didn't want to use the credit card for that very reason, only, as I said, I was thinking about Ms. Vermeer, not the police."

"Mr. Sanders, you said you didn't install the cameras in your hotel room and you weren't aware there were photos of you and Ms. Vermeer. Do you think Mr. Hawkins had the cameras installed prior to your arrival?"

"I don't know, Detective, but I guess it's reasonable to think he did because he's the only one I know of who was involved in this crazy mess other than me, so who else could have done it?"

"Mr. Hawkins is the only one whom you know of, but there may be other people involved."

"I wouldn't know anything about that, Detective."

"Mr. Sanders, have you had any contact with Mr. Hawkins since you returned from San Jose?"

"Yes, he called me the evening of the day I returned to ask me how things went, if I was able to get her to read the articles. He was very pleased when I told him how receptive she was to looking at the articles. Now, in hindsight, it seems what he was really pleased about was that she was in my hotel room and for quite some time. I feel used."

"Mr. Sanders, people who are used are generally not paid $8,000 for a luxurious trip, but you were misled and deceived to a point. As I said to you differently a bit ago, if it seems too good to be true, it probably is. Do you know if David is in town today?"

"No, he isn't. I ran into him last night at a local market and he told me he was leaving today for Philadelphia to spend the weekend at his mother's house because it's her seventieth birthday. He's returning to town on the train on Monday morning and he told me he was going to work straight from the train."

"Thank you, Mr. Sanders, for your help. While you were duped by Mr. Hawkins, you still misrepresented yourself and operated under false pretenses. I'm not sure if the prosecutor will have an interest in pursuing any type of a charge against you or if it would solely be a civil matter should Ms. Vermeer choose to proceed down that road. You are free to leave now, but I'll need you to stay in town in case I need any further information from you."

"No problem. I have no plans to leave town and I'll cooperate fully with your investigation. What do I say to David if I see him?"

"Mr. Sanders, I intend to pick Mr. Hawkins up as soon as he arrives at his office, so he'll know immediately that we've questioned you. Therefore, he may try to contact you to coordinate your stories. You shouldn't talk with him regarding this matter, at least until it's resolved and we know exactly who's done what and what charges will be issued. If he comes knocking on your door, then I suggest you don't open it and inform him I've instructed you not to discuss the matter with him at this time."

"Fine. Would you please tell Ms. Vermeer I'm sorry for the role I played in this scheme and that I never intended her to be harmed in any way?"

"Yes, Mr. Sanders, I will. I will have an officer escort you to the door. I'll be in touch should I need anything further from you. Good-bye." Mr. Sanders left with the officer and Detective Thomas headed straight to Detective Garza's office.

"Cat," she said, "now that we know Mr. Sanders didn't install or uninstall the cameras, we know there's at least one other person involved besides the one who cleaned the room after he checked out. Would you please call Chief Sorenson and ask him to review the surveillance recordings for five days before Mr. Sanders checked in to see if there is evidence of someone going into the room who could have installed the cameras? Also, ask him to look at the recording after 8:12 a.m. on April 4 to find the person who came in to clean the room. Maybe we can identify one or two more people who were in on this scam, and maybe one of them will be Mr. Hawkins. I'd like to know that before I interview him on Monday."

"I'll call the chief right away, Quinn. It's highly unlikely Mr. Hawkins did the camera installation himself when he had accessible cash to pay for those services. He knew he was more likely to insulate himself from this matter if he never set foot in San Jose," suggested Cat.

"I agree. Would you also please find out what time the early morning trains arrive in DC from Philadelphia on Monday? Can you please check that before you call Chief Sorenson?"

"Yes, I'll check now and get right back to you."

"Thanks, Cat."

Ten minutes later, Detective Garza walked into Detective Thomas's office with a printout of the train schedule.

"Quinn, five trains get in between 8:15 a.m. and 9:47 a.m. The train that arrives at 9:47 leaves Philly at 8:12, so Mr. Hawkins could get in at 9:47 unless he's an early riser or unless he has a pressing meeting."

"Let's plan to leave the office Monday morning with an officer so as to arrive at Mr. Hawkins' office at 10:00 a.m.," said Detective Thomas. "That way, we shouldn't have to wait for him in the event he comes in on the 9:47 train. Before we leave, we can review the report you receive from Chief Sorenson regarding the surveillance recordings. I also need to check where Mr. Hawkins works on Capitol Hill so we know where to go. Let me look him up now while you're still here."

Detective Thomas turned to her keyboard and accessed a directory of Congressional staff. She momentarily stared at the screen and then looked up at Detective Garza.

"Cat, Mr. Hawkins is the legal assistant to Representative Sylvia Rossman."

"Representative Rossman was present at the fundraiser dinner where Ms. Vermeer was poisoned," Detective Garza said.

"Yes, she was, Cat. Ms. Vermeer indicated to me that Representative Rossman chastised her at the fundraiser. Since she was at the fundraiser, Representative Rossman had the opportunity to lace the cherries with the poison."

# *Chapter Thirteen*

On Monday morning, Detective Thomas went directly to Detective Garza's office to learn if Chief Sorenson had reviewed the surveillance recordings Detective Garza had requested. The report was in and it was not good. Other than housekeepers and guests, no one entered the hotel room in the five days leading up to Mr. Sanders' stay. Also, no one entered during his stay, meaning that a person disguised as a housekeeper or one of the room's previous occupants had planted the cameras. The recordings showed no clear views of faces, except for the room's occupants, whom the hotel staff already recognized.

On the morning Mr. Sanders checked out, two housekeepers entered the room—one was likely the cleaner and the other the camera remover. No distinct image of their faces appeared. Chief Sorenson indicated he would have a detective interview all the housekeepers to determine if anyone saw any suspicious behavior or had conversations with the faux housekeepers.

"The chief told me he'd call if he learns any helpful information," said Detective Garza. "Further, he intends to interview the two occupants of the room during those five days, although it's highly unlikely that the cameras were planted then because no one knew at that point in which room Mr. Sanders would be staying."

As planned, Detectives Thomas and Garza walked into Representative Rossman's office at 10:00 a.m., accompanied by a uniformed officer. The young man sitting closest to the door was taken aback by the policeman, but quickly regained his composure. "How may I help you?" he asked.

"We're here to see Mr. Hawkins. Is he in?" asked Detective Thomas.

"Yes, he is. May I ask who you are and what this is regarding?" asked the young man, regaining his authority and confidence.

"I'm Detective Thomas and this is Detective Garza and Officer Pembrooke. We're from the Metro Police, and you can tell Mr. Hawkins we're here regarding Glenn Sanders. He'll know what that means."

Without any comment, the young man left his desk and walked down a hallway, clearly electing prudence and discretion over an awkward public telephone conversation with Mr. Hawkins. A couple of minutes later, he returned to his desk. "Mr. Hawkins will be right with you," he announced. "You may take a seat over there."

He pointed to a bank of cushioned chairs along the wall adjacent to the door and began typing away on his keyboard. The detectives and police officer remained standing. Five minutes later, Detective Garza expressed concern that Mr. Hawkins may have exited the office through a back door. Just as she was about to ask the young man to call Mr. Hawkins, Mr. Hawkins appeared. He was a tall, well-dressed man with wispy blond hair and a slim figure. After a brief introduction, he invited them to his office.

Detective Thomas turned to Officer Pembrooke. "Please wait here while Cat and I speak with Mr. Hawkins in his office. I'll call you if we need you." Officer Pembrooke nodded and sat down. The detectives walked in silence down the hallway to Mr. Hawkins' office. Once there, he offered them his two chocolate-brown leather wing chairs, which were separated by a square walnut table with a small drawer and a sleek shaded lamp. Once the group sat down, Mr.

Hawkins immediately took control.

"What is it I can help you with regarding Mr. Sanders?"

"Mr. Hawkins, Mr. Sanders says he's your neighbor and you asked him to fly to San Jose to entice Annalisa Vermeer into joining him in his hotel room to read various articles written about her, her book and her work. Did you, in fact, do that?" demanded Detective Thomas.

For just a moment, Mr. Hawkins showed a glint of surprise, making it clear he had not spoken with Mr. Sanders lately. Like the young man in the outer lobby, he recovered his emotions quickly and attempted to regain control.

"Why would you be speaking with Mr. Sanders, who is, yes, one of my neighbors?"

"Mr. Hawkins, we're here to ask you questions, not the reverse," said Detective Thomas firmly, as Mr. Hawkins raised his eyes toward the ceiling in disgust. He wasn't in the least bit intimidated by the detectives. Detective Thomas continued, "Mr. Hawkins, please answer the question."

"Yes, I did ask Mr. Sanders to meet Ms. Vermeer in San Jose. Why is that a police matter?"

Ignoring his question, Detective Garza asked, "Why did you want Mr. Sanders to coerce Ms. Vermeer into his room? We know it wasn't to read the articles; that was just an excuse to entice her there."

"I knew Ms. Vermeer doesn't exhibit the pristine character she wants everyone to believe she possesses, and I suspected if she was put in a compromising position she would show her true colors," declared Mr. Hawkins.

"Why do you care about Ms. Vermeer's character?" asked Detective Thomas.

"She and her holier-than-though attitude are threatening the occupants of this building. I couldn't allow her to destroy people whom I care about, including me, by presenting herself as a credible, responsible and moral authority on our legislative process," insisted

Mr. Hawkins.

"Setting aside why you believe Ms. Vermeer has less integrity than appears on the surface, why do you think she's threatening you and others in this building?" asked Detective Garza.

"Have you been living under a rock, Detective? She wants to eliminate political parties, lobbyists and the job description of all legislators here and throughout the country. If the legislators aren't making laws, then what are they supposed to do? Their power, influence and accomplishments will all disintegrate, and ultimately the citizenry will decide they aren't needed as the major movers and shakers of this country."

"We have no intention of debating the merits of Ms. Vermeer's advocacy with you," said Detective Thomas. "Our only concern is what action you've taken against her. Did you have the cameras installed in Mr. Sanders' hotel room?"

"Yes, I did. It was the only mechanism for memorializing her actions with Mr. Sanders," defended Mr. Hawkins.

"You seem to be seeing salacious activity on Ms. Vermeer's part that nobody else who's seen the photographs has observed," said Detective Thomas. "Given she remained clothed, she and Mr. Sanders never touched and she was reading in all the photos, how is it you believe publishing the photos will discredit her and destroy her reputation?"

"I don't believe publishing the photos will knock her off her pedestal. That's where my plan failed. I spent all that money to protect Sylvia and the rest of us, and it was for naught because she didn't show her true colors. I can only assume she was so enamored reading about herself that she didn't take advantage of the ambience and the available man. By the way, in contradiction to your prior statement, nobody but the photographer and I have seen the photos."

"Did you ask Mr. Sanders to seduce Ms. Vermeer, Mr. Hawkins?" asked Detective Garza.

"No, I honestly thought *she* would seduce him and he would

fall right into her arms, given her beauty and his availability. However, that didn't occur, so the photos are worthless."

"If you believe the photos are worthless and that publishing them won't destroy her reputation, then why did you send them to the *Press* for publication?" asked Detective Thomas.

"What? I didn't send the photos to the *Press*," insisted Mr. Hawkins. "I just told you only two people have seen the photos. What are you talking about?" Mr. Hawkins' tone was more sincere than controlling.

"Sixteen photos, along with a one-page writing addressing the photos, were mailed to the *Press* for publication. Is it your position that not only did you not mail the package, but you weren't even aware the photos had been mailed?" Detective Garza asked with an air of skepticism in her voice.

"That's correct. How could the photos be mailed, as they're here on my desk?" Mr. Hawkins picked up a stack of files on the far right corner of his desk and shuffled through them until he reached the bottom file. He looked confused, and for the first time since starting the interview he genuinely lost his self-assured demeanor. "I don't understand," he said. "The photos were here the last time I had them. There was no writing, so I don't know what you're talking about with that, but the photos were in an envelope right here near the bottom of this pile of files." Mr. Hawkins appeared truly perplexed.

"When exactly did you last look at the photos?" asked Detective Garza.

"Well, after my contact in San Jose removed the cameras, he printed hard copies for me and overnighted them so I could receive them at my home on Saturday morning. I came into the office that afternoon to work on a project for Sylvia and I put them aside in the pile because they were of no use to me. I should have just thrown them away, but I was preoccupied with my project. When I left on Saturday, I left the envelope where I'd put it. I've had no reason to look at the photos since then."

"The *Press* received the photos on Tuesday, the eighth, and the postmark shows the envelope was mailed on Monday," said Detective Thomas. "So, sometime between Saturday afternoon when you were in your office and Monday before 5:00 p.m., someone took the envelope off your desk, prepared the writing and mailed the photos to the *Press* in a new envelope. Any idea who did that, Mr. Hawkins?"

"Absolutely not. It makes no sense for anyone to send the photos to the *Press* since they didn't accomplish their purpose. Even if the *Press* published them, Ms. Vermeer wouldn't be discredited because the photos are innocuous—there was no wrongdoing on her part."

"Well, Mr. Hawkins, someone believes the photos will destroy Ms. Vermeer, if made public. That someone asked the *Press* to publish the photos and asserted she was unfaithful to her husband and was a dishonest person. Did you orchestrate this entire charade per the instructions of your boss, Representative Rossman?" asked Detective Thomas.

"No, Sylvia wasn't privy to this mission. I acted solely on my own using my personal money to fund it. Sylvia never saw the photos or even knew they were taken. I understood the clandestine nature of my actions and didn't want Sylvia to ever suffer or incur negative repercussions because of them. So, I kept her in the dark to protect her. She would only have become aware of what I did if I was successful and brought Ms. Vermeer down. I failed Sylvia and for that I am sorry."

"Mr. Hawkins, you staged a play with Mr. Sanders. He was your lead actor, Ms. Vermeer was your puppet and you secretly filmed the play while pulling the strings from a distance. The basis of all your actions was false pretenses, yet all you're sorry for is failing Representative Rossman. You have a distorted view of reality and your motivations and actions are severely misplaced," insisted Detective Thomas. Mr. Hawkins made no response, declining to defend himself or exhibit additional remorse. His silence moved Detective Thomas to continue.

"Who had access to your office between the time you left on Saturday and Monday?"

"Everyone who works in this office. When the outside office door is locked on the weekend, none of the internal offices are generally locked, with the exception of Sylvia's, whose is always locked when she's out of the office. She insists upon it, as she has a fear of intruders and is always suspicious that her detractors are out to ruin her. As for Monday, everyone in the building potentially had access, particularly while Gerald, the young man you spoke with in the lobby area who is Representative Rossman's administrative assistant, went to lunch, the bathroom, on deliveries, and on and on. We have no cameras within our office, only out in the hallways. So it's impossible to know who took the envelope of photos unless that person openly carried the photos in his or her hands and the camera caught view of it."

"So, you're claiming this entire scheme from conception to completion was solely yours and that Representative Rossman had no knowledge of or complicity in it?" probed Detective Thomas.

"That's correct. Sylvia knows nothing about this because it was a bust. Now, are we finished here? I have work to do and I've committed no crime with my flawed little plan," asserted Mr. Hawkins.

"Don't be so quick to assume you haven't committed a crime either here or in California," said Detective Thomas. "We'll leave any possible charges that can be asserted against you in California to San Jose's chief of police, who's been an active part of this investigation. We fully intend to inform our prosecutor of every aspect of your scheme involving false pretenses and secret surveillance. Our prosecutor can decide what, if any, charges to bring against you. The only interest Detective Garza and I have is in solving the attempted murder of Ms. Vermeer. To the extent you were involved in that, we will hold you accountable."

Mr. Hawkins, with a grim look on his face, stared squarely at Detective Thomas. "I had nothing to do with the attempt on her life.

"I wasn't even at the fundraiser that night, and I think it would be impossible to poison someone from afar."

"Mr. Hawkins, you've already proven you can attempt to harm someone from afar," asserted Detective Thomas. "We need to talk to Representative Rossman now. Would you please take us to her office?"

"Why would you need to talk to Sylvia?" Mr. Hawkins asked. "I already told you she knows nothing of my efforts at the San Jose event. She's not a part of this. Plus, I'm certain she's in a meeting at the moment."

"Mr. Hawkins, either you can go and end her meeting in a diplomatic fashion and escort us in to interview her or we can just go in there ourselves and end the meeting abruptly. Which do you think she would prefer?" demanded Detective Garza.

"Fine, fine. Just give me a few minutes to arrange it. Please stay here until I return for you," said Mr. Hawkins, who'd become less self-secure at the mention of them interviewing Representative Rossman. He left his office, leaving the two detectives to ruminate over the best approach to use with the representative.

Mr. Hawkins entered Representative Rossman's office to find her deep in discussion with two of her assistants. She ignored his presence. After a couple of minutes, he interrupted the meeting and indicated an emergency had arisen.

"What kind of an emergency, David? We're really busy here, can't it wait?" implored Representative Rossman.

"I'm afraid not, Sylvia." The look in Mr. Hawkins' eyes conveyed his concerns and moved Representative Rossman to dismiss her aides. As they left, Mr. Hawkins closed the door.

"Sylvia, there are two police detectives in my office who've been questioning me about the San Jose fiasco. Now they want to interview you. I tried to deter them by stating you were in a meeting, but they're insistent. If I don't bring them in here, then they intend to come in on their own. They have a uniformed officer in the lobby should they need him."

"Calm down, David. Guilty people exhibit frayed nerves and aren't able to maintain their composure, so you need to be stoic or they'll know something is amiss," demanded Representative Rossman.

"I know, Sylvia, I know," said Mr. Hawkins. "I was self-assured in our interview, at least until they questioned me about mailing the photos to the *Press*. Since I didn't mail the photos anywhere, I could only assume you mailed them after I showed them to you on Saturday. Did you mail the photos and some writing to the *Press*?"

"Yes, but we have no time to discuss this now. If you're in here too long, then they'll suspect we're colluding. Just tell me one thing. Did you maintain I had no knowledge or involvement in any aspect of the San Jose affair?"

"Yes, Sylvia, you need to act surprised about the entire event and take the position that I acted entirely on my own. I have one question for you before I go get the detectives. What were you thinking when you decided to mail the photos to the *Press* when they're not in the least bit incriminating?"

"My dear, in this town all it often takes to bring someone down is the mere appearance or even suggestion of impropriety," said Representative Rossman. "We are surface people in this town; nobody digs down deep to find the truth when the surface is covered with potential wrongdoing. Reputations fall every day in DC based on nothing more than speculation, as long as it's supported by the media. Now go get the detectives and bring them to me. I'll take care of everything."

As Mr. Hawkins walked toward the door, he turned around. "You should know they're also investigating the attempted poisoning of Ms. Vermeer."

"I've got this, David," Representative Rossman assured him as she waved him out of the room.

Meanwhile, Detectives Garza and Thomas realized Mr. Hawkins was gone far longer than necessary to adjourn the meeting and get Representative Rossman. Clearly, Mr. Hawkins was giving her the play-by-play and they were strategizing their next move. Neither woman believed for a second that Representative Rossman was isolated from the events in San Jose. Proving that was another matter, and they hoped to trip her up in the interview. As they discussed this possibility, Mr. Hawkins returned and asked them to follow him to the representative's office.

When they arrived, Representative Rossman was nowhere to be found. Mr. Hawkins offered them seats in two red velvet antique chairs facing her desk. As he turned to leave, he said, "Sylvia will be here momentarily. She is quite busy, as you know."

"Mr. Hawkins," said Detective Thomas, just as he was about to close the door, "as we told Mr. Sanders, please don't leave town until this investigation is concluded." Without a response, he closed the door.

A minute later, a side door to the office opened and Representative Rossman strutted in, plumage in full array. It was obvious to the detectives this was yet another staged event. As she sat in her black leather wing back chair, she turned to the detectives and stated, "It's a pleasure to see you, but I hardly know how I can be of any assistance to you. David told me of your investigation into some matter in California, which he just told me he orchestrated, but I know nothing of that. Nor do I know anything about the attempted murder of Ms. Vermeer, and I told an officer that when I was interviewed the day after her unfortunate poisoning." Her grasp of controlling the conversation was even more powerful than Mr. Hawkins' grasp, yet the detectives ignored her attempt to control them.

"Representative, how long has Mr. Hawkins worked for you?" asked Detective Thomas.

"A long time, but as for definitive dates we would have to ask my human resources director. Would you like me to call her?" offered Representative Rossman, feigning cooperation.

"That won't be necessary. It is sufficient, at least for now, to know he has been here many years. It partially explains his loyalty and devotion to you, as well as his over-the-top initiative in plotting an elaborate scheme to promote you at the expense of destroying the reputation of Ms. Vermeer," asserted Detective Thomas.

"Yes, David is loyal and devoted to me, as he should be, but he only exposes bad people on my behalf—he doesn't create immorality where it doesn't already exist. Now, I have a meeting to get to, so you must excuse me." With that, she stood up and opened her hand toward the door, dismissing the detectives.

"Representative Rossman, your meeting will have to wait, as we're not finished here," volleyed Detective Garza, causing the representative to sit down. Detective Garza continued, "Did you play any role in the planning, implementing or financing of Glenn Sanders' actions in relation to Ms. Vermeer in San Jose on April 3, or mail photographs of them to the *Press*?"

Without skipping a beat, Representative Rossman retorted with, "Who is Glenn Sanders? He doesn't work here for me."

"Glenn Sanders is the man who met with Ms. Vermeer in his hotel room at The Fairmont in San Jose, California," explained Detective Thomas.

"I don't know any Mr. Sanders, but it seems highly inappropriate for Ms. Vermeer to be meeting any man in his hotel room, other than her husband, whom I know quite well and respect fully. I'm saddened to hear Ms. Vermeer would betray her husband. He doesn't deserve such treatment. Possibly I can refer him to an outstanding divorce lawyer."

"Thank you, Representative, for your time," said Detective Thomas. "I believe these are all the questions we have for you now. Mr. Hawkins has admitted to some serious actions, some of which may be legally actionable under criminal law. Therefore, if you're making lawyer referrals, then you may wish to refer Mr. Hawkins to an outstanding criminal defense lawyer. We can find our way out."

Detective Thomas knew Representative Rossman wouldn't admit to any liability on her part and was fully protected by Mr. Hawkins, who would be happy to fall on his sword for her.

As they drove back to the station, Detective Garza said to Detective Thomas, "Representative Rossman is a savvy woman who is trained in the art of deception and political gamesmanship. She won't overtly incriminate herself, but she did make one mistake that tells me she's the one who mailed the photos to the *Press*."

"I agree, Cat. She said Ms. Vermeer betrayed her husband. That was the same phrase used in the writing to the *Press*. She clearly holds Mr. Vermeer in high regard and is quick to assume any wrongdoing on Ms. Vermeer's part is true. That, coupled with her prior verbal attacks on Ms. Vermeer's advocacy, make me wonder if it's enough to give her a motive to murder Ms. Vermeer."

"She was at the fundraiser and has made no qualms about opposing Ms. Vermeer's positions," said Detective Garza. "Now we learn the San Jose smear campaign was instigated and financed by one of her employees. Though we can't prove she was the driving force for this operation, she is connected to the admitted puppeteer. I think there's indeed a reasonable basis for your suggestion she may be the one who attempted to murder Ms. Vermeer."

# *Chapter Fourteen*

After the trio departed, Representative Rossman immediately summoned Mr. Hawkins into her office. He was impressed with how fast she'd completed her interview with the detectives.

"David, I took care of the situation, which was easy considering I never had contact with your neighbor. They can't connect me to the San Jose affair or to the attempt on Ms. Vermeer's life at the fundraiser. The thread is too thin in that while you do in fact work for me, you have the intelligence, connections, motive and funds to have carried out the San Jose affair strictly on your own, without any involvement on my part. Given I took no action regarding the matter, I am safely insulated from liability," Representative Rossman asserted with confidence.

"I agree, Sylvia," said Mr. Hawkins. "I'm fully capable of planning and carrying out such a mission without your assistance. They'll never figure out, let alone prove, that you devised the San Jose event and I merely put it into action. I'm still unclear, however, as to why you sent the photos to the *Press*. I understand you believe the mere appearance of impropriety is enough to destroy her, but frankly, aside from the hotel room venue, the photos appear to be merely of a business meeting. You grasped too far in believing the *Press* would publish the photos and propose they prove an adulterous affair."

"I beg to differ, David. I think that had the police not caught wind of the matter, the photos would have been published and Ms. Vermeer's reputation would be irreparably destroyed. At the very least, Brad would have become aware of his wife's betrayal and would be preparing to divorce her. She simply doesn't deserve him," said Representative Rossman, sounding like a mother.

"Sylvia, I understand you want to protect Brad from his wife, but I believe it's time for you to stop your efforts against her," said Mr. Hawkins. "The surveillance cameras we had installed inside their home have given us no dirt with which to smear her. The man who initially cased their home saw no problems with either her or Brad. They get along famously; plus, she's made no incriminating telephone calls and no man has set foot in her house. In fact, instead of gleaning negative information from our surveillance, we learned she's being honored by ASSIST. Her reputation is improving over time and you simply have to acknowledge she's not cheating on her husband or otherwise betraying him. Simply put, she's not exhibiting behavior that can justify any attacks."

Mr. Hawkins rose from his chair and began pacing the room, clearly exasperated at what he viewed as the representative's obsession with Annalisa. Normally, he was quite effective at influencing her position on matters, but he was completely incapable of moving her mindset regarding Annalisa. Her attitude frustrated him immensely.

"Be patient, David, and, for heaven's sake, sit down." Mr. Hawkins immediately returned to his chair, but the expression on his face didn't change, especially in light of her next statement. "We haven't been observing her for that long. Eventually she'll reveal her true nature and I will be there to save Brad from her."

"Sylvia, Brad can take care of himself. You have to let this go and forget about her."

"Never, David, never. You men never see the evil side of your women. You think with your penises instead of your brains when it comes to women, and so you men fail to discern the betrayal going on before your eyes. Brad needs me to protect him. Just keep watching the footage from the cameras in her house and let me know if you learn anything I can actually use. That's it for now, David. I'm going to lunch with Harry Gibbs."

Without a word, Mr. Hawkins left her office, well aware that Representative Rossman would never deviate from her path of destruction unless *she* determined on her own it was prudent to do so. That afternoon, Detective Thomas met with Annalisa at her home to report all they had learned about the San Jose setup. Annalisa was shocked to hear Mr. Sanders was from DC; she found his proximity a bit disconcerting.

"Ms. Vermeer," said Detective Thomas, "I don't believe you need to worry about Mr. Sanders bothering you. He was almost as much in the dark as you were about this charade. He needed money and so he accepted the task of getting you to his hotel room to read the articles. He had no knowledge of the hidden cameras or Mr. Hawkins' hope that you would seduce him. He wasn't asked to harm you in any way and he indicated more than once that he found you to be a very nice person. He also asked me to tell you he never meant to harm you and he's sorry."

"Well, that's a relief. I'm still quite bothered that he lives close by—maybe Mr. Hawkins will be able to influence his behavior again and cause him to try to hurt me. What will happen to Mr. Hawkins, whom I don't think I've ever met?"

"I've referred this matter to the prosecutor for further investigation and he will determine whether or not there are grounds to arrest Mr. Hawkins," said Detective Thomas. "As for Representative Rossman, we have no evidence connecting her to Mr. Hawkins' efforts, other than that Mr. Hawkins works for her. He's devoted to her and so I believe he'll go to his grave protecting her."

"I hope the representative appreciates Mr. Hawkins' loyalty toward her, despite how misplaced it is," said Annalisa. "Do you think he'll continue to harass me behind closed doors?"

"That's a tough call, but I believe he will. It's not so much that he personally wants to destroy you, but I believe Representative Rossman is pulling all his strings and will continue to direct his actions against you. Though we can't prove it, we believe Representative Rossman has dedicated herself to protecting your husband from you, and I fear she'll continue to try to destroy you until she's either caught or she accomplishes her purpose. She's the one you have to be wary of whether you're in DC or traveling the country. The problem is, she doesn't do her own dirty work, so you won't know which strangers to steer clear of and which ones to trust."

Annalisa trembled at the detective's words. She stood and walked over to the window, staring out, searching for anyone loitering on the sidewalk or sitting in a nearby parked car. She now did not even feel safe in her own home.

"I knew Representative Rossman despised my advocacy work, but I never would have suspected she hated me more because of her devotion to Brad. I wonder if Brad even realizes she feels protective of him. Do you think Brad should talk to her?" asked Annalisa.

"That's another tough call. I suggest you ask your husband what he thinks, given he knows Representative Rossman better than we do. Also, he should only speak to her if he can remain calm and not overtly offend her, as she believes she's protecting him and may feel he doesn't know what's best for him. This is personal for her, so he needs to tread carefully."

"I'm speaking only twice this week and both times are in DC, so I won't be traveling," said Annalisa. "I'll be with Brad each evening and so maybe I'll be less at risk. Thank you for letting me know about Mr. Hawkins and Representative Rossman in relation to my meeting with Mr. Sanders. Can you connect either of them to the attempt on my life?"

"No, not yet. Mr. Hawkins wasn't at the fundraiser, although we know he farms out his schemes. As for the representative, she was, as you know, at the fundraiser, but we haven't been able to connect her any more than anyone else to the poison placed on your food. Now that we suspect she may be the person who tried to kill you, we'll be watching her at any public function you attend where she's present and we otherwise already have officers there. Our purpose will be twofold. First, we'll want to discourage her or any of her entourage from attempting to murder you again, and second, we'll want to witness her efforts should our presence not deter her."

"I'll be mindful of her presence and I'll watch her every move if she's near me," said Annalisa. "If Brad is with me, he can keep an eye on her too. Plus, we'll show a photo of her to Michael so he can identify her as well."

"That sounds like a good approach," said the detective. "This shouldn't go on for much longer. She'll either make another move on you and we'll catch her in the act or she'll grow tired of failing and move on to some other cause she creates." Annalisa walked Detective Thomas to the door and then reviewed her speaking schedule for the next few weeks, wondering where and when she would next be attacked.

When Brad came home that evening, Annalisa recounted her conversation with Detective Thomas. He was shocked to hear Representative Rossman was likely connected to both the San Jose setup and the attempt on Annalisa's life.

"I've had a friendly professional relationship with Sylvia for many years," he said. "We're not personal friends and we only occasionally discuss personal matters, including our spouses. What she does know about you from me is all positive, so she has no basis from my comments to believe you're hurting me in any way."

"Brad, my own belief is this: Had she not initially felt personally threatened by my speeches and my book, she wouldn't have latched onto deciding you were also threatened by me. Possibly at a subconscious level, she really is acting to protect herself, but on a conscious level she's convinced herself she's protecting you," suggested Annalisa.

"That makes sense because we've worked together for years and you and I have been married for years, yet only since your book came out and you've become visible has she decided you're out to hurt me. I'll talk to her and try to get her to understand you love me and have my best interests at heart."

"I talked to Detective Thomas about the possibility of you speaking to Representative Rossman," said Annalisa. "Detective Thomas believes Representative Rossman may feel you don't really understand what is best for you, so she must take action herself to protect you. The detective said you need to remain calm if you decide to discuss this with her because if you make her feel you are criticizing her, she may retaliate further against me in an effort to justify her actions."

"I'll be careful with my words and my demeanor," said Brad, "but I can't sit by and let her hurt, possibly kill, you when she's misguided, acting irrationally and—frankly—bordering on insanity. She isn't even a relative of mine, so why is she taking such an interest in my marriage?"

"Brad, as I said, I think her concern for you is an outlet for her hatred of me and my ideas. It's more palatable for her to attack me based on protecting you than on protecting herself. So, she's taken on a motherly interest and is determined to make sure I don't damage you."

"Funny you should mention that because she has no children. More than once she's expressed regrets about her and her husband never being able to have them."

"Do you know if they ever tried to adopt?" asked Annalisa.

"No, I don't know the answer to that. We never discussed the subject in detail, as I felt it may be too sensitive and personal for her and so I didn't make much of an inquiry."

"Maybe if she had children, then she wouldn't feel compelled to protect you or to use you as the excuse to protect herself," suggested Annalisa.

"It's way too late for that," said Brad. "Either way, attempted murder and public campaigns to destroy your reputation are crazy methods to protect me, especially when there's nothing from which to protect me."

"It may not make sense, but that doesn't mean it isn't real to her," said Annalisa. "A person's perceptions are his or her reality. I'm glad I'm in town this week and that we'll be spending our evenings together."

"Let's spend our evenings at home, cooking dinner and relaxing afterward," said Brad. "It will give us both a break from worrying about what's waiting for you around the corner."

"I like the sound of that. Speaking of dinner, I made Swedish meatballs and noodles. Come help me get the table set and dinner served," requested Annalisa. Brad grabbed her hand and they headed to the kitchen, both silently wondering what harm might come next.

# *Chapter Fifteen*

The next morning, David Hawkins walked into Representative Rossman's office immediately after getting to work. He found her talking on the telephone; she waved him toward a chair. Once she hung up, he relayed the video and audio that had been captured on the cameras in Annalisa's home from the day before. Given his devotion to her, he did not share the comments regarding her mental state or her failure to have children. As he had conveyed the previous day, he believed she should walk away from her efforts to destroy Annalisa. He felt she would only be more infuriated at Annalisa if she knew the full extent of the conversations Annalisa had with Detective Thomas and her husband.

"So, David, the police and the Vermeers believe I masterminded the San Jose affair and Ms. Vermeer's poisoning. Now that all eyes will be on me, we'll have to be cognizant of our activities and who is watching us. This is most inconvenient, but not an impassable obstacle."

"Sylvia, the police think you tried to kill Ms. Vermeer and they have convinced Ms. Vermeer and her husband you are the culprit. "You have to stop all further action against Ms. Vermeer. Let me have the cameras removed from their house and let us move on to issues that actually affect you," pleaded Mr. Hawkins.

"David, we've been through this. I will not abandon the cause. You should understand how I feel. After all, you are loyal to me and, consequently, will do anything to protect me. I feel the same way about Brad," asserted Representative Rossman.

"You are making a huge mistake," said Mr. Hawkins, "and if you continue on this path you may find yourself walking off a cliff to your demise. Don't say I didn't warn you, Sylvia." Mr. Hawkins shook his head, still exasperated at her attitude. He left her office without another word. Representative Rossman made no response to his warning and lifted the receiver to make a call.

Late that afternoon, Gerald called Representative Rossman to announce Brad's arrival. Though Brad did not schedule an appointment, Representative Rossman expected him, given the conversation he had with his wife the prior evening. She was anxious to see him and hoped to get him to understand she was acting in his best interest. She asked Gerald to escort Brad to her office, and while she waited she poured two cups of coffee, adding a spoonful of sugar and a dollop of milk to Brad's cup, just the way he drank it.

As Brad entered her office, she smiled broadly while inviting him to sit. On her desk was the steaming coffee, which he thanked her for as he sat. Gerald closed the door and returned to his desk. The representative moved toward her chair and coyly said, "Brad, it's so good to see you. What interesting political issue are you writing about now for which you want my advice?"

"Sylvia, I'm not here on journalistic business. Rather, the nature of my visit is personal."

Representative Rossman feigned surprise. "Brad, you intrigue me. You know I'm always happy to see you, so what can I help you with today?" Despite her deception, she was sincere in her interest in seeing and helping him.

"Sylvia," said Brad, "Detective Thomas of the Metro Police Department informed Annalisa that an employee of yours arranged a scheme in San Jose, California in an attempt to manipulate and discredit her. I'm aware Detective Thomas discussed this matter with you yesterday. What do you plan to do to ensure this employee will take no further action to harm my wife?" Since Brad fully suspected that Sylvia was the mastermind and director of the scheme, he showed that he too could practice deception.

"Brad, I was shocked to hear Mr. Hawkins took such action, but he perceived a threat to me and was merely expressing his loyalty. I'm very sorry for the pain he caused you and your wife and I assure you we have talked and he will not be taking such action again."

"Are you keeping him in your employ, Sylvia?"

"Yes, of course, Brad. He may have acted inappropriately, but he didn't do so with malice. I reprimanded him and I believe that was enough."

"Sylvia, of course he acted with malice," insisted Brad. "He orchestrated a meeting with a man acting under false pretenses to influence my wife into acting in a certain manner. He did so in order to coerce her into acting inappropriately so the *Press* would publicly expose her to destroy her reputation." Brad's voice rose as he spoke.

"Brad, given you broached the subject, I feel I must be honest with you. Your wife went to another man's hotel room. Do you not see she betrayed you, that she isn't good enough for you?" Representative Rossman implored.

"Sylvia, I don't consider the mere presence of my wife in a man's hotel room a betrayal. She was having a meeting with the man, and I don't care where they had the meeting. If you'd seen the photos, then you would have seen there was no improper conduct by either of them." Brad was certain she did, in fact, see the photos.

"Brad, appearances can be deceiving and we have no knowledge as to what may have transpired had they stayed together in the room longer than they did," explained Representative Rossman.

"Sylvia, they didn't stay in the room longer," said Brad. "Annalisa voluntarily left without expressing any interest in this man. She did nothing wrong. You and I have known each other for many years and I'm asking you as a close colleague to please stop attacking my wife, either directly or through your employees," Brad firmly stated to show her he felt she was a part of the scheme.

"Brad, I haven't acted inappropriately and I'm offended you believe I did. I already told you Mr. Hawkins won't take such action again, so you have no reason to be short and demanding with me." Representative Rossman sounded hurt—the result Brad was cautioned to avoid. Not wanting to induce further retribution against his wife, he recanted.

"I'm sorry, Sylvia, to have accused you of acting to hurt Annalisa. I'm just so upset Mr. Hawkins tried to hurt her. Plus, someone has already tried to murder Annalisa, probably twice. I love my wife and she loves me. I trust her implicitly and I know she will never betray me. I appreciate your friendly concern for me, but you have nothing to worry about. I know you wouldn't hurt my wife, which would indirectly hurt me, but I'm concerned one or more of your employees may attempt again to hurt her. I ask you to please prevent that from happening," Brad pleaded with sincerity in his voice.

Representative Rossman arose from her chair and walked over to Brad, putting her hand on his shoulder. She looked deep into his eyes. "Brad, I promise you I'll make sure you aren't hurt. I will speak with my employees and make it clear what behavior I expect from them. Please don't worry. Everything will be fine."

She patted his shoulder and returned to her chair. Brad found no comfort in her words, knowing full well she believed causing harm to Annalisa would not hurt him, but would ultimately be best for him. He concluded she was unbalanced and dangerous and that continuing the conversation was useless and probably counterproductive.

"Sylvia, thank you for your time and your assurances. I appreciate your friendship and your understanding. I will call you the next time I need your professional advice." He rose from his chair and moved toward the door.

"You are most welcome, Brad. I'm happy to assist you at any time. Don't be a stranger, and have a great rest of the day." Representative Rossman smiled. Brad smiled back and left her office with chills running throughout his body.

The remainder of the week was uneventful for Brad and Annalisa. Annalisa's two local speeches brought many familiar faces. As expected, she was welcomed by supporters and denounced by the usual detractors. The tenor of the detractors' statements was becoming routine and, consequently, the statements lost much of their sting. She and Brad enjoyed their evenings together, as well as the weekend, and she began to dread the upcoming travel the following week to St. Louis, Chicago and Indianapolis, despite the open minds and respectful welcomes that would mostly greet her in those cities.

* * *

Annalisa and Michael flew to Chicago on Tuesday morning, April 22, where she spoke to a large crowd late that afternoon. No suspicious activity occurred and they flew that evening to Indianapolis where she was scheduled to speak on Wednesday at noon. Talks at that time generally brought in an extra large crowd because people could attend during their lunch hour. She was invigorated by the thunderous applause during the speech and knew her publisher would be thrilled at the number of books sold at the end. Michael and Annalisa were in St. Louis by dinnertime and she dined with a group of six people who formed the board of a new grassroots support group there. By the time her head hit the pillow on Wednesday night, she was content and excited with her listeners' responses, as well as the steps the grassroots group had taken to meet with their local legislators. She had finally witnessed her ideas being put into action and it motivated her to advocate more vigorously.

On Thursday, Annalisa spoke to a group of 400 people at two in the afternoon at a St. Louis hotel. Supportive spectators held banners outside the auditorium before her speech and many walk-ins showed up. They were always welcome, and Annalisa hired a local person to sell tickets and otherwise ensure the event went smoothly.

One of the walk-ins was a woman wearing sunglasses whose head was covered with a powder-blue silk scarf. She wore a beige raincoat with a just-above-the-knee dress that barely showed below her coat hemline. She drew no one's attention beyond those wondering why she was wearing sunglasses indoors. She completed the registration form and purchased her ticket with cash, then slipped silently into the auditorium, selecting a seat in a rear corner just as Edward would do when he attended Annalisa's speeches.

As Annalisa spoke, the woman listened intently, but, unlike Edward, she took no notes. With the usual lights shining in her eyes as she spoke, Annalisa could see people, but not their faces as they sat in the crowded auditorium. When Annalisa's speech concluded, the woman politely joined in the applause and exited the auditorium. Rather than joining any of the small groups gathered in the lobby area to discuss the speech, she spoke to no one and immediately left the hotel, heading toward the parking lot.

# *Chapter Sixteen*

"Edward, as you know, we failed at proving that Annalisa Vermeer was guilty of instigating acts of anarchy and terrorism through her speeches. Further, Sylvia failed miserably in painting Ms. Vermeer as an adulterous tramp. In fact, she may even be responsible for the failed attempt on Ms. Vermeer's life," suggested Senator Dobbins.

"Don't you *know* if she's responsible?" asked Edward.

"No, I don't know because she's been unwilling to share her plans with me, telling me it's best if I don't know. That sounds like an admission of guilt to me, but I can't prove it. Either way, Sylvia can't be counted on, as she's thinking with her emotions instead of good judgment and common sense. We both know decisions driven by emotion usually turn out badly."

"If you can't count on Representative Rossman to eliminate this problem, then do you have a plan?" asked Edward.

"Our only option at this point is to take action on Ms. Vermeer's behalf that she won't take herself," declared Senator Dobbins.

"What do you have in mind, Senator?" asked Edward.

"Given that the public, and even our government, is inclined to instantly denounce anyone accused of terrorism, before irrefutable proof is even, or ever, presented, we'll destroy Ms. Vermeer by exposing a terrorism plot she's devised," Senator Dobbins said with disdain in his voice.

"Terrorism? What kind of plot?" asked Edward.

"Since her advocacy is directed at changing Capitol Hill, we can create a plot in which she intends to bomb Capitol Hill, killing all the senators, congressmen, congresswomen and congressional staff."

Edward did not immediately respond, but instead stared blankly into Senator Dobbins' eyes. Senator Dobbins smiled at Edward and shook his head up and down, as if to assure Edward that he had heard correctly.

"I intend no disrespect, Senator, but how can this plan possibly work? Nobody will believe Ms. Vermeer intended to blow up the Capitol and everyone in it. Nobody even believed she cheated on her husband. It's a far greater leap of faith to believe she's a terrorist," explained Edward.

"Adulterers are commonplace these days, Edward. While adultery may lead to divorce in some cases, society overall has accepted adultery as an act without moral turpitude. Sylvia's plan was flawed from start to finish. Terrorists, on the other hand, are deemed by society to be more deviant, dangerous and immoral than anyone else, save for pedophiles, although the reach of their crime is limited. Terrorists, as we know, can wipe out thousands with one act," declared Senator Dobbins.

"You believe all it will take for the public to revile Ms. Vermeer is framing her to look like a terrorist, even if there's no proof?" asked Edward.

"Oh, there will be proof, Edward. One of my contacts has arranged for ten bombs to be made of sufficient strength to destroy the Capitol. These bombs will be complete, but they won't be activated to detonate. After all, if they blow up her house and her neighborhood, then the police will assume the bombs were placed there by someone else in an effort to kill her. Therefore, the bombs can't go off," explained Senator Dobbins.

"That's comforting," said Edward, with confusion and disbelief in his voice.

"Edward, relax, no one will be harmed by the explosives," said Senator Dobbins. "They must be built to completion so that when they're found by the authorities they'll be deemed a legitimate threat. Certainly Ms. Vermeer wouldn't activate them to go off until she placed them at the Capitol, so the authorities will understand this when they find the bombs ready, but not set."

"You've definitely thought this through, Senator, I will give you that. However, I still believe the police, Homeland Security, the FBI and any other oversight agency will conclude the bombs were a setup by one of Ms. Vermeer's many enemies," Edward firmly stated.

"These agencies will have no option but to pursue her. The media and the public will assume she's guilty, and the zero-tolerance policy will result in her prosecution, even when she denies responsibility and is believed by a few cops," Senator Dobbins assured Edward.

"I can see there's no convincing you your plan is flawed, so I'll waste no more energy debating this with you," said Edward. "I'm heading back to my office now. Call me if you need me."

"You'll see in the end my plan is flawless and will fully effectuate my intent," said Senator Dobbins. "On your way out would you please send Jonah Culver into my office? He should be sitting in the lobby."

"Have you involved Jonah in this plot?" asked Edward.

"As a matter of fact, yes, as he'll take care of creating and securing the hiding place for the bombs in Ms. Vermeer's garage. For obvious reasons, it's imperative that neither Ms. Vermeer nor her husband stumble across the bombs while they're searching for gardening tools," explained Senator Dobbins.

Exasperated, Edward shook his head and left the room. Upon entering the lobby, he saw Jonah Culver sitting in a chair reading documents in a file folder. Mr. Culver was a middle-aged man of average appearance without any distinguishing features. He looked up after noticing movement in his peripheral vision. He saw Edward walking toward him.

"Edward, it's good to see you again," Mr. Culver said. "It's been weeks since our paths have crossed." Mr. Culver rose to shake Edward's hand.

"Good to see you too, Jonah. I've been traveling a great deal the last few weeks and haven't seen much of anyone here in DC. Dobbins asked me to tell you to go into his office. I'll see you later." Edward opened the door to leave. Mr. Culver gave a quick nod and moved down the hallway to the senator's office.

"Jonah, thanks for coming so soon," said Senator Dobbins.

"No problem, sir. What can I do for you?" asked Mr. Culver.

"I need a job done—one that demands complete secrecy, as only you, Edward and I are privy to this plan. Your discretion and abilities are the reasons I brought you on board and I need your assurance that all that is said in this room shall remain completely confidential," directed Senator Dobbins.

"Certainly, sir, I shall never speak of our activities outside our circle of confidentiality. How may I serve your purposes?" Mr. Culver asked deferentially.

"Annalisa Vermeer has become a problem that must be eliminated. A colleague of mine has attempted to address this issue, but has failed in her efforts. I intend to succeed in mine. Ms. Vermeer seeks to incite anarchy through nonviolent means, which means she is striving to destroy the lives of all of us who work in legislative government. She won't destroy us, if I can first destroy her by proving violent action is her actual intent," explained Senator Dobbins.

"Is violent action her actual intent, sir?" asked Mr. Culver.

"Not yet, but I won't wait for that to become her agenda because by then it will be too late for all of us," said Senator Dobbins with urgency in his voice.

"Pardon me, sir," said Mr. Culver, "but from what I've heard from Ms. Vermeer, she appears to pose no threat to our status quo.

Yes, she proposes significant changes to the system, but she has no power and so her words have no power behind them. Is she really worth even a second thought to you?"

"Jonah, you sound like Edward. Have you two been talking and joining forces to oppose me?" demanded Senator Dobbins.

"Sir, of course not. We would never oppose you. You should know our loyalty is always to you. I didn't mean to offend; I merely wanted to raise the notion that Ms. Vermeer isn't an actual threat, so there's no need for you to devote your thoughts and energy in her direction. I'm sorry you felt Edward and I were against you."

"I'm the brains here, a senator of the great commonwealth of Pennsylvania, and I know who the true enemies in this country are. Ms. Vermeer is definitely one of them. She is intent on destroying the senators, congressmen and congresswomen of this great nation. Her words may not declare this mission directly because she's too smart to advocate anarchy overtly, but I know that secretly she wants to destroy me, my family and those similarly empowered. So, are you on my side or are you on her side?" demanded Senator Dobbins.

"I am on your side, sir. How can I help you complete your mission?" asked Mr. Culver, realizing Senator Dobbins was not to be reasoned with when it came to Ms. Vermeer.

"Good. I'm glad you came to your senses. Now, I need you to enter Ms. Vermeer's garage by whatever surreptitious means necessary to enable you to create a hiding place for ten relatively small bombs. You need not fear for your safety in that these bombs won't be activated and can't explode. My thought is this: if there are cabinets in her garage, you should saw out the bottom of one of the base cabinets. This will give you access to the empty space between the bottom of the cabinet and the garage floor. If you do it properly, then you can brace the cut-out bottom to the cabinet from underneath. That way, no one scrounging around in the cabinet would by happenstance ever realize the bottom of the cabinet had been cut out and was removable. Do you understand, Culver?" asked Senator

Dobbins.

Initially, Mr. Culver said nothing and stared at the floor. For the first time ever he was concerned that Senator Dobbins had suffered a mental break. What Mr. Culver believed he heard from the senator was strong paranoia, not sensible concern and reasoned action. He had also just seen firsthand that the senator could not be swayed from thinking that Annalisa was an enemy of the United States. He turned his gaze from the floor to the senator.

"Yes, sir, I understand," said Mr. Culver, finally. "As instructed, I'll gain access to Ms. Vermeer's garage and, if there are base cabinets present, I'll remove the bottom of a cabinet to create the storage area for the bombs. Do you have any specific instructions should there be no base cabinets in the garage?"

"Actually, no. If there are no base cabinets, then you'll simply have to devise another means to conceal the bombs. When you've completed your mission, call me, and I'll direct you to where you will retrieve the bombs so you can return to Ms. Vermeer's garage to plant them. I need you to do this as quickly as possible, so start surveillance of the Vermeer house today to learn when she and her husband are normally away. You'll know when it's safe to enter the garage without being detected. By the way, Ms. Vermeer travels extensively, particularly during the middle of the week, which may be your best time for accessing her property." There was an air of delight in the senator's voice as he imagined his plot coming to life.

"Fine, sir, as you wish. Is there anything else before I go?" asked Mr. Culver.

"No. I believe I've given you all the necessary instructions. I will await your call," said Senator Dobbins.

"Thank you, sir. I'll be in contact shortly." Mr. Culver stood and then walked through the doorway, closing the door behind him.

For the next week, Mr. Culver observed the Vermeer residence each day to determine their general schedule. On the first day that he saw Annalisa leave with a suitcase and Brad head out to work, he entered their garage—a simple task, given there was an unlocked door on the side. Wearing latex gloves, he flipped the light switch on and gazed around. Along one wall was a bank of cabinets—base cabinets covered by a Formica counter and upper cabinets hanging above. He could not help but think this job was too easy, almost as if Senator Dobbins had been in the garage and knew there were base cabinets.

Wasting no time, Mr. Culver unzipped his duffel bag, removed some power tools and selected a base cabinet that abutted a wall. He opened the cabinet door and pulled out a notepad and pen from the bag. To ensure that he properly returned items to where he found them, he wrote down the location of each item he removed. Using a power saw, he methodically cut along the sides of the bottom where they met the frame of the cabinet.

Once he lifted the bottom out of the base, he measured the space below and found a height of approximately six inches, just enough space to allow for the bombs and the flush replacement of the removed bottom piece. The cabinet had a twenty-four-inch-wide base, so the two feet of space could easily hold the ten bombs. After snugly securing the bottom piece to the cabinet, he returned each item to its rightful place, turned off the light switch and left the garage.

Mr. Culver drove about a mile and pulled over to the side of the road. He took out his phone and dialed a number. "The cabinet has been prepared to your specifications," he said as soon as his call was answered.

"Good," said Senator Dobbins. "The package we discussed can be picked up from the health club on 1st Avenue near Jameson Street, locker six. You'll find the key to the locker under the doormat at your home. After you access the locker, throw the key away. If you have any questions, call me."

"Consider it done, sir," said Mr. Culver.

Mr. Culver ended his call and drove home to retrieve the key. It was under his mat, as expected. He entered his house and emptied the power tools from the duffel bag. He grabbed the bag, returned to his car and headed to the health club. The club was crowded, but nobody gave him a second glance as he opened the locker and lifted a bag sitting on the lower shelf. It was heavy, but relatively small. As he left the building, he tossed the key into the trash can at the door.

When Mr. Culver reached his car, he placed the bag with the bombs into his duffel bag and drove back to the Vermeers'. He saw the postal carrier on Annalisa's street when he arrived, so he drove past her house and onto an adjoining street. Ten minutes later, he returned to her street, parked several houses away, and once again put on gloves to protect his identity. He entered the garage, seemingly unseen.

Mr. Culver removed the items in the cabinet and lifted the bottom piece with the end of a flat screwdriver, as if he were opening a can of paint. He dug deep into his duffel bag and removed a bag, stuffing it into the space between the cabinet and the floor without removing the contents. It was easy to return the contents of the cabinet to their places, having done so once already that day. He glanced around the room, verifying he had left no evidence of his break-in. He switched off the light and left.

Mr. Culver drove home and sat down at his dinette table. He pulled his phone from his pocket and called Senator Dobbins.

"I thought you'd want to know my work is done," he said.

"Excellent," said Senator Dobbins. "It was smart to complete the tasks all in one day. I will contact you if I need your services again."

"Thank you, sir," said Mr. Culver. He hung up and gazed across the room with a vacant stare, lost in thought regarding his actions that day.

# *Chapter Seventeen*

Hannah Garian, a server in the Gathering Room at the DC Women's Literary Club, opened her oven at home to remove a dish of bubbling lasagna. She placed it on a stove burner to set and cool, and turned to tearing apart romaine lettuce for a Caesar salad. It was a rare Friday evening when Hannah did not have to work, and she looked forward to her boyfriend, Derrick Lowell, soon arriving at her apartment. She and Derrick viewed this weekend evening together as a special time.

The telephone rang and Hannah set down the parmesan cheese and cheese grater. "Hello," she said, matter of factly.

"Hello, Hannah. How are you this evening?" The voice was strange and Hannah did not recognize it.

"Who is this?" asked Hannah.

"That isn't important, Hannah. What is important is what I need you to do for me." Hannah said nothing. "Hannah, are you still there?"

"Yes, I am, but why are you using a voice changer? I can't even tell if you're a man or a woman."

"I'm using a voice changer because I don't want you to ever recognize my voice should you hear me speak at some point in the future," explained the caller.

"Why would it be a problem for me to recognize your voice?" a confused Hannah asked.

"Forget about my voice. Are you alone?"

"Yes, I am for now, but my boyfriend will be here in a few minutes," Hannah said.

"Well, then, let me get to the point. In two weeks, on the tenth, there will be a function in the Gathering Room and I need you to work that night. The function is an ASSIST Honoree Dinner where a woman named Annalisa Vermeer will be recognized. I need you to put an aphrodisiac liquid into her coffee or tea at the dinner. She needs to be embarrassed in front of the senators, their wives and her husband."

"Why would you want this woman to be embarrassed?" asked Hannah.

"She's made life hell for many people, including people whom she professes to care about. It's time for her to pay for what she's done," insisted the caller.

"Why me? Why do you need me to spike her drink? Why can't you do it yourself?"

"Hannah, you serve food and drinks at the Literary Club. You are expected to be handling the patrons' meals, including their beverages. I don't work there, so I don't have complete access to the kitchen. This woman has a bodyguard who watches over her food preparation, so nobody can touch her food or drink other than those employed for that purpose. That's why you must do this."

"I don't know why you thought I'd be interested in helping you with this practical joke, but I have no intention of getting involved. You have to find some other employee to do this for you," asserted Hannah.

"No, Hannah, you're the one who's going to do this for me. You see, I know you worked as a prostitute until last year and I'm certain you wouldn't want your parents, your employer, your friends and especially your boyfriend to become aware of your little secret. You do this for me and your secret stays a secret."

Hannah slumped down onto a chair, stunned that this stranger knew about her prior secret life—a life she had mostly forgotten and that was unknown to others. She had been so discreet, servicing men strictly through an escort she had met in college. The men always booked the hotel rooms and she arrived separately so no one would know where she was going, whom she was seeing or what she was doing. Tears welled up in her eyes as she realized she was being blackmailed. She made every effort to compose herself.

"I've never been accused of being a prostitute," she said. "Why do you think I was a prostitute?"

"There's no point in arguing with me. I have access to facts in ways you could never imagine. There are no secrets from those of us who have unlimited power to be in the know. Yes, there may be no police record of any arrests or any person who claims you operated as a hooker, but I still know you were accepting money in exchange for sex, and I can prove it beyond all doubt should you force me to do so. Do you really want to test me?"

"No, I have no interest in testing you, but I do want you to know I did it to pay for college. I'm in my last year of school now and my tuition is fully paid, so I no longer work as a prostitute. I need less money now, so I started working at the Literary Club. I'm not an immoral person, but people sometimes have to take actions they would prefer not to take."

"I understand, and this is another one of those times when you will have to undertake a certain course of action when you would prefer not to, but your choice is quite clear. Either you embarrass Ms. Vermeer for me or I will embarrass you. It's entirely up to you," declared the caller.

"Fine, I'll do what you demand. Tell me about the aphrodisiac that I'm putting in her coffee or tea."

"It's an herbal concoction that admittedly is experimental, so I'm not certain it will achieve the desired result. However, there has been some promising research that proves in most women tested there is a marked increase in sexual desire and a significant decrease in sexual inhibition. In addition, sexual sensation is anticipated to be beyond the best that can be imagined. If it works, then Ms. Vermeer should be all over not only her husband, but every man in the room."

"Wow, it sounds like the manufacturer could make a fortune by offering it to the general female population," said Hannah. "What woman wouldn't want to have every aspect of her sexual being stimulated and satisfied?"

As upset as she was, Hannah found the aphrodisiac exciting. She had never heard of a true aphrodisiac and the thought of it bringing such satisfaction and stimulation to a woman was intriguing. A part of her looked forward to seeing the aphrodisiac's effects on Annalisa. The caller's answer to her rhetorical question interrupted her mind's wandering.

"Yes, but such a potent potion is best used in the privacy of the bedroom, not at a public function with a bevy of men at her beck and call." The caller chuckled, clearly finding great pleasure in anticipating Annalisa's predicament.

"Will it work soon after she drinks it because these types of dinners often finish soon after coffee and dessert?" offered Hannah.

"Oh, yes, Hannah. If its efficacy exists, then it will produce the desired effect within five to ten minutes. The attendees will all still be there to witness her sexual display."

"Fine, then. You'll be happy to know I'm already scheduled to work that function, but I won't know until I arrive if I'm assigned to her table. That could be a problem. Normally I serve the four tables closest to the windows, but I have no control over where she's seated. If I'm her server, then how do I go about accomplishing your goal?"

"About three days prior to the event, you'll receive in the mail a small vial of liquid containing the aphrodisiac. Take the vial with you that night, but don't add it to her drink until you've left the kitchen because her bodyguard will be watching her food and drink. Once you're in the Gathering Room, very discreetly pour the contents into her drink and serve it to her. The vial will be tiny and clear, so you can easily carry it with just your pinky finger curled tightly against your hand and nobody will notice. Make sure you take the vial home with you and destroy and dispose of it, so it's never found at the Literary Club and traced back to you because your fingerprints will be on it. Do you understand?"

"Yes, I understand," said Hannah. "It sounds simple enough, but since the aphrodisiac works so quickly, isn't there a chance the servers will be searched before we all go home to see if any of us added the toxin to her food or drink?"

"No, there's no chance that anyone will even become suspicious at the event, as she won't be sick, just unbelievably amorous. Everyone will more likely assume she simply drank too much alcohol."

"If she's not seated at one of the window tables, then I won't be serving her," said Hannah. "I have no control over that, and I can't bring her a beverage if she's at another server's table. If that happens, then should I just throw the vial and its contents away when I get home?"

"There will be no issue with the seating. She will be seated at one of your tables," assured the caller.

"You *are* powerful," said Hannah. "If I do this for you, how do I know that you won't blackmail me again; that you won't demand that I commit an illegal or another otherwise questionable act?"

"I assure you," said the caller, "if you successfully complete this for me, I won't need your help in the future and your secret will be forever safe. In fact, I'll reward you for your efforts with a bonus. When you arrive home after the event, you'll find another vial of the aphrodisiac for your own personal use. I believe you and your boyfriend will be quite pleased with its effect on you."

"OK, fine, I'll take care of this for you, but then I don't ever want to hear from you again."

"Agreed, Hannah. Be certain to watch for the package containing the vial and follow the instructions precisely so all goes according to the plan. Good-bye."

Without waiting for a response from Hannah, the caller hung up. Hannah stared at the wall, thinking about the commitment she had unwillingly made to a powerful and dangerous stranger. The excitement of the idea of the aphrodisiac had worn off and she felt only fear: fear she would get caught pouring the liquid into Annalisa's drink, fear the caller would tell the world she had been a working girl, fear the caller would find cause to blackmail her into doing some other nefarious actions again and again. Would she ever be free of this stranger? The doorbell startled her out of her thoughts. When she opened the door, she was relieved to see Derrick. She fell into his arms in a lingering embrace, searching for a sense of security and protection from the monster that she could not even tell him about.

* * *

Just as the caller had said, three days prior to the Annual Honoree event Hannah found a small brown box in her mailbox with no return address on it. She took it into her apartment, cut the tape and opened the box. Resting on a bed of white tissue paper that crinkled when she touched it was a small glass vial with a rubber cap firmly sealing the clear liquid inside. At the bottom of the vial were small, dark shards she could not identify. Next to the vial was a folded-up piece of white paper that she lifted out of the box and unfolded. The writing on the paper said:

> Hannah, take care not to break the vial, as the aphrodisiac is a combination of ingredients that must marinate together for at least one week to reach its full potency. Remember the aphrodisiac must be added to her coffee or tea after you leave the kitchen and before you reach her table. Do exactly as I instruct or you won't find your bonus waiting for you at the door. Instead, you'll find the

*Washington, DC Press* with your photo plastered on a page with a full exposé of your past profession.

Hannah tore the paper into four pieces, threw them in the box and set the vial on the coffee table. She took the box to the building's trash chute, sending it sailing to the basement Dumpster. Returning to her apartment, she hid the vial behind one of many books stacked on a shelf and memorized the book title so she could easily retrieve it in three days. She stared at the book for several minutes as she contemplated the devious task she was about to do.

# Chapter Eighteen

The Gathering Room was decorated with strings of tiny white lights draped over the valances atop large windows and French doors facing the rear garden of the Literary Club. Purple and pink long-stemmed roses filled tall, clear glass vases on each of the eight round tables laden with pink tablecloths and cloth napkins. A white name placard sat on each white china plate, indicating in black calligraphy the name of the guest assigned to sit at that place. The room was inviting even when not decorated for a function, with built-in wooden bookcases lined with books and comfortable tufted light green velvet chairs beckoning readers to sit and enjoy a good book. The rear garden was fully visible through the large expanse of windows and French doors covering one entire wall. The vista showcased rosebushes, lilac trees and dogwoods meandering along a brick walkway leading to a gazebo. The gazebo was lined with benches for enjoying outdoor reading or relaxation.

Eighty guests attended the ASSIST Annual Honoree event. Many ASSIST member wives and their senator husbands, along with Annalisa and Brad, were in attendance. The men were traditionally dressed in suits with a variety of colored ties and the women covered the fashion spectrum from elegant pantsuits to floor-length gowns. Annalisa found middle ground in wearing a gray-blue sleeveless and V-neck, tea-length dress made of sequined burnout chiffon and trimmed with a beaded lattice fringe. Draped over her upper arms was a matching shawl also trimmed in lattice fringe. Her hair was pulled back into a ponytail, held by a sequined hair clip that matched her dress. She was beautiful and exhibited understated elegance.

While Annalisa and Brad stood near the doorway admiring the beauty of the room, Jennifer Hampton and Daphne Wagner approached, smiling. Ms. Wagner touched Annalisa's arm.

"Ms. Vermeer," Ms. Wagner said, "it is a great privilege to honor you this evening. Thank you both for permitting us to do so."

"It's our honor to be here, and please call us 'Annalisa' and 'Brad,'" insisted Annalisa.

"Thank you, Annalisa," Ms. Hampton chimed in. "Would you mind accompanying me, as I know our board members would enjoy seeing you before the dinner begins?"

Brad held his hand in an open gesture, indicating that Ms. Hampton should lead them as she pleased. Ms. Wagner followed behind as they headed for a group of four women. Ms. Hampton interrupted the conversation between Dolores Williams, Patty Witt, Marian Dobbins and Genevieve Holmes so they could include Brad and Annalisa.

"It's nice to see you again, ladies," Brad said, addressing the three women he had previously met. He turned to Patty Witt and extended his hand. "It's nice to meet you, Ms. Witt, and thank you all for the honor of joining you."

Brad possessed the perfect personality for socializing in groups. He naturally bonded with strangers immediately and his journalistic mind found interest in any subject and any person with whom he spoke. Those around him were drawn to his sincere nature.

"Ladies," said Annalisa, "I am anxious to announce to the group the results of the continuing fundraising from my ticket sales since you designated me as this year's Honoree. I am really excited about how many foster children will be able to reach their full potential through the generosity of others."

"I am excited too," exclaimed Ms. Witt. "As I explained during our nominations discussion, the long-term effect of these scholarships is immeasurable. As college graduates, these young adults will be contributing members of society for their lifetimes. They will have an impact on others as well, an impact that will likely extend beyond their own lifetimes."

"I couldn't agree more, Patty," Ms. Wagner said. "The continuing nature of Annalisa's ticket sales means scholarships can continue as long as she does. Perhaps there will even be enough revenue raised to form an endowment fund for the scholarships."

"This is why I agreed to seek out donations through my ticket sales," said Annalisa. "There's potentially so much benefit to be gained for individuals who so often feel forgotten, as well as for our overall society. In addition, the fundraising efforts are spread out nationally so no one particular person or group is continually asked to donate, other than those who attend more than one of my speeches. Given the request for donations is made on my website, it makes it more amenable for a person who chooses not to donate since they are spared from having to account to a voice over the phone or a face looking at them."

"Another benefit is that your system permits each person to determine the amount to be donated," said Ms. Williams, "so a person can give $1.00 or $10,000 and be comfortable in doing so."

"From a practical standpoint," said Ms. Holmes, "as the treasurer of this organization, I must say it's simple for me to account for and process all cash, check and credit card donations either from the copies of your ticket order forms or from the walk-in registration forms. The records for the transactions are handed to me, which makes my work easy. Thanks for that, Annalisa."

"You are most welcome, Genevieve," Annalisa said with a warm smile on her face.

Ms. Dobbins remained silent during the exchange among the women. They all knew she despised Annalisa for her message. Annalisa hoped Ms. Dobbins would exhibit restraint and focus on her fundraising, not on her advocacy regarding the political system.

The attendees were asked to find their tables and sit to enjoy dinner. Brad and Annalisa were seated at the table of honor, which was placed in front of the French doors leading out into the garden. At their table were Senator and Ms. Hampton, Senator and Ms. Wagner, Senator and Ms. Holmes and Senator and Ms. Witt.

Unbeknownst to the attendees, other than Ms. Hampton, who, as president of the organization, made the necessary arrangements, Michael was stationed in the kitchen to watch Annalisa's meal being prepared. He was as unimposing as possible, careful not to insult the chef and staff or to interfere with their work. Hannah and the other servers scurried throughout the kitchen and Gathering Room serving the guests. Hannah was, in fact, assigned to serve Annalisa, as Annalisa and Brad were seated at a table along the wall of windows.

Initially, Hannah was concerned because the caller had not described Annalisa to her. However, given Annalisa was the guest of honor, it was a needless concern, as it was clear to all exactly who she was and where she sat. Hannah remained uncomfortable with her mission, wondering if the caller was there and watching her every move.

The dinner was decadent, offering a rich selection of lobster tail, filet mignon and curry eggplant with sweet potato au gratin as the main dishes. Each main course was accompanied by delectable side dishes, as well as warm focaccia bread and a fresh greens salad. Conversations were chatty and light and laughter was abundant. While all appeared to be having a wonderful evening, Senator Dobbins and his wife sat at the opposite end of the room from the head table and scowled throughout most of the dinner. They seldom visited with their tablemates, choosing instead to quietly talk only to each other.

"Sid, I don't know how all these people can compartmentalize the misguided thinking of this Vermeer woman," said Marian Dobbins. "How can they separate her efforts at fundraising from her efforts to destroy our lives?"

"Because they are dolts, Marian, complete and utter fools," said Senator Dobbins. "It's like the wealthy big business owners in the nineteenth century who made their fortunes by abusing their workers and our political and social systems. Then, in their later years they became philanthropists, donating huge sums of money for worthy causes. Most people focus on the philanthropy and are blind to the initial source of the funds. These people believed the end justified the means. These men would never have had these huge sums of money to donate had they not been such selfish and greedy entrepreneurs."

"I understand completely, Sid, and I agree with you. Dolts, every one of them."

At that moment, Jennifer Hampton walked to the podium and asked for quiet, thanking the Literary Club and its staff for the delicious dinner and promising a most tasty dessert at the conclusion of Annalisa's acceptance speech.

"Ladies and gentlemen," she said, "again, welcome to the 2014 Annual Honoree Dinner. I hope you all are enjoying yourselves." A big round of applause broke out, causing Ms. Hampton to beam.

She continued, "This year we have chosen to honor a nonmember of our organization, which is the first time we have done so. This is also the first year a nonmember has raised funds to support a cause of this organization. As you all know, in the past we have made modest inroads in our efforts to raise funds for high school foster children—children who can't afford the cost of college and have no parents to cover any of the costs. On a large scale, these children are literally abandoned by society at age eighteen and are often unprepared to thrive as adults on their own. College gives them not only the education to become productive members of society, but also at least four years to develop as adults, to mature, to cope, to interact with others on the same journey into adulthood and to be mentored by adult faculty members before they actually enter into society all on their own.

"Until Annalisa Vermeer offered to assist our efforts, our inroads were, as I stated, minor. She has changed all that. As of the beginning of April, after only one month of fundraising, she had collected over $15,000 for college scholarships. I understand she has more exciting news for us tonight about the fundraising that has occurred in the last six weeks, so we can all look forward to that. Without further ado, I present to you this year's Honoree, Annalisa Vermeer."

Applause rang out as Annalisa rose from her chair and walked to the podium, where Jennifer Hampton presented her with a plaque that stated: "2014 ASSIST Honoree for stellar fundraising efforts for the benefit of foster children college scholarships." Applause filled the room again after the reading of the plaque and after Jennifer Hampton took her seat, leaving Annalisa alone at the podium. Annalisa waited for the applause to end, smiling broadly and perusing the crowd.

"First," Annalisa said, "I would like to thank all of you from ASSIST for honoring me in this way. I appreciate the acknowledgment of my efforts and I am grateful to be in a position to raise these funds for this marvelous and worthy cause. Jennifer summed up the worthiness of our mission succinctly and completely. A foster child is often at a disadvantage. Once he or she reaches age eighteen, there may be no adult present who can function as a parent would in giving guidance as to college and career options and helping to obtain loans and scholarships, prepare college applications and finance the cost of college.

"We are now only working on one aspect of the problem, the financing aspect of college. I hope one day this organization can create a college counseling center not only for high school foster children, but also for all high school juniors who feel they have no adult to guide them through the process of evaluating and selecting colleges and applying to them. Potentially, one day there could be centers in other cities lacking them as well."

With that statement, applause again filled the room. Annalisa had not told anyone about her idea, including Brad, who was now heartily applauding his wife and smiling with great pride in the person that she was and he always knew her to be.

"Thank you. For now, my focus remains on funding college scholarships. As Jennifer said, more than $15,000 was donated in the first month I created a line item on my ticket order form for donations. I'm very pleased to announce that in the six weeks since then, an additional $27,744 has been raised, for a grand total, to date, of $42,953."

Applause rang out yet again, but this time the audience stood. Their gratitude was sincere, and even Senator Dobbins and his wife rose and joined in the applause. They too had either compartmentalized their feelings regarding Annalisa or had succumbed to peer pressure. As the crowd sat, she continued.

"As you can see from the numbers, we've not seen ticket purchasers lose interest in the cause. Online donations are also being made on my website separate from ticket orders. I intend to maintain the ability to donate to this cause by making the line item on my ticket order form and the website donation option permanent."

Applause started again, but this time Annalisa extended her hands to silence the crowd.

"While I realize I'm the conduit in this fundraising, I wish to emphasize the money is coming not from me, but from my patrons—patrons who are ordinary citizens who care about each other and about the future of our American society. I would like us to take a moment to honor the many generous and caring donors with our applause. In addition to those donating to the ASSIST program, there are other donors contributing to other nonprofits similarly collecting funds for college scholarships for foster children in this country and those programs are also making huge inroads for these children. I am proud of ASSIST for being one of these worthy organizations helping these young adults."

The entire crowd joined her in applauding and rising to their feet to thank the myriad of people who stepped into the financial role that parents, organizations and institutions seldom fill for these children.

"Finally, I'd like to announce that ASSIST will be forming a scholarship committee. This committee will administer the donated funds and start the application process for foster children. Beginning this fall, this money can be used to pay for these children to attend college. So, if any of you ladies have an interest in serving on the college scholarship committee, then please let Jennifer know. As for me, I will continue in my efforts to collect funds for the committee to give away. Thank you again and enjoy the rest of your evening."

As she walked from the podium to her table, the crowd again stood, applauding her accomplishments. They all then sat to enjoy dessert, which was mint chocolate soufflé nestled next to vanilla bean ice cream drizzled with hot fudge. Hannah served the table coffee and tea—Annalisa had requested hot green tea with honey. Hannah prepared this in the kitchen and carried it out into the Gathering Room with a pot of coffee on her tray. She set the cup of tea before Annalisa, who promptly began sipping it, remarking to Brad how refreshing green tea was, whether served hot or cold.

After an hour or so of enjoying the quartet play smooth jazz, most of the guests left and Hannah and her fellow servers finished picking up the dishes. Annalisa had not shown any sexual inclinations toward her husband or any other man, and she and Brad had left with her full wits about her. Hannah paid no mind to Annalisa as she left, as Hannah was anxious to finish her tasks and go home.

On her way home, Hannah called Derrick and invited him to her apartment, telling him she was not tired and was most anxious to spend the night with him. He agreed to meet her there in an hour. When she arrived home, an identical vial to the one she received in the mail was lying against the door. Had she not known to expect it, she likely would have stepped on it, breaking the glass and causing the liquid to soak into the carpet. She clutched the vial and quickly unlocked the door.

When she entered her apartment, she sat on the couch, opened her purse and took out the vial the caller had sent her three days before. The rubber cap was still in place and the liquid and shards remained inside. Hannah had defied the caller and had not added the concoction to Annalisa's tea, which explained why Annalisa maintained her normal decorum at the conclusion of dessert. Hannah set both vials down on the table, fingering them as if not quite sure what step to take next.

After a minute, she took the cap off the vial meant for Annalisa and drank it down quickly, shards and all. She followed that with the contents of the second vial, treating it as a chaser and thinking that double the potion meant double the pleasure with Derrick. She threw the two vials in her kitchen wastebasket and entered her bathroom where she took a quick shower and put on a red lace teddy for Derrick.

Hannah was already feeling amorous, confident the aphrodisiac was affecting her libido. She put on make-up and dried her blond hair only partway so there would be curls when it fully dried on its own. She dug her pink six-inch heels out of the back of the closet and put them on, practicing walking in a "come hither" fashion while she waited for Derrick. Forty minutes after Hannah drank the potion, Derrick knocked at the door and was happily surprised to be greeted by his salacious girlfriend, who was dressed like a hooker.

"Wow, Hannah, what's going on with you tonight?" asked Derrick.

"I'm turned on and I want you to rev my motor hard. So, baby, have I turned you on yet?" Hannah strutted a few feet back and forth in front of Derrick and then turned around full circle so he could see all of her. Her pouty red lips drew him in and he felt himself becoming aroused.

"Oh, yes, Hannah, I'm feeling it. Why haven't I ever seen you in that teddy and those shoes before?"

"I forgot I had them, but they seemed the perfect things to wear for you tonight. Of course, I wouldn't want to wear them too long 'cause that wouldn't be any fun." With that, she stretched out her legs one at a time and flung each shoe off into the air. She lied down on the couch and unsnapped the crotch of her teddy, exposing herself to Derrick, who remained standing. He stared at her in sincere disbelief.

"Hannah, have you been drinking since you got home from work?"

"No, silly, but we can have some wine, if you want. I'll get the glasses, but we have to drink fast because I can't wait to get you inside of me."

"No, I don't need any wine, forget that. Come here."

Hannah immediately embraced Derrick and they kissed passionately. She took his hand and led him into the bedroom where she undressed him and he removed her teddy. They pleasured each other for the next hour, and then Hannah rolled off Derrick and lied quietly on the bed.

"Hannah, did I do something wrong to make you stop?" asked a perplexed Derrick.

"No, you've been doing all the right things, couldn't you tell? All of a sudden my mouth started to burn inside and it really hurts."

"What kind of burn—like a rug burn from rubbing the inside of your mouth against me?"

"No, nothing like that. It's more like acid has been poured on the inside of my cheeks and they really hurt."

"I promise you, Hannah, I have no acid in me, so I didn't do this to you. Why don't you go drink something or rinse your mouth out? Did you eat or drink something at work you've never had before? Maybe you're allergic to something, but not to me."

Hannah rose from the bed, threw on a terrycloth robe and left the room. Derrick could hear her open the refrigerator and take out a can of soda. He put on his pants and joined her in the kitchen.

"Is your mouth feeling any better now that you're drinking?"

"I can't quite tell yet, Derrick. I'm sorry I just stopped like that and left you in the lurch. Are you OK?"

"Don't worry about me. I think the hour we just spent together in there may have been the most pleasurable hour of my life. I'll just look forward to the next time we experience that much passion together," exclaimed Derrick.

"Derrick, I don't know if there will be a next time," Hannah said with sadness in her voice.

"What do you mean? Why not? Are you mad at me?"

"No, Derrick, I'm fine with you. The thing is, I didn't become that amorous and passionate on my own. I had help. I took a magic potion someone concocted, an aphrodisiac that made me act like a sex-starved nymphomaniac, and I doubt I can recreate that mood on my own without the potion," explained Hannah.

"Can't you just get some more of the potion from the same place where you got this potion? I'd love it if you would take some again tomorrow and maybe the next day too."

"Yes, Derrick, I'm sure you would," Hannah said, "but I have no way to contact the person who gave it to me. In fact, I'd be hesitant to reach out to the person because I was supposed to give most of the love potion to someone else, but at the last minute I decided to keep it for us. If I hear from the person, then I'll just say the aphrodisiac simply didn't work on the intended victim. The person who gave the potion to me will never know I took it all. After all, I was told it was experimental and may not be effective." Hannah put a hand on her stomach and bent slightly forward. "Oh, my stomach is starting to hurt. I think I drank the soda too quickly and now I'm full of air. I think you'd better go. I'm really not feeling well and I want to lie down in bed and try to sleep. Maybe when I wake up my mouth will feel better too."

"Maybe the aphrodisiac is making your mouth burn. What's in it anyway?" asked Derrick.

"I have no idea, but wouldn't my mouth have started to hurt before now because I took the potion almost two hours ago?"

"I wish I could tell you, but I know nothing about aphrodisiac potions and I bet the pharmacist doesn't either," said Derrick. "OK, I'll go and let you sleep. Are you sure you don't want me to stay with you and sleep here tonight to keep an eye on you?"

"No, Derrick, that isn't necessary. I'd feel better if I wasn't making you watch over me. Just go home and do whatever you would have been doing if I hadn't called you tonight. I'm sorry I lost my libido, but my mouth is just killing me. Goodnight, honey, and thanks for the mind-blowing sex."

"Right back at you, Hannah. Feel better and call me tomorrow."

Derrick quickly finished dressing and left the apartment as Hannah went to her bedroom to sleep. She took some aspirin for the mouth pain; it subsided enough for her to sleep for a couple of hours, but then she woke up and rushed to the bathroom to vomit. She lay on the cool bathroom floor, resting as much as she could between bouts of vomiting. At last, she fell asleep on the floor.

The next morning before Derrick left for work, he called Hannah to see how she was feeling. There was no answer, so he left a message, thinking he would hear from her later that day after she woke up from what he hoped was a long and restful sleep. By the time he left work that day, she had not returned his call. He could not call her in the evening because she had to work at the Literary Club for another dinner event, so he planned to call her late that night. At midnight, when she still did not answer, Derrick drove to her apartment and began knocking on the door. When she did not answer, he knocked frantically and yelled her name at the door.

Given the lateness of the hour and the noise he was creating, the nearby neighbors opened their doors to ask for quiet. Derrick quickly explained the situation and the neighbors all acknowledged they had not seen Hannah that day. One neighbor was quite close with Hannah and had a key to her apartment, so she and Derrick went in to see if Hannah was there. Derrick immediately checked the bedroom, then rushed to the bathroom where the neighbor joined him.

There on the floor was Hannah. She did not respond to their calls, but Derrick did detect a weak pulse. The neighbor called 911 while Derrick watched Hannah's chest shallowly rise and fall. As they waited for the paramedics, Derrick noticed Hannah had soiled herself and her robe was stained with feces, urine and vomit. He was certain she was dehydrated from all the fluid loss and that once she was given fluids at the hospital she would be fine. However, he remained terrified until the paramedics arrived.

When medical help arrived, Derrick told them Hannah had become ill about twenty-four hours before and that her mouth burned and her stomach hurt. The paramedics saw the vomit and other fluids and started intravenous fluids to hydrate her. As they were moving her onto the gurney, Derrick told them about the potion and that maybe that was the cause of her illness. However, since he could not produce the potion or list the ingredients, the information was of limited utility.

Derrick followed the ambulance to the hospital. Once there, he sat in the waiting room of the emergency room until a physician came and sat down next to him.

"I am Dr. Fanelli. Are you the young man who came in with the comatose young woman about thirty minutes ago?" asked the physician.

"Yes, as I told the lady at the desk, her name is Hannah Garian and she's my girlfriend. I'm Derrick. How is she, Doctor? Will she be OK?"

"We don't know yet, Derrick. She's in a coma and we're trying to determine what caused it. She was severely dehydrated and we're pumping her full of fluids to hydrate her and rebalance her electrolytes. We've also drawn blood to see what toxins, if any, are in her system. If we find a toxin, then we may know how to treat her, and we'll do so as quickly as possible. She is very sick. Can you tell me anything about how she became ill?"

Derrick described all that had happened the previous evening and the symptoms Hannah had before he left for home. He told Dr. Fanelli about the aphrodisiac and how it had turned Hannah into a different woman. The physician expressed doubt to Derrick that she had taken an actual aphrodisiac, given medical science had not yet recognized any substance as a true aphrodisiac. He explained that some cultures truly believe in them and sell substances purporting to be aphrodisiacs, but there was no scientific proof that aphrodisiacs existed. When Derrick insisted Hannah was sexually aggressive and stimulated beyond anything he had ever seen, the physician remarked that the mind is a powerful thing and if Hannah believed she consumed an aphrodisiac, then she could behave as if she had consumed one.

"Derrick," said Dr. Fanelli, "I'm calling the police so they can search her apartment and look for signs of what Hannah took, as well as any medication, food and drink she might also have consumed. Whatever she had must still be there because it certainly appears she didn't leave her apartment after you left. Before they go there, I'm going to ask them to talk to you, so you can tell them what you've told me. Is that fine with you?"

"Yes, Dr. Fanelli, I will do whatever it takes to help Hannah. Please just save her life," pleaded Derrick.

"We'll do all we can for her, Derrick. Please wait here for the police to talk with you. I will let you know if there's any change in Hannah's condition," explained Dr. Fanelli.

Derrick sat still as tears rolled down his cheeks. He kept thinking that if he had just stayed with Hannah that night, then he would have been able to get her to the hospital sooner and maybe she would be better by now. The guilt crushed him and he bent over in his chair, sobbing so loudly that a nearby nurse came to comfort him. There was no solace for him, so the nurse took him to an unoccupied patient room and asked him to lie down to try to compose himself.

When the nurse returned to her station, she found Detectives Thomas and Garza.

"May I help you?" asked the nurse.

"Yes, I'm Detective Thomas and this is Detective Garza. We're here to speak to a young man named Derrick—we don't yet know his last name—who brought in Hannah Garian to the emergency room earlier this evening. Do you know where we can find him?"

"Yes, despite it not being our normal protocol, I just escorted him to that empty room over there." The nurse pointed to the room where Derrick was resting. "He was so upset that I felt it was best for him to lie down for a bit and to have some privacy until he could compose himself. You can go in if you'd like."

"Thank you," said Detective Garza. The detectives walked toward the room. As they entered, Derrick looked at them from the bed. His eyes were red and wet and he quickly wiped them.

The detectives introduced themselves. "Derrick," said Detective Thomas, "we've come to help determine if someone has hurt Hannah. We know you've recounted the facts to the paramedics and Dr. Fanelli, but we need you to tell us everything you can think of about Hannah's illness and her activities around the time she became sick. Can you do that for us?"

"Yes, I would do anything to help Hannah. I am so sorry. I just hope Hannah will forgive me," lamented Derrick.

"What are you sorry about, Derrick?" asked Detective Garza.

"I should have stayed with her last night instead of leaving when she asked me to go home," said Derrick.

"Derrick, you did the right thing in leaving, if she asked you to go. For now, let's focus on what you know. Please take us through it," said Detective Thomas.

Derrick explained the events since he had met Hannah at her apartment the previous evening. The detectives were intrigued by the claim that she had consumed an aphrodisiac, although it would be impossible to determine the mode of consumption until they searched her apartment. More intriguing was that the aphrodisiac was meant for someone other than Hannah, that Hannah's mouth burned and that at some later point she vomited and had diarrhea. The symptoms sounded exactly the same as the initial symptoms experienced by Annalisa on the night she was poisoned. Just as the detectives were leaving to investigate at Hannah's apartment, Dr. Fanelli walked into the room. He asked everyone to sit down.

"How is Hannah? Did she wake up? Can I see her, please?" pleaded Derrick.

"I'm sorry, Derrick, but sadly Hannah just died. We did all we could, but we were unable to properly adjust her electrolytes before significant damage was done to her heart. Her heart stopped and it was too damaged to start again. She never came out of the coma," explained Dr. Fanelli as he walked over to Derrick and rested his hand on Derrick's shoulder.

Derrick stared at Dr. Fanelli in shock, unable to say a word. Still lying on the bed, he curled up in the fetal position and started crying, getting louder and louder until he began screaming. Despite valiant efforts from Dr. Fanelli and the two detectives, there was no calming him, so Dr. Fanelli had the nurse sedate him. He instructed her to keep him under watch until he woke up and Dr. Fanelli could speak with him again.

Detective Thomas introduced herself and Detective Garza to Dr. Fanelli. "Doctor," she said, "we're investigating the illness, and now death, of Hannah Garian. Have the results of Ms. Garian's blood test come back yet?"

"No, not yet, but I'm expecting them later today. It takes extra time because of the extensive list of items I requested her blood be tested for, given the circumstances of her illness and the question of the alleged aphrodisiac," explained Dr. Fanelli.

"I understand," said Detective Thomas. "The reason I'm asking is that a few months ago we investigated the attempted murder of a woman by poison. She exhibited many of the same symptoms as Hannah—burning of the mouth, vomiting and diarrhea. If there's a connection, then we'll want to investigate it."

"I'll let you know the test results the minute they come in," said Dr. Fanelli.

"Did Derrick give you the names of any of Hannah's family members whom you've been able to contact?" asked Detective Thomas.

"Yes, we have the contact information for her parents, but last I asked, the nurse hadn't been able to reach them," said Dr. Fanelli. "I believe she left a message for them to call the hospital."

"Fine," said Detective Thomas. As she handed him her card, she said, "Please let me know once you've heard from her parents, as Detective Garza and I will need to speak with them. In the meantime, we're headed over to her apartment to search for signs of the purported aphrodisiac and any other substances that may help explain her death. Please have Hannah's body sent to the medical examiner's office, unless her parents are able to get here soon. In that case, hold her body here until they've seen her."

Dr. Fanelli nodded. He gazed at Derrick with sadness in his eyes, as he felt that Derrick truly loved Hannah. He grieved for them both. While Derrick remained asleep, the detectives went to Hannah's apartment to find evidence to explain her illness and death.

# *Chapter Nineteen*

It was 5:00 a.m. when Detectives Thomas and Garza arrived at Hannah's apartment building, far too early to disturb her neighbor for the key. Instead, they knocked on the manager's apartment door, waking him from a sound sleep. As he opened the door, he greeted them with a scowling face and half-opened eyes.

"What's going on here? Do you have any idea what time it is?" he asked.

"Yes, it's just past 5:00 a.m.," said Detective Thomas. "We're sorry to disturb you, but we're detectives from the Metro Police and we're here to see Hannah Garian's apartment. I'm sorry to tell you this, Mr. Wisnie, but she died this morning after she was hospitalized." She and Detective Garza showed him their badges.

The news fully woke him and his eyes quickly became moist, yet not enough for tears to fall. Without a word, he moved back into his apartment and sat in a chair, too dazed to immediately speak. The detectives followed him and silently took their seats on the couch facing the chair.

"We're sorry for your loss. Did you know Hannah well?" asked Detective Garza.

"Thank you, yes," said Mr. Wisnie. "This is a small building, so I know all the tenants, sometimes better than I want to or should.

Hannah lives at the opposite side of the building, but since we both live on the same floor, we cross each other's path regularly. She's a nice college kid—pays her rent and doesn't cause any trouble. I really like her. She's young, too young to die. What happened to the poor girl?" At that, a tear fell onto his cheek. He made no move to wipe it away.

"We're not completely sure yet, and won't be until her blood test results are in," said Detective Thomas, "but we believe she consumed what she thought to be an aphrodisiac. The alleged aphrodisiac was in some way toxic to her. We need to examine her apartment to see if we can find traces of the aphrodisiac and any other substances she may have consumed. We would appreciate it if you would let us into her apartment now. We have two crime scene investigators waiting outside her apartment so they can help us determine exactly what happened to her."

"Before we go to her apartment, Mr. Wisnie, can you tell us if you saw Hannah during the last couple of days?" asked Detective Garza.

"Yes, I saw her late in the afternoon on Saturday, about 4:30 or so. She was leaving for work. I knew that because she had on her uniform."

"Did you speak with her?" asked Detective Garza.

"Yes, but only briefly because she wasn't her usual friendly self. She was pensive. I don't know where her mind was, but it wasn't there with me. She covered her distraction with the excuse she had to hurry because she was late for work. I know her schedule though, and she had plenty of time to get to the Literary Club before 5:00," explained Mr. Wisnie.

"She works at the Literary Club? Which one, do you know?" asked Detective Thomas.

"Yes, she's a server when there are dining functions at the DC Women's Literary Club. In addition to her job, she's a senior at a local college, although I'm not sure which one—there are so many of them here in DC."

"Was she alone when you saw her on Saturday afternoon?" asked Detective Garza.

"Yes, as I said, she was rushing off to work."

"Have you seen her since?" asked Detective Thomas.

"No, she would have returned here Saturday night after I went to sleep, and I never saw her in the building yesterday."

"How about her boyfriend, Derrick Lowell? Did you see him since you saw Hannah on Saturday afternoon?" asked Detective Thomas.

"Derrick's a great guy. He seems very attentive to Hannah when he's here, but they're both so busy I seldom see him. No, I didn't see him at all this weekend. Was he here?"

"He says he was here both Saturday night after Hannah came home from work and again last night when he found her unconscious on her bathroom floor," explained Detective Thomas.

"I didn't see him either night. I go to sleep pretty early and I'm up by six o'clock each morning. Occasionally, I'll see him in the morning after he's spent the night, but I didn't see him at all yesterday. Would you like me to let you into her apartment now?"

"Yes, Mr. Wisnie, we'll let you know if we have any further questions for you later. We may after we search Hannah's apartment," said Detective Thomas.

Mr. Wisnie grabbed a ring of keys hanging on a hook in his foyer. He opened his door and led the detectives down the hall to Hannah's apartment where Greg Dallison and Julia Markum were waiting. Mr. Wisnie unlocked the door, leaving the four to enter the apartment alone. It was dark inside, the lights were off and the drapes were drawn. After putting on gloves, Detective Garza flipped the light switches on in the kitchen and living room and the four began to process the scene.

Detective Thomas examined the living room while Detective Garza entered the kitchen. Greg moved to the tiny bathroom and turned on the light. Meanwhile, Julia opened the curtains in the bedroom and inspected the bed. Detective Thomas first noticed the pink heels Hannah had kicked off her feet. They were lying about two feet apart near the wall facing away from the couch, just as Derrick had described.

Hannah's purse was standing on the coffee table in front of the couch. Detective Thomas sat on the couch and picked it up. Inside were the usual innocuous items: makeup, mirror compact, pack of tissues, hairbrush, keys, wallet, credit card receipts and two ink pens. None of these items could be construed in any fashion to be an aphrodisiac or the container for one. Detective Thomas placed the purse back on the table and glanced around the room, hoping the room would talk and direct her to the toxin that took Hannah's life.

She heard Detective Garza call out to the others, "I've got something here."

The three others moved to the kitchen where Detective Garza was holding two small glass vials sealed with stoppers. They were empty, but all four investigators agreed they were not standard containers for food and drink, so their presence in the kitchen was telling.

"I found these in the wastepaper basket, so it seems whatever was in them was consumed by Hannah here in the apartment," Detective Garza proposed. "Greg, can you please bag them and we'll have them analyzed by the lab? Since they're sealed, possibly some of the contents are still inside."

"Sure, Cat, and I'll take the entire contents of the wastepaper basket and the basket itself to be analyzed too," said Greg.

"Cat, have you found anything else that may be pertinent to the case?" asked Detective Thomas.

"Possibly, Quinn. There's a partially drunk can of soda on the counter. Derrick explained that Hannah drank a soda to relieve the burning sensation in her mouth, so it's not likely the source of the aphrodisiac, but there may be some traces of the aphrodisiac on or in the can. Nothing else here stands out."

"Julia, Greg, have either of you found anything in the bedroom or bathroom?" asked Detective Thomas.

"Other than the red teddy Derrick described, the floor was clean," said Julia. "The bed has clearly been used, but until we test the sheets we won't know what all we've got. I also found a bottle of aspirin on the nightstand, which we'll test for toxins, but I suspect the aspirin was ingested only once Hannah was already sick. There's no sign of vomit in the bedroom and no empty containers lying about."

"The vomit that wasn't in the bedroom is in the bathroom," said Greg. "There's some on the floor and more in the unflushed toilet. I've already collected samples. There was a pillow on the floor, so I think she was in there for quite a while, bouncing between trying to rest and regurgitating."

"Since Hannah appears to have not left her apartment after Derrick did, the apartment probably holds all the clues from Saturday night and Sunday," said Detective Thomas. "However, we don't know when, where or how Hannah took possession of the aphrodisiac—it may have been before Saturday. Cat, will you please go ask Mr. Wisnie when the garbage gets picked up for this building? If it's still here, then we need to search through it. Also ask him if there are any cameras inside or outside of this building."

Detective Garza nodded. "I'll be right back." While she was gone, the three did a final sweep through the apartment for any unturned clues, but none were found. When Detective Garza returned, she was beaming.

"Good news—Mr. Wisnie said the garbage is still here in the basement. It won't be picked up until tomorrow," she said.

"Let's go down there now. We're finished here, at least for the time being," said Detective Thomas.

"Mr. Wisnie also said this building is too small to justify the cost of cameras, so there are none inside or outside," declared Detective Garza.

The four went down the stairs briskly into the dank and smelly basement. They were grateful the building was small, as it limited the quantity of garbage. The garbage chute hung over a large black metal collection bin, which took up approximately one-third of the room. Detective Garza opened the doors at one end of the bin to expose an assortment of stuffed black and white plastic garbage bags. The garbage bags were intermixed with plastic grocery store bags, paper bags and loose garbage not worthy of being bagged at all. When the doors opened, the bags were freed and began rolling about on the ground, as if to say, "Search through me."

Beyond wearing gloves, the group was not dressed for Dumpster diving and was soon dripping in the dredges of the tenants' waste. They opened bag after bag, including a bag with junk mail addressed to Hannah. This showed they had found Hannah's garbage, yet there was no sign of the aphrodisiac or how it came to be in Hannah's possession. As they sifted through the loose garbage that filled in the spaces between the garbage bags, Julia came across a small brown cardboard box addressed to Hannah.

"Hey, I just found a box that was mailed to Hannah," she announced as she stumbled through the garbage bags, moving toward solid ground. She found an open space and set the box down to examine it. The other three turned their attention to Julia as she spoke.

"Hannah's address is typed and there's no return address. The postmark is from this area, so it was sent from just down the street, unlike the material sent to the *Press*. Just as with the *Press* package, there are stamps on the box and probably more than the postage rate requires. So, it was probably dropped in a box, rather than mailed at the counter with a postal clerk."

"It's the smart approach if your goal is to avoid surveillance cameras," observed Detective Garza.

"Right, Cat," said Julia. "There are no other markings on the outside and it's a typical cardboard-type shipping box." She lifted the unsealed flaps of the box, which were at one point bound with packing tape. Remnants of the tape still remained on the box. Julia noticed pieces of white paper inside. She lifted each of the four pieces out, carefully setting each piece on top of the box. She was pleased to find writing on the puzzle pieces and she put them together in order to read the writing to the others. When Julia finished reading the instructions, Detective Thomas was the first to speak.

"We now know the container for the aphrodisiac was a vial, so it was likely one of the two vials Cat found in the kitchen. If there's just one vial for the aphrodisiac, then what was in the second vial? The vials were identical, so both had to have come from the same person."

"Possibly the second vial was the bonus the note references, the reward for giving the contents of the first vial to the intended victim," suggested Greg.

"That makes sense, Greg, given what Derrick told Cat and me," said Detective Thomas. "He said she was supposed to give 'most' of the aphrodisiac to someone else, which means she was given some for herself. The first vial came in the box and was meant for some yet-to-be-identified person. The second vial, the bonus, was waiting for Hannah at her door when she came home Saturday night. That vial was for her to ingest."

"Does that mean the supplier of the aphrodisiac intended to kill two people— first the victim and then Hannah, so people would think she was the killer, and that she had committed suicide just before being apprehended?"

"It would make sense," said Detective Garza, "because then Hannah could never speak about what she'd done or that she'd done it for someone else. We would stop at Hannah and not investigate a third party."

"That sounds like a Representative Rossman approach, Cat— getting a subordinate to act on her behalf so she can keep her hands clean as she hides behind an alibi. Certainly she couldn't have David Hawkins poison Ms. Vermeer, if she was the intended first victim, since we've already determined he instigated the San Jose matter. She would need another lackey to make this attempt to kill Ms. Vermeer," asserted Detective Thomas.

"The note does narrow down the intended first recipient to a female and the female would have ingested the poison by drinking it. That's different than the berries that Ms. Vermeer ate, although that attempt was a failure. So it would seem an alternative poison and method of ingestion would make sense," suggested Greg.

"Yes, one would think so," said Detective Garza, "but think about it. Ms. Vermeer had a burning mouth, severe stomach pains, vomiting and diarrhea, followed by dehydration, just as Hannah did. It sounds like the same poison, just in a different form. Possibly the killer decided that since the berries didn't work, he or she would try some type of liquid concoction."

"It should be simple enough to determine if Ms. Vermeer was the intended first victim," said Julia. "We know it had to be a woman whom Hannah was serving at the DC Women's Literary Club on Saturday night."

"I think we're done here," said Detective Thomas. "Greg and Julia, I hate to ask you this, but would you please throw the garbage back in the container before you get the box, note and other items we've bagged back to the lab? Cat and I will go to Ms. Vermeer's house and see if she's home. We'll find out if she was at the Literary Club on Saturday night."

Greg and Julia reluctantly nodded their heads while Detectives Thomas and Garza headed up the stairs. Once in the car, Detective Thomas noted Annalisa was often in town on a Monday and tended to stay at home, at least until Brad returned from work. When the two detectives rang the doorbell, Annalisa quickly answered. Detective Thomas introduced Annalisa to Detective Garza. Annalisa invited the two detectives into the living room where they sat facing her.

"Unfortunately, another person has been poisoned with a substance that causes the same symptoms as the poison you ingested.

We're still waiting for a number of test results, but we do know this woman wasn't the only one who was intended to ingest the poison. We believe it may have first been intended for you," explained Detective Thomas.

Detective Thomas paused for a moment to give Annalisa time to absorb this new information. Annalisa remained silent as she thoughtfully gazed at the floor. In an unconscious effort to release stress, her hands pressed the fabric of her pants down firmly against the skin of her thighs.

"We believe the intended victim was a person who was at the DC Women's Literary Club for a dining event on Saturday evening. Were you there then?" asked Detective Garza.

"Yes, Brad and I were there for an awards dinner for ASSIST, which is a group comprised of wives of senators. The group named me its Annual Honoree for my work in raising college scholarship money for high school students in the foster care system," explained Annalisa.

"Did you have a female server?" asked Detective Garza.

"Yes, I did. Her name was Hannah and she was an excellent server and very friendly," said Annalisa.

"We're sorry to tell you this, but Hannah was instructed by someone to poison you or another woman at one of her tables. While she didn't follow the instructions, she ingested the substance herself and died," Detective Thomas quietly stated.

Annalisa looked at the detectives and started to cry. "That poor girl, so young and vibrant. She said she was about to graduate from college. She was just starting her life, and now you tell me she's died. How heartbreaking."

"Yes, I know," said Detective Garza. "What we gather from the evidence, including statements from her boyfriend, is that a few days before the event someone gave Hannah a vial of liquid. She was supposed to pour it into a cup of coffee or tea, depending on what the intended victim drank. Hannah had no knowledge the liquid was a poison. She was told it was an aphrodisiac, which means that if it worked, it would have made the victim lose any sexual inhibitions she might have otherwise had in public. We don't know this for sure, but we believe Hannah thought the purpose of the aphrodisiac was to embarrass you in front of the other attendees. We suspect had the perpetrator told Hannah the liquid could kill you, Hannah wouldn't have initially been willing to give it to you."

"Why didn't she give me the poison?" asked Annalisa.

"According to her boyfriend, she wanted them to enjoy the benefits of the aphrodisiac," said Detective Garza. "The person who wanted you dead told Hannah the aphrodisiac may not work, so Hannah planned to use that as an excuse for why you didn't become sexually promiscuous at the dinner, in case she was questioned by the supplier. This person had to tell Hannah this because clearly you wouldn't have had a sexual reaction if you ingested the liquid since it wasn't an aphrodisiac. It's not entirely clear whether Hannah's death was an intended result of the poison's supplier."

"Annalisa, I should interject an important fact here," said Detective Thomas. "We don't yet actually know the liquid Hannah consumed was poisonous. The information we have leads us to believe that, but without any concrete information about the liquid's chemistry, we can't be sure."

"Yes, we're still waiting for all the medical and forensic test results," said Detective Garza. "However, we felt you should be aware your life might have once again been threatened. Also, we wanted to determine if you were at the Literary Club on Saturday night. It's reasonable to conclude you were the intended victim Saturday evening, given the similar attack on you in February."

"I completely understand and I appreciate you letting me know the person who is trying to kill me has likely tried again," Annalisa said, trying to hide the fear in her voice. She rubbed her hands together, as if to dissipate the sweat developing on her palms. Were it not for Hannah coveting the aphrodisiac, she may be dead. She was terrified and convinced she was entirely vulnerable to all threats against her.

"Annalisa, did you notice anything out of the ordinary that evening? Did anyone verbally or otherwise attack you or make you feel uncomfortable?" asked Detective Thomas.

"Yes, I did notice something unusual that night in that nobody attacked me verbally or raised the issue of my advocacy work. Mr. and Mr. Dobbins certainly scowled at me throughout the evening, but they didn't speak to me and even stood to applaud at the end of my speech. Now *that* was unnerving. As for Hannah, she was initially quite reserved and even seemed somewhat nervous, but she relaxed after a while. I decided once she felt comfortable with those of us at her tables, she became more confident in her service. Other than that, the evening was filled with frivolity, delicious food and great conversation."

"How many tables did Hannah serve that night?" asked Detective Thomas.

"Well, I can't be sure, but I believe three. There was my table and the tables on either side of my table. I don't know if she served any tables further away, but I do know there were three servers there that night."

"We will interview the director of dining at the Literary Club to determine all that," said Detective Thomas. "Who were the other women at your table?"

"There were ten people at each table and at our table there were five couples, so five women. Besides me, there was Daphne Wagner, Jennifer Hampton, Genevieve Holmes and Patty Witt. So, I guess they were all potential targets," said Annalisa.

"It's possible, but not likely," said Detective Thomas. "In cases like this, coincidences seldom exist, so for you to be poisoned in February and then for someone at your table other than you to be the target of a poisoning in May is highly unlikely. The reasonable likelihood is you were the intended target in both cases."

"Yes, that makes sense. So, I have Hannah's desire to consume the aphrodisiac to thank for me not being dead," said Annalisa, shaking her head in grief.

"That's how it appears," agreed Detective Garza. "We suspect Representative Rossman is behind this latest attempt, only she was using Hannah instead of David Hawkins. As you know, she's determined to protect your husband from you, as she has this bizarre thinking that you're betraying him and she's his savior. It's difficult to tell if she's doing this simply because of her misplaced feelings and concerns for Brad or because she feels you're betraying her and her fellow politicians by your advocacy. Either way, if she's behind this latest attempt, then she's dangerous."

"I don't understand what motivation Hannah would have for even trying to embarrass me in public. What would she have to gain by helping Representative Rossman carry out this scheme?" asked Annalisa.

"We found a note in the box containing the vial of liquid," said Detective Thomas. "The note indicated that if Hannah didn't do as she was instructed, then there would be a full exposé of her past profession in the *Washington, DC Press* with her photo plastered on the page. Our impression is that Hannah possibly worked as a prostitute at one point. So, Hannah was being blackmailed. In exchange for silence, she was willing to help the perpetrator."

"We believe the threat to publish in the *Press* points us yet again to Representative Rossman, despite her and David Hawkins' claim that they weren't involved in sending the *Press* photos of your meeting in San Jose. Again, we don't see this as a coincidence," explained Detective Garza.

"We'll also need to talk to your bodyguard, Michael, to determine if he noticed anything suspicious that night with Hannah," said Detective Thomas. "He may have noticed her speaking to one of the guests other than as a server. I realize Representative Rossman wasn't at the event, but the supplier of the vial didn't need to be present because, as we said, the vial was sent to Hannah days before the event."

"Certainly—I'll ask Michael to call you, Detective Thomas," said Annalisa. "What do I do now, Detectives? I'm becoming afraid to eat or drink outside of this house, and even then I suppose someone could get into this house to poison my food, if they wanted to badly enough."

"I think we're close to solving this case, and the person who's been trying to kill you will soon be behind bars," said Detective Thomas. "We have tests being done on Hannah, as well as on numerous items we retrieved from her apartment, several of which the perpetrator touched. We're hoping to make a definitive connection between Hannah's death and the attempt on your life, and we may find fingerprints or DNA from Representative Rossman that will wrap up this case." Detective Thomas hoped her comments would bring Annalisa some comfort.

"In fact," declared Detective Garza, "Quinn and I are going to Representative Rossman's office tomorrow morning to question her and David Hawkins. We also expect to receive test results later today. Believe me, we're doing all we can to find out who killed Hannah and who tried to kill you as well."

"Thank you. I know you and your team are making every effort to find the killer. I just hope you find him or her soon," said Annalisa as she walked the detectives to the door.

Detectives Thomas and Garza returned to the station feeling confident they were closing in on Hannah's murderer. After a day that had started in the middle of the night, they were each exhausted and went to their respective homes to get a long night's sleep. The rest would hopefully invigorate them for the next day's interrogation of David Hawkins and Representative Rossman.

# *Chapter Twenty*

Just before arriving at Representative Rossman's office on Tuesday morning, Detective Thomas received a call from Michael. He said he observed only normal activity in the kitchen during the Literary Club event. He and Hannah had never exchanged more than a few casual comments and he found no reason to be concerned with any of her actions.

When the detectives entered Representative Rossman's office, Gerald stood up to greet them.

"Hello, Detectives," he said, expressing no surprise to see them. "Who are you here to see today?"

"Good morning. We're here to see Representative Rossman and David Hawkins," replied Detective Thomas.

"David is in his office, but Representative Rossman is in a meeting in another part of the building. So, I will tell David you're here," said Gerald. As he walked down the hallway, the detectives discussed the faux aphrodisiac ploy, wondering if the perpetrator's intent was to kill both Annalisa and Hannah. David Hawkins then appeared, visibly surprised to see them.

"Detectives, why are you here?" he asked.

"We have some questions about Hannah Garian and Annalisa Vermeer as it pertains to Saturday evening's event at the DC Women's Literary Club," said Detective Thomas.

"I don't know who Hannah Garian is nor do I know anything about the activities at the DC Women's Literary Club. In case you haven't noticed, I am a man, and so I'm not a member there," retorted Mr. Hawkins with disdain in his voice.

"Mr. Hawkins, might we discuss this matter more privately in your office?" asked Detective Thomas.

"Look, I'm very busy today and I don't really have time to discuss matters that don't pertain to me or to this office," he firmly stated.

"We can either talk to you in your office or you can accompany us to our office. It's your choice. Which is it?" asked Detective Thomas.

"Fine, fine, come with me." The detectives followed him to his office where they sat facing him on the other side of his desk.

"Have you taken any action in the last several days intended to target Ms. Vermeer?" Detective Thomas asked, intending to cover all the bases.

"No, of course not, why would I?"

"Last we knew, Ms. Vermeer was still traveling the country advocating the same messages she was advocating in April—the time when you tried to destroy her reputation in order to protect Representative Rossman. Ms. Vermeer hasn't changed, so why would we expect you to have changed?" asked Detective Garza.

"Look, I told you I was done with her when the photos from San Jose weren't incriminating. I have important work to do in this office and for the country, and I'm not thinking about that woman any longer. She is not worth one more ounce of my energy," declared Mr. Hawkins convincingly.

"Mr. Hawkins, are you certain you don't know Hannah Garian?" probed Detective Thomas.

"Absolutely. What is this about anyway?" Mr. Hawkins sincerely seemed mystified by the questions. Deciding to follow his line of ignorance, Detective Thomas answered his question.

"Hannah Garian was a server in the dining room of the DC Women's Literary Club," she said. "On Saturday evening, she ingested a poisonous liquid that caused her to exhibit the same symptoms Ms. Vermeer exhibited when she was poisoned. Hannah was the server at Ms. Vermeer's table that evening, and we have evidence indicating the poison was also intended for Ms. Vermeer. Unfortunately, Ms. Garian wasn't as fortunate as Ms. Vermeer because she died."

Mr. Hawkins stared at Detective Thomas in utter disbelief and shock, digesting her words in silence. If he was responsible for Hannah's death, then he was expert at hiding it. The detectives remained silent as well, waiting for him to respond. As their eyes bore down on him, he shifted uncomfortably in his seat. Possibly feeling compelled to speak, he coughed and responded.

"That's terrible. I am very sorry for that woman's death, but I assure you I had nothing to do with it and neither did Sylvia. I have repeatedly told you I wasn't involved in the attempt on Ms. Vermeer's life in February either. Yes, I tried to hurt her, but with photos, not poison."

At that moment, his office door opened and Representative Rossman came in. She ignored the presence of the detectives and unabashedly started speaking.

"David, I need the report on current agricultural subsidies that came out of Senator Williams' office. Please find it for me." Despite the word "please," her request was clearly a demand.

"Yes, Sylvia. I'll find it immediately," said Mr. Hawkins. He stood up to look for the report, but when his eyes met Detective Garza's eyes, he just as quickly sat back down.

"Well, what are you waiting for, David?" demanded Representative Rossman.

Rather than waiting for him to respond, Detective Thomas turned toward Representative Rossman.

"Representative, please sit down. We have some questions to

ask you."

"Young lady, I am very busy running the affairs of this country and I don't have time for unscheduled meetings. If you wish to speak with me, then please make an appointment with Gerald."

"Representative Rossman, I will make you the same offer I made to Mr. Hawkins," said Detective Thomas. "You can either talk to us here and now or you can accompany us to our office. Which do you prefer?"

Representative Rossman stared at Detective Thomas as if she was trying to determine if the detective was bluffing. Without comment, she moved next to Mr. Hawkins and stood looking down on the detectives.

"Thank you, Representative Rossman. We were just speaking with Mr. Hawkins about the death of Hannah Garian yesterday and how it relates to another attempt on the life of Annalisa Vermeer," explained Detective Thomas.

Representative Rossman made no facial movement upon the mention of Hannah's death, but when she heard about the attempt on Annalisa's life, her eyes opened further and her eyebrows rose, piqued with interest.

"Did you say someone attempted to murder Annalisa Vermeer yesterday?" she asked, an eerie smile surrounding her words.

"Not yesterday, but yes," answered Detective Garza.

"Did she die?" asked Representative Rossman, just a bit too quickly and with hope in her voice.

"No, she didn't, thankfully. Ms. Garian was instructed to taint Ms. Vermeer's coffee or tea with a purported aphrodisiac, so that Ms. Vermeer would embarrass herself. Ms. Garian wasn't aware the substance was poison, so instead of giving it to Ms. Vermeer she took it herself, hoping to experience the aphrodisiac's anticipated effects," explained Detective Garza. With that, Representative Rossman's eyes and eyebrows fell.

"Well, if Ms. Vermeer didn't die, why are you here?" demanded the representative.

"We are investigating both the death of Ms. Garian and the attempted murder of Ms. Vermeer, and that investigation has brought us straight to you," said Detective Thomas.

"Why here?" asked the representative with defiance in her voice.

"Representative Rossman, do you know Hannah Garian?" asked Detective Garza.

"No, I've never heard of her. Let me save you some time. I had nothing to do with any attempt on Ms. Vermeer's life, although I wouldn't be sad to see her go."

"Sylvia," said Mr. Hawkins sternly. "That kind of comment isn't helpful, especially to you."

"I'm sorry, David. I don't want anyone to die, but it's no secret I feel Ms. Vermeer hasn't treated her husband properly."

"Are you a member of the DC Women's Literary Club?" asked Detective Thomas.

"Yes, I am, but how is that relevant?"

"Ms. Garian was a server at the club, so you must have known her from when you've dined there," insisted Detective Thomas.

"Do you really think the members get to know the servers? I'm there to talk to the people I'm dining with, not to the help. I might recognize her face if I saw her, but I certainly wouldn't know her name," insisted the representative.

"If you're lying to us, then we'll find out and we'll be back here. If you enlisted the aid of Mr. Hawkins, then we'll discover that as well," declared Detective Thomas.

"Knock yourselves out, Detectives." The representative glanced down at Mr. Hawkins and left his office, closing the door behind her.

"Detectives, Sylvia would never be involved in killing anyone, no matter how much she may despise them. You really should be traveling down a different path," insisted Mr. Hawkins.

"The perpetrator threatened Ms. Garian with publishing some incriminating information about her in the *Press.* Doesn't that sound just a bit familiar, Mr. Hawkins? Further, Hannah was working for the perpetrator, as the perpetrator doesn't take care of matters personally. Doesn't that too sound just a bit familiar?" asked Detective Thomas.

"It may sound familiar, Detective Thomas, but there is a substantial difference between killing a person's reputation and killing the person. Sylvia wouldn't do either of those things, and I would never murder even my worst enemy."

"That remains to be seen," said Detective Thomas as she and Detective Garza stood to leave. "We will reserve final judgment until the forensic evidence is fully analyzed."

Mr. Hawkins escorted the detectives to the lobby, where Gerald strained to hear their conversation. Afterward Mr. Hawkins went directly to Representative Rossman's office, where he found her writing furiously at her desk. She looked up when she heard him enter.

"David, are the detectives gone?" she asked.

"Yes, Sylvia, I just saw them out, but they're very suspicious of us, believing we blackmailed this Garian woman in order to intimidate her into humiliating and embarrassing Ms. Vermeer in public. Frankly, I can see their point, although I know I had nothing to do with it."

"David, did you watch the surveillance tapes of Ms. Vermeer in her home over the weekend?"

"Yes, and she was fine. She and her husband had a normal, nothing special weekend, but I do know they were gone for several hours on Saturday evening, which is when they were at the Literary Club event. I haven't yet watched any of the tapes from yesterday, but the detectives made it clear Ms. Vermeer wasn't harmed."

"Yes, what a pity," the representative quietly stated. She stared pensively past Mr. Hawkins.

"Sylvia, did you blackmail that woman so she would cause Ms. Vermeer to be embarrassed in public?" probed Mr. Hawkins.

"I can't believe you're asking me that, David," said Representative Rossman. "You know the instructions to embarrass Ms. Vermeer were a ploy, a deception proffered to that woman so she would unknowingly poison Ms. Vermeer, causing her death, not her public humiliation. Death would only convert Ms. Vermeer into a martyr for her cause, and her followers would become a patch of pricker bushes for us, while she herself is only now a thorn in my side. Besides that, Brad would be forever in love with her, grieving her death while never understanding she was not the wife he truly deserved. Oh, and by the way, pricker bushes and thorns aren't poisonous, David."

"I get your point, Sylvia, and I'm sorry I momentarily suspected you of trying to kill Ms. Vermeer," said Mr. Hawkins. "I did my best to defend you to the detectives, but your words, tone and mood a moment ago made me question myself."

"David, I'm a politician, so I'm used to being verbally attacked and accused of a multitude of vile acts. The truth is my goal is to see Ms. Vermeer divorced, not dead."

"Someone is definitely trying to kill her, so the Vermeer marriage may end soon," said Mr. Hawkins. "Whoever is doing this hasn't confronted Ms. Vermeer in her home because there hasn't been one word of conflict uttered in that house. Sylvia, I believe, despite your protestations, that Mr. and Ms. Vermeer are a happily married couple." Not wanting to incite a lecture on the error of his belief, Mr. Hawkins left the room and returned to his office.

# *Chapter Twenty-One*

An hour later, Edward received a telephone call from an assistant to Senator Dobbins summoning him to the senator's office. As Edward walked down the hallway and stood in the doorway to the office, the senator called his name.

"Yes, Senator?" Edward asked.

"Edward, it's time. Please contact Jonah Culver and ask him to make the anonymous call through the appropriate channels to Homeland Security to tip them off to Ms. Vermeer's plan to bomb the Capitol," instructed Senator Dobbins.

"Yes, sir," Edward said, despite being appalled at and disturbed by the senator's desperate attempt to destroy Annalisa, who was no more than a baseless perceived threat. He returned to his car and called Jonah.

"Jonah, this is Edward. The senator asked me to instruct you to move forward with the next step in his plan against Ms. Vermeer. Using the correct channels, he wants you to alert Homeland Security of her terrorist plot."

"Fine, Edward, no problem. I'll make the call immediately and start the ball rolling," said Jonah.

"Let me know what your sources tell you after they investigate the claims," directed Edward.

"I'll call you as soon as I hear the official word," replied Jonah.

They hung up and Jonah looked down at his cell phone. He pressed a number on speed dial. The call was quickly answered, and Jonah began speaking without identifying himself.

"I have credible chatter to report, sir. This relates to Annalisa Vermeer. She has changed direction, moving from writing and speaking about changing the legislative process to purchasing bombs to blow up the Capitol to force legislative change via violent means. She has transitioned from a nonviolent advocate to a terrorist in order to more quickly accomplish her purposes."

"Who is this?" demanded the listener.

"Jonah Culver, sir. I was instructed to call you by the person whose code-name is 'The One.'"

"I understand, Mr. Culver. I didn't recognize your voice, but I recall your name. We've talked several times, have we not?"

"Yes, sir, on behalf of 'The One' I have reported security breaches and informant information to you on numerous occasions," said Jonah.

"Who is Annalisa Vermeer and what evidence do you have to support your assertion?"

Jonah smiled to himself, understanding the irony of the question. Despite Annalisa's highly acclaimed book, public presence and controversial message, Homeland Security, or at least this one man, had taken no notice of her. She was of no significance, yet Senator Dobbins perceived her as a dangerous threat whom he was bent on destroying. Mr. Culver explained Annalisa's mission and message and carefully described the location of the bombs.

"What is your source, Mr. Culver, for the intelligence regarding the explosives in her garage? We receive more warnings of imminent threats than I can count, so we will only pursue those that are provided by credible sources."

"I understand, sir, but 'The One' didn't provide the source of the chatter. He clearly found it credible, however, or he wouldn't have instructed me to contact you," stated Mr. Culver in attempting to convince the listener to act on the information.

"I acknowledge we have received significant credible information through 'The One' in the past, so there is no reason to doubt his sources now, especially when we can easily determine the threat's validity within the hour," explained the listener.

Jonah silently breathed a sigh of relief. He asked the man if he could call him later to learn if Annalisa had been taken into custody. The man said yes, and Jonah hung up. Two hours later Jonah made the call.

"Culver, do not contact me again with information provided by the source that informed on Ms. Vermeer because the facts were inaccurate," demanded the Homeland Security officer.

"How so, sir?" asked Jonah.

"I sent investigators to Ms. Vermeer's residence and there was no one home. So, based upon the information you supplied, the investigators entered her garage to locate the bombs. They discovered the false cabinet bottom per your informant, but there were no hidden bombs. What they found were a dozen bricks. Other than breaking a few windows, there is little damage the bricks could do to the Capitol. How does your informant misconstrue bricks as bombs? Why would the cabinet contain a false bottom and why would bricks be hidden there? It seems to me your informant has been playing with 'The One,' which leads me to yet another question: Why would he or she do that?"

Smiling a smile the listener could not sense, Jonah responded, "Bricks, not bombs, how strange. I share your curiosity as to the true nature of the situation, but I assure you that since I had no direct contact with the informant I have no answers to your understandable questions."

"I strongly suggest if 'The One' desires to retain his credibility with this agency that he interrogate his informant to determine the basis for the misinformation," said the listener. "If he doesn't derive a satisfactory explanation from the source, then he should dismiss the source as being wholly unreliable and should no longer entertain any information he offers. Have I made myself clear, Culver?"

"Yes, sir, you have. I will convey all you said to my contact so he can communicate it directly to 'The One,'" assured Jonah.

"You do that, Culver, as I don't want you to waste one more minute of my time or that of my investigators. Don't call me again unless you have information I can actually use."

The line went dead and Jonah leaned back in his chair. His smile faded as the reality of his fate set in. He knew that soon Senator Dobbins would learn he had disobeyed orders and placed innocuous bricks where deadly bombs were to be hidden. Senator Dobbins was not a forgiving man and there would be serious consequences for his actions. Jonah had carefully considered his options and their consequences before acting, and he was confident he had acted appropriately, yet accepting the consequences would not be pleasant. Being aware that delaying was of no value, he called Edward.

"Edward, it's Jonah. As you instructed, I contacted Homeland Security and they paid Ms. Vermeer's garage a visit."

"Jonah, this is crazy. How could you plant bombs in her garage? She's not a legitimate threat. Dobbins is imagining that which isn't there, don't you see?" urged Edward.

"Yes, of course, I see," said Jonah. "Just as I see the imaginary threat, I also see the senator believes it to be entirely real. Perceptions are real to those who possess them, despite reality perhaps being quite to the contrary. The reality is that Homeland Security didn't find any bombs in Ms. Vermeer's garage and they don't view her as a threat. In fact, I had to explain to my contact there who she even was, as he hadn't heard of her."

"I don't understand, Jonah—how could it be that the bombs you planted were removed by someone? Did you tell someone what you'd done?" asked Edward.

"No, I didn't speak to anyone about my actions," Jonah said.

"Only you and the senator were privy to my mission. I did take the bombs, but I never planted them in her garage. I destroyed and disposed of them so they'll never be found and activated. Instead of the bombs, I placed bricks in the false bottom I created. I wanted Ms. Vermeer's name cleared and I wanted to discredit the supposed source who divulged information to the senator. Homeland Security will question any information it receives through Senator Dobbins for quite some time to come."

"I'm impressed, Jonah. It took real guts to stand up to the senator like you did. I spoke my mind to him, but my courage ended there. You do realize he'll be furious when I tell him what you did?" asked Edward.

"Yes, and I'm prepared for the consequences," said Jonah. "I'm no longer enamored with the type of work I've been doing for the last twenty years. It's time for a change, a monumental change. I intend to resign my position tomorrow and leave DC."

"You *have* thought this through. What will you do?" asked Edward.

"No idea, other than I plan to visit my brother in Maine for a few weeks. I'll decide while I'm there the direction I want to go in from here. I have to be free of the paranoia and power that permeates this town. I'll think clearly once I leave."

"I envy you, Jonah," said Edward. "I wish I could break free of this town, this way of life, but I don't know where I'd go or what I'd do. I've been here so long it's wormed its way into my very soul, although I'm grateful I still know right from wrong, even if my conduct isn't always consistent with my knowledge."

"I'll look for you in the office tomorrow when I come to resign in case you're there. I assume you'll share the news with the senator now?" asked Jonah.

"Yes, although I don't relish being the bearer of it. He may just shoot the messenger, especially since he knows I didn't support his scheme to destroy Ms. Vermeer," said Edward.

The two men ended their call. Jonah opened a suitcase and began to pack while Edward grabbed his keys and headed for the door. Thirty minutes later, Edward entered Senator Dobbins' office to find the senator engrossed in perusing a document. When Edward knocked on the door, the senator looked up and gestured for Edward to come in.

"You must have news," said Senator Dobbins with a smirk.

"I do, but you won't like it. Jonah decided not to plant the bombs at the Vermeer residence, so Homeland Security found a stack of bricks he left instead," Edward said, deciding it best not to mince words.

Senator Dobbins stared hard at Edward, trying to digest the shocking news.

"Is this your idea of a joke, Edward? If it is, then I'm not laughing."

"No, I wouldn't joke about this. I'm serious. Jonah felt it was wrong to destroy Ms. Vermeer when she hadn't exhibited any terrorist activity and wasn't a true threat to anyone," explained Edward.

"You agree with him. You made your feelings crystal clear on the subject. Did you encourage him to betray me in this way? Was it your idea?" grilled the senator.

"No, sir, I had no knowledge of his activity until this evening when he revealed what he'd done. He will be here tomorrow morning to speak with you and can explain himself then. Yes, I do agree with him that Ms. Vermeer isn't an actual threat, but he's entitled to full credit for his actions," said Edward, feeling a bit guilty he lacked the courage of his convictions.

"Tomorrow morning? He must be insane. Call him and get him in here now. His treasonous activity will be addressed today, not tomorrow," asserted Senator Dobbins.

Edward went to his office and called Jonah, explaining that Senator Dobbins demanded to speak with him immediately. Not surprised, Jonah agreed to meet with the senator. When he arrived a short time later, he found the senator's door wide open with the senator facing the doorway, as if lying in wait.

"Get in here, Culver, and shut the damn door!"

Jonah entered the office, closed the door and sat down in a chair directly across from the senator. He made no effort to keep his distance or avert eye contact. He was ready to defend his actions and stand by them with no apology. Senator Dobbins spoke immediately.

"Have you lost your mind? Have I not taken good care of you and your interests all these years? How could you betray me as you have?"

"Sir, my mind is functioning just fine and you've taken excellent care of me over the last twenty years. My actions were not a betrayal of you, but an expression of what I view as the immoral and unethical course of action you have undertaken in relation to Ms. Vermeer," said Jonah with confidence and conviction in his voice.

"Ms. Vermeer will destroy us all, but you won't be here to see it. You're fired! I want you to leave this building immediately. I never want to see you again. Have I made myself clear, traitor?" the senator yelled.

"Yes, your position is obvious, but you can't fire me because I've already resigned. Here is my letter of resignation, which is effective immediately. I'll be gone within five minutes. I'm sorry we have to part this way, as you've been good to me for many years, but we no longer are on the same honorable path we once walked together, so it's best I move on," Jonah said with a mix of sadness and hope in his voice.

"Good riddance to you, traitor. Close the door on your way out," Senator Dobbins ordered as his face reddened and he rose slightly from his chair. Jonah said no more as he left the room. Senator Dobbins dropped back into his chair and stared across his desk at the envelope containing Jonah's letter of resignation. The look in his eyes conveyed an evil intent.

# *Chapter Twenty-Two*

WHEN DETECTIVES THOMAS AND GARZA returned to their office after interviewing Mr. Hawkins and Representative Rossman about Hannah Garian, they found a message from Dr. Fanelli. Hannah's blood work had been completed and the doctor had the cause of death. Detective Thomas immediately returned his call.

"Hello, Detective Thomas. Sorry I did not call you yesterday, but we received the results from Hannah's blood tests after I left the hospital, so I could not contact you until this morning. The results prove Ms. Garian was poisoned. There was such a high level of mezereon toxin in her system over a span of twenty-four hours that it caused, among other things, severe dehydration and cardiac arrest due to the imbalance of her electrolytes," explained Dr. Fanelli.

"That's the same toxin that poisoned the person I previously mentioned to you, although that person lived. Berries were the source of the mezereon toxin for her, however."

"Yes, well, from what we saw in her vomit and other fluids on her robe, there were no berries in Ms. Garian's system. Yet we were never able to do gastric lavage on her because she was too weak and dehydrated, and even in her comatose state we detected heart damage. This convinced us she wasn't strong enough to survive the procedure, at least until we stabilized her electrolytes and assessed the heart damage. The main problem was she was left for too long with the poison in her body before she was brought here. I suspect the other person who was poisoned sought treatment much earlier."

"Yes, she's married and her husband took action after only a few hours of her falling ill, so that's the difference—that and the berries. Did you find the source of the mezereon toxin, Doctor?" asked Detective Thomas.

"Yes, we did. "In the vomit we found a needle-thin piece of bark from the shrub. The bark is as toxic as the berries, if not more so. The bark wasn't in its natural condition, however. Normally, the bark would have broken off from the twig or branch just as any other bark would, and would have retained its entire thickness with uneven edges and contours. In this case, the bark has clearly been altered by carving. It's been thinned along all edges and sharpened on both ends. It's actually in the shape of a needle, with definite sharpness. The ends have been dipped in a substance that reinforced the strength of the tips without compromising their piercing ability," explained Dr. Fanelli.

"Do you think the ends were sharp enough to pierce the esophageal or stomach linings as the bark was swallowed?" asked Detective Thomas.

"Yes, I do. I believe when your medical examiner gets a look inside, he or she will find more pieces of bark lodged in the linings. This means that even if we had been able to perform the gastric lavage, much of the bark may have remained intact inside her esophagus and stomach. By the way, Hannah's parents were here yesterday and they identified the body—a routine step since Derrick had already identified her when he brought her in. They were, understandably, in deep pain over their daughter's death, but Derrick was inconsolable, so they reached out to him and convinced him to go home with them. I suspect they need Derrick right now as much as he needs them, especially since he was the last one to spend time with her."

"I doubt Derrick is going to want to share with Hannah's parents what happened between him and Hannah during their last night together," said Detective Thomas, "but since a purported aphrodisiac supposedly caused her death, I can't see him avoiding it." Detective Thomas spoke with sadness in her voice, as Derrick would have to continue to retell his story and relive his pain.

"Poor guy," said Dr. Fanelli. "He's been through so much, and now he has both grief and guilt plaguing him. He's correct that Hannah would still be alive if he'd stayed with her, but it's not his fault he wasn't with her because she asked him to leave. Speaking of leaving, after Hannah's parents left with Derrick, I sent Hannah and her robe to the medical examiner's office for the autopsy. I also sent the bark needle to be further analyzed by your people."

"Thank you, Dr. Fanelli," said Detective Thomas. "I appreciate your professional and compassionate care and concern for Hannah and her loved ones. If you think of any other pertinent information, then please call me."

"I will. Good-bye, Detective." They hung up and Detective Thomas headed directly to the crime lab, hoping for some results on the vials, the box and the note. She found Greg sitting at his desk hovering over a stack of papers next to the two glass vials found in Hannah's apartment.

"Hi, Greg, do you have anything yet on the Garian items we brought in from her apartment building?" asked Detective Thomas.

"Yes, we do. I've been waiting for you to get back to the office to update you. The two vials each contained water and carved pieces of bark. Since Ms. Garian drank the contents of the vials, there were only traces of the water and one piece of bark in each vial stuck to the inside of the rubber cap. I'll get to the carving in a minute, but first you should know the contents of the vials are different, despite looking the same."

He continued, "One vial contains bark from a forsythia shrub and water. The forsythia bark isn't toxic to humans, so the contents of this first vial wouldn't have made Ms. Garian ill. The bark in the second vial, however, is from a mezereum shrub and it's extremely toxic to humans. Just as the note Ms. Garian received stated, the bark 'marinated' with the water for a while, so the water trace in the second vial is heavily saturated with the toxin from the shrub. The second vial contained the placebo aphrodisiac and it's what I believe the medical examiner will determine killed Ms. Garian."

"Greg, is the toxin in the second vial the same toxin that was in the mezereon berries that Ms. Vermeer ingested?" asked Detective Thomas.

"Yes, Quinn, it is. I can understand the question because each plant is known by more than one name and it gets confusing. Mezereon is a more common name for the shrub, but mezereon and mezereum both refer to the same shrub," explained Greg.

"So, we're looking at the same perpetrator using the same toxin," Detective Thomas said. "Possibly the killer realized Michael was monitoring Ms. Vermeer's food and decided berries wouldn't slip past him or that Ms. Vermeer wouldn't eat any berries given her poisoning. It would be reasonable to think Michael wouldn't notice anyone pouring a small amount of liquid carrying tiny slivers of bark into a cup of coffee or tea. This is especially true since Hannah was instructed to pour the poison in the dining room, outside of Michael's sight."

"That makes sense," said Greg. "The killer must be watching Ms. Vermeer, and so knows her schedule and that Michael is her bodyguard. He or she must be from the DC area or it would be difficult to know Ms. Vermeer's every move."

"You're probably correct that the killer is from the area, but at the same time, her presence at two of the three functions where she was targeted were well publicized. Her speaking schedule is posted on her website, so the public knew she'd be in San Jose. Also, the ASSIST website displayed the announcement about her being the Annual Honoree for weeks. As long as the killer had access to a computer, he or she would know Ms. Vermeer would be at those two events. The guest list for the journalists' fundraising dinner was likely not hard to latch onto either. Then, it was just a matter of recruiting help to pour on the poison," suggested Detective Thomas.

"I had a thought, Quinn, about the perpetrator's knowledge of Ms. Vermeer's activities," said Greg. "If Ms. Vermeer's house was laced with surveillance devices, he or she could easily know Ms. Vermeer's whereabouts. I think it's worth having her house inspected. What do you think?"

"I think I know why I like working with you so much, Greg. If you're available, then I think you should call Ms. Vermeer and ask her if you can come over to sweep her house for surveillance equipment. I'm certain she'll be agreeable, as she wants us to find the culprit as quickly as we can."

"As soon as we're done here, I'll call her and get over there. As for the bark in the vials, it wasn't hunks or chunks as one might expect. Rather, the bark had been carved down into thin shards. In the vial containing the mezereum bark, the shards were sharpened to give them pointed ends. Someone had dipped the ends in clear base fingernail polish, presumably to strengthen them so they wouldn't bend and break when they encountered resistance. In the vial containing the forsythia bark, the ends of the shards were blunt with no polish on them, but because the shards were so similar to those in the other vial, the naked eye couldn't notice a difference," explained Greg.

"That's consistent with what Dr. Fanelli told me they discovered at the hospital, although he didn't know what substance coated the ends of the shards," said Detective Thomas. "He also only found one shard, and it was from the vial containing the poisonous bark. He believes the shards were sharp enough to become embedded in the linings of the stomach and esophagus. The autopsy should confirm this."

"Moving on to the box and the note inside of it . . ." said Greg. "Other than Hannah's prints, we didn't find any fingerprints on the note or the box, or the vials for that matter, so it appears the killer wore gloves. I hoped to find fingerprints on the tape used to seal the box, but there were none, confirming that the killer likely used gloves. However, I do have some good news: I found a long dark brown hair stuck to the tape between the tape and the box. The entire strand of hair was present, including the hair root and the follicle in which it was encased, so it was likely pulled out of the person's scalp. It probably got caught on the tape, and in moving the tape the person ripped out the hair. It's likely the person was unaware that the hair stuck to the tape."

"Great, Greg. That feels like our first real break in finding evidence to identify the perpetrator. Did you get DNA?"

"Yes, Quinn, I did," said Greg. "Fortunately, I had both the hair root and follicle because that's where nuclear DNA is best found. It's also good this person wasn't using hair dye because dye degrades the DNA. Unfortunately, though, this DNA isn't in our system. Given the hair length, I believe our killer is a woman, although some men wear their hair long, so I can't be certain of that." Greg lifted a clear bag off a nearby table to show the hair inside to Detective Thomas.

"At least there's a good chance we have the perpetrator's DNA," said Detective Thomas. "Now we have it to match against the DNA of any suspects. We have one-half of the equation. I wish I had Sylvia Rossman's DNA, as she's our primary suspect, is local and has fairly long, dark hair. Plus, while I've so far resisted the stereotype, female murderers use poison more often than men."

"From what Cat's told me, Representative Rossman insists she's innocent, so maybe she'd be willing to give you a hair or other DNA sample so we can rule her out as a suspect. It can't hurt to ask her. What about Mr. Hawkins—is his hair dark like this hair?" asked Greg.

"No, his hair is blond; plus he wears it short, so he's not our culprit. It would be most imprudent for Representative Rossman to use his services for any actions against Ms. Vermeer given we have him on our short list of suspects. As a politician, she has a multitude of minions at her beck and call, so she could call on any number of them, including a male or female with dark hair," asserted Detective Thomas.

"It's good we can rule out at least one of our suspects, but I agree Representative Rossman can still be the main perpetrator, merely pulling the strings of another of her puppets," said Greg. "It's time for me to give Ms. Vermeer a call. Julia is analyzing the robe the hospital sent over, so you may want to touch base with her."

"Thanks, Greg, I'll go talk with Julia now. Please let me know if you find anything of interest at Ms. Vermeer's house," said Detective Thomas. When Detective Thomas entered the part of the lab where Julia was working, Julia put down the robe and walked in her direction.

"Hi, Quinn," she said with exasperation in her voice. "This poor girl went through hell. Her robe has vomit, diarrhea, saliva, urine, phlegm and tears covering it, and this all happened within one day. Traces of the liquid she thought was an aphrodisiac are also on the robe, mixed in with the vomit. Within the traces of liquid, we found two shards from the vials, one forsythia and one mezereum."

"Dr. Fanelli called me with Hannah's blood test results," Detective Thomas said, "and your findings agree with his in that Hannah ingested the liquid in both vials. The vial for Ms. Vermeer was filled with the toxin and the vial intended for Hannah contained plain water and innocuous forsythia bark. If Hannah hadn't decided to ingest the 'aphrodisiac,' then Ms. Vermeer would have spent another night in the hospital. She possibly would have died once the shards became embedded in her digestive tract, which is what Dr. Fanelli believes is the case with Hannah. We'll know if that occurred once the autopsy results are in."

"Quinn, I've studied the shards in great detail and the effort that went into making them was substantial," said Julia. The creation of them, while diabolical, was done with artistry, patience and a total commitment to causing Ms. Vermeer's death."

"We're dealing with a narcissist whose vanity and self-importance are so fragile that Ms. Vermeer's advocacy is perceived as a threat that must be destroyed by destroying her," said Detective Thomas. "The question is, has Representative Rossman only pursued destroying Ms. Vermeer's reputation or has she moved to the next level by trying to destroy her physically? Is she so protective of Brad and her own ego that she would try to kill Ms. Vermeer?" Julia shrugged her shoulders and Detective Thomas left the lab.

Three hours later, Greg walked into Detective Thomas's office carrying a small cloth bag bulging at the sides. Without a word, he unzipped the bag, lifted it and turned it over. Numerous miniature cameras with attached microphones spilled onto Detective Thomas's desk.

"I found these in Ms. Vermeer's house, in every single room except the bathrooms," said Greg. "A few were also attached outside with views of all sides of the yard and house. The only places where the Vermeers had privacy were in the bathrooms. Otherwise, they were being watched and listened to every minute of the day and night for who knows how long. Ms. Vermeer is in shock over this, and I didn't leave her until she had called her husband and he came home."

"This has David Hawkins' and Representative Rossman's signatures on it," said Detective Thomas. "We already have Mr. Hawkins' admission that he had cameras planted in San Jose, so how far of a stretch is it to believe he had his installer pay a visit to the Vermeer residence?"

"I'd say it's time to get David Hawkins to confess," said Greg.

"Yes, but it's too late to go today. I'll head over there first thing tomorrow morning. You have a good evening, Greg. While I'm meeting with David Hawkins in the morning, please inspect all the surveillance equipment for prints and DNA. Call me if you find anything. I'll haul both of them in here if you can definitively connect them to those cameras."

"Sure thing, Quinn. I'll get right on it in the morning," said Greg. He walked toward the door, then stopped and turned toward Quinn.

"While you're there, take a look for any stray hairs lying around in the representative's office," said Greg facetiously.

Detective Thomas smiled as he left, returning to the lab.

* * *

The next day, when Detective Thomas walked into Representative Rossman's office lobby, Gerald looked up and immediately spoke.

"Hello, Detective Thomas," he said. "I'll let Mr. Hawkins know you're here."

"Thank you," said Detective Thomas. Gerald lifted the receiver to call Mr. Hawkins. A moment later, Mr. Hawkins appeared. His face had an irritated look and he stared intently into Detective Thomas' eyes.

"What do you want now, Detective?" he asked.

"I have some additional questions for you. Could we take this conversation to your office?" asked Detective Thomas.

Silently, Mr. Hawkins turned and led her down the hallway to his office. He sat in his desk chair and stared at her while she closed the door.

"I already told you— I had nothing to do with killing or attempting to kill anyone. At this point, I believe you're harassing me, Detective," asserted Mr. Hawkins.

"Mr. Hawkins, yesterday we found a multitude of cameras and microphones inside and outside the Vermeer residence. Given you admitted you orchestrated the installation of the cameras in San Jose, my first thought was that you are responsible for the surveillance at the Vermeers' home." Detective Thomas thought she detected a slight flush in Mr. Hawkins' face, but his facial expression remained unresponsive to her statement.

"Is there a question in there, Detective?" he demanded.

"Yes. Did you install or arrange for someone else to install cameras and listening devices at the Vermeer residence?"

"No," insisted Mr. Hawkins.

"What is the name of the person who installed the cameras for you at The Fairmont?" asked Detective Thomas.

"How is that relevant to your current interest in the cameras at the Vermeer residence?"

"Why get a new installer when the first one did competent work?" asked Detective Thomas rhetorically.

"I don't know his name. I found him online and all our communications were handled online. I cleaned the hard drive so I can no longer access any pertinent information," asserted Mr. Hawkins.

"How did you pay him for his services?"

"I sent cash with the cameras to pay half of his fee. After he sent me proof the cameras were installed, I left cash for him for the remainder of the fee on a park bench in a local park. Before you ask me his address, I don't have it. I sent the cameras and the first fee installment directly to The Fairmont, addressed to Glenn Sanders, and the installer picked up the package posing as his associate."

"It sounds as if you thought of everything, Mr. Hawkins, in order to keep your operative's identity secret. It's hard to believe he would ask you to leave cash sitting on a park bench for anyone to take, but if that's true, then we know he resides in this area. Excuse my skepticism, but I believe you know far more than you're inclined to admit."

"Believe what you want, Detective. I really don't care. Now, I must get back to work. Are we done here?" asked Mr. Hawkins.

"You and I are, but now I need to speak with your boss. Before you tell me Representative Rossman is otherwise engaged, let me remind you I can find her and take her to my interrogation room to question her."

"Fine, fine, I'll get her." Mr. Hawkins left his office and didn't return for five minutes. This told Detective Thomas they were responsible for the Vermeer surveillance and were discussing damage control as to the San Jose affair. When Mr. Hawkins returned, Representative Rossman accompanied him and warmly greeted Detective Thomas.

"Hello, Detective Thomas. I'm always happy to assist where I can. So, how can I help you today?" she asked, barely disguising her disdain.

"Thank you, Representative, I appreciate your willingness to cooperate. On that note, before we get to the issue of the surveillance of the Vermeer home, as I'm sure Mr. Hawkins has shared with you, I'd like to accept your offer of assistance. Would you be so kind as to give me a sample of your DNA?"

Representative Rossman looked perplexed and momentarily did not respond.

"Why would you want my DNA?" she asked. "I had nothing to do with any surveillance of the Vermeers."

"Giving me your DNA is very simple. All I need is a strand of your hair. It's virtually painless, and you did ask how you could help me today," said Detective Thomas, boxing the representative into a corner.

Representative Rossman reflected for a moment, wondering why the detective wanted her DNA and whether it was prudent to deliver it. She elected to cooperate, knowing her DNA could not incriminate her because she was not personally involved in surveilling Annalisa. She opened the center drawer of her desk and drew out a pair of scissors.

"Representative Rossman," said Detective Thomas, "we may not be able to get your DNA from a snipped-off piece of hair. We need the entire strand, so I'd appreciate it if you'd pull a strand out of your head, which is why I said the process is 'virtually' painless."

The representative stared at the detective as she reevaluated her decision. After a moment's pause, she carefully separated a strand of her hair, took hold of it next to her scalp and gave it a firm jerk away from her head. She returned the scissors to the drawer and handed the hair to the detective, who pulled a clear evidence bag from her pocket and placed the hair inside. Detective Thomas could not help but smile, thinking of what Greg's expression would be when she handed him the hair.

"Thank you, Representative. Now, you stated a moment ago you had no involvement in installing the surveillance equipment in the Vermeer residence, correct?" asked Detective Thomas.

"Correct. I know nothing about the matter."

"Have you seen any of the camera feed or listened to the recorded audio?"

"No, I haven't," said Representative Rossman with growing irritation in her voice.

"Fine. Those are all my questions for now. I'll let you know if I have any further inquiries," said Detective Thomas.

"You do that, Detective," Representative Rossman said sarcastically as Detective Thomas left the room.

When Detective Thomas returned to the station, she went to the lab to give Greg the representative's strand of hair.

"Greg, I have some evidence for you to analyze," she said. He looked up from his work and smiled.

"What do you have, Quinn?" Detective Thomas pulled the bag out of her pocket and handed it to him. Once he saw there was a hair inside, his smile immediately broadened.

"How did you get her to give this up?" Greg asked.

"A bit of manipulation and distraction. She was focused on surveilling Ms. Vermeer and also presented an air of cooperation. So, I combined the two to convince her it was prudent to give me the sample. I'm certain she wasn't connecting the hair to Hannah's death or Ms. Vermeer's attempted murder," explained Detective Thomas.

"Great, I'll get right on this. By the way, I just finished dusting the cameras and, as usual, there were no prints. There also weren't any hairs or other DNA, so it's another dead end."

"OK, Greg. I have another idea for how to identify the installer. I'll let you know if my idea pans out. Meanwhile, please let me know as soon as you've compared the two hairs." Greg nodded and Detective Thomas headed to Detective Garza's office.

# *Chapter Twenty-Three*

"CAT, DID GREG BRING YOU up to speed on the cameras he discovered in the Vermeer residence?" asked Detective Thomas.

"Yes, Quinn, he did. It's lunacy how much effort is being put forth to destroy Ms. Vermeer."

"Lunacy is the right word. I'd also add "narcissism" to the mix because someone is so enchanted with himself or herself that the perceived threat to that ego has been enough to drive that person to destruction," said Detective Thomas.

"That and *self-destruction*," added Detective Garza.

"David Hawkins told me his hired gun in San Jose picked up the cameras and the first payment from the hotel desk before Mr. Sanders checked in," said Detective Thomas. "Would you please contact Chief Sorenson and ask him to revisit the surveillance tapes he obtained, focusing on several days before Mr. Sanders arrived? Ask him if he can get a good look at the face of the person who picked up the package. Chief Sorenson will also have to touch base with the front desk clerk who handed the package to the man to see if he or she has any information as well. The clerk may be able to pinpoint the date and time when the package was delivered to the installer, as well as give a description of the package."

"Sure, Quinn, I'll call him right away."

"Thanks, Cat. Let me know what you find out." Detective Thomas left the office and Detective Garza picked up the phone to call Chief Sorenson. Once he answered, she explained the new information they had obtained and he agreed to review the tapes and interview the desk clerk.

Greg walked into Detective Thomas' office and announced he had compared the two hairs.

"They don't match," he said. "They're from two different people. The color is similar, but the DNA is not."

"So, that means Sylvia Rossman didn't herself package the box to Hannah. She still could have hired someone else to send the package," asserted Detective Thomas.

"That's true, Quinn," agreed Greg. "I doubt she does much herself. She certainly can't get her own hands dirty."

"Cat has asked Chief Sorenson in San Jose for some assistance that could potentially move us forward on the surveillance issue. Hopefully, she will hear from him tomorrow. We should also be hearing from the medical examiner in a day or two, which may give us additional evidence toward finding our killer."

"Good, Quinn," Greg said as he walked toward the door.

* * *

The next afternoon, Chief Sorenson called Detective Garza.

"Detective," he said, "I spoke with the desk clerk who delivered the package to your camera installer. Fortunately, the young man was working when my detective went to the hotel and he recalled the delivery. The desk clerk said a man picked up the package in the afternoon of the day Mr. Sanders checked in and was in a very big hurry. The clerk was working on the computer when the man approached him and demanded the package immediately, despite the clerk indicating he was almost completed with his task. The man paced the floor while waiting and rushed away once the delivery was made. This recollection made it easy for my staff to locate the event on the tape."

"Great," Detective Garza said. "I've never understood why some criminals don't realize that flying under the radar is far more beneficial to their interests than creating a scene. Those scenes become unforgettable, and that is far more beneficial to us."

"I completely agree, Detective. The scene was located on the tape and the man made no effort to conceal his face from the camera at the front desk. We used our facial recognition databases to identify him. He's former CIA and his name is John Kasmo. He's not from San Jose, however. You'll likely not be surprised to hear he lives in DC. He's probably a freelance security officer for hire," suggested Chief Sorenson.

"That makes sense. He's probably well known among our local government officials. He wouldn't be hard to find for someone who holds substantial power and is heavily connected. Would you please forward a copy of the tape to me, as well as the identification data you obtained?" asked Detective Garza.

"Certainly. We'll get it out to you today. We also viewed the tapes covering the door to Mr. Sanders' hotel room and never saw Mr. Kasmo entering the room. Aside from Mr. Sanders and Ms. Vermeer, only housekeepers entered Mr. Sanders' room after the package was picked up. So, we think either a housekeeper impersonator or a bought housekeeper must have installed the cameras. Given it takes some skill to hide cameras from view when installing them, I believe Mr. Kasmo disguised himself as a housekeeper. Let me know if I can be of any further assistance."

"Thanks, Chief. I agree with your assessment and believe the same approach was taken in removing the cameras since the tapes after Mr. Sanders left show only maids entering the room. Therefore, as you stated, either a different person, a woman, removed the cameras or Mr. Kasmo disguised himself as a woman. I appreciate your help and will get back to you if I need anything else." They hung up and Detective Garza went to Detective Thomas's office to deliver the news of the identification of John Kasmo.

"Let's find Mr. Kasmo's address and pay him a visit," said Detective Garza. Detective Thomas started typing on her keyboard until she located his address in one of their various directories and databases.

"Mr. Kasmo lives in the Anacostia Waterfront neighborhood," said Detective Thomas. "Let's see if he'll admit to working with Mr. Hawkins and Representative Rossman."

The two went to Mr. Kasmo's apartment and knocked on the door. They were pleased he was home and opened the door. Before them stood a man of average height with a salt-and-pepper beard and gray hair surrounding a balding head. He appeared to be about sixty years old and smiled at the detectives as he said, "Hi. How may I help you, ladies?"

"Are you John Kasmo?" asked Detective Garza.

"Yes, I am. Who are you?" asked Mr. Kasmo.

"I'm Detective Catalonia Garza and this is Detective Quinn Thomas. We're from the Metro Police Department and are here to ask you a few questions regarding David Hawkins and Sylvia Rossman."

"Come on in, ladies, and make yourselves comfortable," Mr. Kasmo said as he fully opened the door. They thanked him and stepped inside. He led them to his living room where he offered them chairs. "So," he said, "what questions do you have for me?"

"First, Mr. Kasmo, we want to ensure you're the Mr. Kasmo who was formerly employed by the CIA," said Detective Thomas.

"Yes, that's me. I worked for the agency for thirty-two years and retired last year. Now I consult for various parties who can benefit from my services," explained Mr. Kasmo.

"Exactly what type of services do you provide?" asked Detective Garza.

"Numerous services—anything from security to surveillance. It's kind of funny—one day I'm guarding people and their secrets and the next day I'm following them to discover their secrets," admitted Mr. Kasmo.

"Did you place some cameras in a room at The Fairmont Hotel in San Jose, California, in early April?" asked Detective Thomas.

Mr. Kasmo, who until then had been so willing to discuss his work, suddenly fell silent and squirmed, as he appeared to be pondering the question before him. He began tapping the fingers of his right hand on the arm of his chair. At last, he spoke.

"My clients and the work I do for them are confidential. I cannot discuss any specifics with you," he said.

"Mr. Kasmo, I'm going to cut to the chase. We have you on tape at the front desk of the hotel picking up the package containing the cameras and cash. Therefore, there's no point in you hiding behind confidentiality or pretending you didn't work for David Hawkins," explained Detective Thomas.

"Fine—he did retain my services to install cameras in the hotel room, but what's the problem? Mr. Hawkins was investigating a possible terrorist and needed to listen to his conversations and watch what transpired in the room. These are services that government personnel don't always have the time to handle, particularly when the risk hasn't yet been fully substantiated. Of what concern is a possible terrorist to the Metro Police and why are you talking to me when Mr. Hawkins knows the specifics of the terrorist?" asked Mr. Kasmo.

"Mr. Kasmo, there was no possible terrorist," said Detective Garza. "You were lied to, as you were in the room of a man sent there by Mr. Hawkins. The purpose of the cameras was to attempt to destroy the reputation of a woman who was in the room meeting with the hotel guest."

"Hey, when a government employee hires me, I believe what they tell me and I have no responsibility to research the backstory I'm given. I trust anyone who works on Capitol Hill and in the Pentagon. After all, they're the ones in charge of this country and they know what they're doing," asserted Mr. Kasmo.

"Did you remove the cameras from the hotel room?" asked Detective Garza.

"Yes," responded Mr. Kasmo sheepishly. "Since it was early in the morning, maids were everywhere. Therefore, the best way to fit in undetected was to pretend to be a maid. Three days before, I bought a wig and borrowed a uniform from the hotel. I disguised myself as a maid to get into the room to extricate the cameras. I obviously didn't have a beard then. I used the same disguise when I installed the cameras while the room occupant was attending some speech at the hotel the day before."

"How did you know where to install the cameras?" asked Detective Garza.

"Mr. Hawkins provided me with a photo of the man who was to be watched, as well as the approximate time he would arrive at the hotel. So I waited in the parking lot until I saw him arrive and then I followed him into the hotel, again disguised as a maid. When he went to his room, he never suspected he was being followed by a maid, so it was easy to get his room number. I left the hotel until the next day when I planted the cameras in the room," explained Mr. Kasmo matter-of-factly.

"What was the reason Mr. Hawkins gave you for installing hidden cameras at the Vermeer residence?" asked Detective Thomas.

"I don't know who those people are, at least not by name. Can you be more specific?"

"They live in Glover Park at 721 Coventry Court. Does that address sound familiar?" asked Detective Thomas.

"Yes, it does. Mr. Hawkins had me install those cameras in February or March. He said there was an arms dealer living there and the government had to watch his every move in order to amass the necessary evidence to prosecute him. Was that a lie too?" asked Mr. Kasmo.

"Yes, it was. Considering you were a CIA agent, you seem pretty gullible, Mr. Kasmo," declared Detective Thomas.

"I wasn't an agent. I was more of an assistant in that I installed surveillance devices where agents needed them, and at times I watched people or things in order to track or guard them. I followed the instructions of the higher-ups and I never gave orders, so discerning truth from fiction wasn't a job requirement," explained Mr. Kasmo.

"So, you listened to Mr. Hawkins' instructions without any consideration for the truth, correct?" asked Detective Garza.

"Right. I figured if the Department of Homeland Security trusted him enough to employ him, then there was no reason for me to question him."

"Mr. Hawkins doesn't work for Homeland Security. He works for Representative Sylvia Rossman. Have you had any contact with her or did Mr. Hawkins indicate she was involved in these operations?" questioned Detective Garza.

Mr. Kasmo put his hands over his face and bent over, as if in pain. He shook his head back and forth several times before he spoke.

"I feel like such a fool. I blindly followed Mr. Hawkins' lead, never questioning him, never even thinking to question him. I wonder if anything he told me was true. As for the representative you mentioned, no, I've never heard of her."

"Have you ever met Mr. Hawkins in person?" asked Detective Garza.

"Sure. I met him when he hired me to do the camera installation in Glover Park, when he gave me the cameras to install, when he paid me for the job and again when I delivered the photos and the cameras from the San Jose hotel and he paid me," said Mr. Kasmo.

"How did he know of you and the services you offer?" asked Detective Garza.

"It is well known in the various governmental departments that a group of us retired guys from the CIA and FBI is available for surveillance and security work. We routinely network ourselves among the current agents so they can refer us if asked for outside assistance.

Our availability is no secret," explained Mr. Kasmo.

"Did Mr. Hawkins ask you to perform any services in addition to the surveillance work you did, such as provide him with any plant material?" asked Detective Thomas.

"Plant material? What do you mean? I don't have any plants here. Mr. Hawkins and I never discussed plants. He was all about the watchful eye on the marks. All I ever did was install cameras for him and clean the San Jose hotel room after the occupant checked out," Mr. Kasmo said.

"So, you're the one who virtually sterilized the room," said Detective Thomas. "Were you in your maid disguise when you did that too?"

"Yes, I was. First, I went into the room and uninstalled the cameras. Then, with the cameras hidden in my cart, I rolled the cart to a housekeeper supply closet, removed the bag holding the cameras from the cart and took the bag to my car. I then returned to my cart and went to the room with bleach and other cleaning supplies and chemicals to sanitize it," explained Mr. Kasmo.

"That explains the presence of two maids separately entering the room the morning of the room occupant's departure," said Detective Garza.

"Mr. Kasmo, these are all the questions we have for you at this moment," said Detective Thomas. "We may need to contact you later, so please don't leave town without first letting one of us know. I suggest that prior to accepting any further work you properly vet the person hiring you and the alleged facts presented to you." Each detective handed Mr. Kasmo her business card and together they left.

Once they returned to their car, Detective Thomas called the district attorney's office and relayed all they'd learned from Mr. Kasmo, substantiating the detectives' position that Mr. Hawkins was behind the surveillance activity at the Vermeer home. The district attorney told the detectives to arrest Mr. Hawkins and bring him to the police station for processing. Detective Thomas contacted Officer Pembrooke and asked him to meet them at Mr. Hawkins' office.

When the detectives walked into Representative Rossman's office lobby, they found Officer Pembrooke waiting for them. Without a word, Gerald stood up and walked down the hallway, returning with Mr. Hawkins.

"What do you want now, Detectives?" asked Mr. Hawkins with exasperation in his voice.

"Mr. Hawkins, you are under arrest for the illegal video and audio surveillance of the Vermeer residence," said Detective Thomas forcefully. She gave him his Miranda rights as he stood silently in shock. Officer Pembrooke handcuffed him. When Detective Thomas stopped speaking, Mr. Hawkins lashed out.

"You have lost your mind, Detective Thomas. I have done nothing wrong and have already explained to you I wasn't involved in surveilling the Vermeers' house. Sylvia will have your badge for this outrage. I will be free of these charges by the end of the day. Lady, you don't realize whom you're dealing with here."

Mr. Hawkins turned to Gerald and instructed him to get Representative Rossman. Gerald sprinted from his desk and returned quickly with the representative trailing close behind him. When she saw Mr. Hawkins in handcuffs, she rolled her eyes in disdain and turned to Detective Thomas.

"What's going on here, Detective?" she demanded.

"Mr. Hawkins hired a former CIA employee to install cameras inside and outside the Vermeer residence to spy on them," said Detective Thomas.

"Oh, that's ridiculous! David certainly had no involvement in that," asserted the representative.

"The CIA employee confirmed that Mr. Hawkins paid him to install the cameras. A search warrant is being issued as we speak to search Mr. Hawkins' apartment for evidence of that," said Detective Garza.

"We're not here to debate this matter with you, Representative.

Officer Pembrooke, please take Mr. Hawkins to the station for processing," said Detective Thomas.

Detective Thomas told Detective Garza that she was going to call to determine if a search warrant had been issued. She learned it had been, and, as she and Detective Garza left the representative's office, Representative Rossman yelled to Mr. Hawkins that she would have an attorney meet him at the station.

After briefly looking at the search warrant, the concierge for Mr. Hawkins' apartment building admitted the detectives into Mr. Hawkins' apartment. They started their investigation in a room dedicated as Mr. Hawkins's office and quickly found a laptop computer that was turned on and fully accessible. Shortly afterward, Jared Willoughby joined them to analyze the computer for any electronic surveillance items.

After a bit of navigating, Jared announced he had found the link to the feed from the cameras at the Vermeer house, which was blank because the cameras had been removed. He also found a file containing the previous recordings. The three of them watched a smattering of them to confirm Mr. Hawkins was a responsible and active party.

"Take the laptop with you back to the lab, Jared, and copy all the recordings," said Detective Garza. "Also, determine if Mr. Hawkins sent any of the recordings to Representative Rossman by e-mail."

"Do you want me to wait here until you're certain there aren't any other computers?" asked Jared.

"We've already combed the entire apartment and there are no other computers and no surveillance equipment present. I think it's fine for you to head back to the lab. Quinn and I will stay to search for other pertinent evidence," explained Detective Garza. Jared nodded and left the apartment.

The detectives spent the next two hours searching every crevice, corner, container, closet and cupboard for evidence of David Hawkins' involvement in the attempts on Annalisa's life, but there was not a single plant in the apartment or glass vial or even a book on botanical life. There also was no outside space dedicated to Mr. Hawkins' apartment where he could grow a shrub. If Mr. Hawkins was the instigator, then he did not conduct any of his actions from his apartment, or he delegated them to other parties.

"We didn't find a shred of evidence connecting Representative Rossman to the surveillance cameras or the attempt on Ms. Vermeer's life," lamented Detective Garza.

"True, but it's not surprising," said Detective Thomas. "Representative Rossman knows better than to have any threads of connection between her and any illegal, improper or unethical conduct. She's far too savvy for that. The only way we'll prove she's involved is if Mr. Hawkins admits it."

# *Chapter Twenty-Four*

Brad and Annalisa were watching a comedy and enjoying popcorn when the telephone rang. Their laughter ceased as Brad paused the film. Annalisa walked over to the other side of the living room and picked up the receiver.

"Hello," she greeted the caller.

"Hi, Annalisa. This is Daphne Wagner. How are you this evening? I hope I didn't interrupt you from anything important."

"Hi, Daphne. Brad and I are watching a movie, but it's paused, so no problem, I can talk," said Annalisa.

"Great. I won't keep you long. I want you to know I volunteered to chair the scholarship committee to administer the scholarship program. I want to thank you again for all the funds you've raised for the program."

"Thank you, Daphne, for the appreciation and for volunteering to chair the committee. I think you'll be a great chairwoman, and with teenagers yourself you'll be a positive representative of ASSIST when interviewing scholarship candidates."

"Thank you, Annalisa. I appreciate your confidence in me. Before the committee meets for the first time, I'd like to meet with you to discuss some thoughts I have and to see if you have any insight into administering the funds. Do you have any time available in the next few days when we could meet for lunch?" asked Ms. Wagner.

"Yes, I do. I'm in town for the next ten days, so would you like to meet on Monday?"

"I'm looking at my calendar and can juggle some other activities around so I'm clear that day. How about 1:00 at the Junction Tavern?" asked Ms. Wagner.

"That's fine, Daphne. I'm looking forward to it."

"See you then, Annalisa."

"Good-bye." Annalisa returned to the couch and snuggled up to Brad, who had been reading a magazine while she talked to Ms. Wagner.

"I'm meeting Daphne Wagner for lunch next Monday at the Junction Tavern to talk about the scholarship program," Annalisa said.

"Yes, I heard. That should be fun and productive. How about we get back to the movie?"

Three minutes back into the movie, the telephone rang again. Annalisa picked up the receiver and, without waiting to learn who was on the line, said, "Hi, Daphne. Did you forget something?"

"Annalisa, this is Quinn Thomas."

"Oh, I'm so sorry, Detective. I was just talking to Daphne Wagner—you may recall she's a member of ASSIST—and I just assumed it was her calling back," explained Annalisa.

"No problem. I'm sorry to bother you so late this evening, but I wanted to tell you that today we arrested David Hawkins for instigating the surveillance of your home. We located the man who installed the cameras and he admitted Mr. Hawkins hired him to put them both in San Jose and in your home," said Detective Thomas.

"A man whom I don't even know has been watching our every move for months. That's so unsettling, and the invasion of privacy is unnerving and embarrassing. To think there was even a camera in my bedroom makes me sick. I've been so upset since I learned about the cameras that Brad finally told me we had to watch a comedy to distract me," said Annalisa.

"The distraction has to be good for you. I completely understand your position, as Mr. Hawkins' actions were reprehensible and illegal. However, he clearly didn't orchestrate such an elaborate surveillance operation here and in San Jose solely for his benefit. He did it for the sake of his boss, Representative Rossman, although he claims to be protecting everyone on Capitol Hill from you," explained Detective Thomas.

"Maybe if they'd discredited or killed me a year ago, my message would have been destroyed with me. I suspect with the current growth of various grassroots organizations, my message can live and thrive without me. Did Mr. Hawkins admit to arranging the attempts on my life?" asked Annalisa.

"No, so far he's maintained his innocence in that regard. Detective Garza and I plan to question him further tomorrow. Unfortunately, but not unexpectedly, Representative Rossman sent an attorney to represent Mr. Hawkins. He arrived at the station almost before Mr. Hawkins. The attorney was able to have him immediately arraigned and released on bond. Mr. Hawkins probably went right back to his office so he and the representative could concoct consistent stories to prevent any further damage. If he doesn't report to my office at ten o'clock tomorrow morning, then we'll go to his office to pick him up," stated Detective Thomas.

"At least for now, Brad and I aren't being spied on in our home, correct?" asked Annalisa.

"Correct," said Detective Thomas. "Greg removed every visible device and thoroughly inspected the entire premises to ensure there were no more surveillance cameras hiding inside or out. In addition, while Mr. Hawkins may have been released, his personal laptop computer from his apartment wasn't. We have it locked away in the evidence room, which means we have all the recordings."

"That's good to know. Thanks also for letting us know you arrested Mr. Hawkins. I'll sleep better tonight knowing he's probably not stupid enough to try to hurt me now that he's facing criminal charges. Please let me know of any new developments," requested Annalisa.

"Certainly—I will contact you as soon as we have any new information. Good night."

"Good night," responded Annalisa. She reported the news to Brad, who was pleased that an arrest had been made, even if it was solely in relation to the surveillance cameras.

* * *

The next morning, David Hawkins and his attorney arrived at the station promptly at 10:00 a.m. Detectives Thomas and Garza questioned him for approximately two hours; still, he would not implicate Representative Rossman in any illegal activity. He continued to insist he was innocent of any attempt on Annalisa's life. It was clear to the detectives he would protect his boss regardless of his predicament. They would have to connect him and the representative to Hannah's death and the attempts on Annalisa's life without his help.

Jared spent the morning analyzing all the information on the hard drive in David Hawkins' computer. There was no evidence proving Mr. Hawkins had e-mailed any of the surveillance recordings to Representative Rossman or to anyone else. There were no e-mails between Mr. Hawkins and any other person discussing Annalisa, making it appear he was solely responsible for the spying efforts. After lunch, Jared reported his findings to the detectives.

"Jared, did you find any research on how to poison a person or information on mezereon or mezereum shrubs?" asked Detective Garza.

"No, no searches were made on those topics. There's no evidence Mr. Hawkins researched any methods for killing a person," explained Jared.

"We didn't find any books on poisonous plants in his apartment and I doubt he would be foolish enough to research the subject on his work computer. Maybe he did his research at a public library," suggested Detective Garza.

"Well, if that's the case, then unless he checked out a book, we'll never know what he read," said Detective Thomas.

"Jared, will you please ask Julia to contact the branches of the public library closest to Mr. Hawkins' apartment and Capitol Hill?" asked Detective Garza. "Have her ask if they have surveillance recordings in the branches and if they still exist back to February. If they have such tapes, then please tell her I'd like her to view them, looking for Mr. Hawkins reading any literature on poisons."

"Yes, Cat, I'll go talk to her now," said Jared. "I believe she's returned from lunch." As he walked away, Detective Garza turned to Detective Thomas and for the first time acknowledged that neither David Hawkins nor Representative Rossman may have been responsible for Annalisa's attempted murder or Hannah's death.

"There's simply no solid evidence to suggest either one of them is a murderer or paid someone to murder for them. They seem more interested in discrediting Annalisa's reputation than in killing her. I suspect they're both savvy enough to understand murdering her could potentially turn her into a martyr, which would strengthen her mission," suggested Detective Garza.

"There's logic in that line of thinking, Cat. I can't say I disagree with you, although they're the only ones who we can prove took overt action to hurt her. If they didn't commit the crimes, then we have to stand back and reassess the entire scene to determine who our most likely suspects are at this point," explained Detective Thomas.

Julia walked into the office. "I have good news," she said. "There are library branches near Mr. Hawkins' apartment and not far from Capitol Hill, and they both have surveillance tapes going back about a year. I'm leaving now and will spend the afternoon watching them, looking for any appearance by him. I'll note any literature he reads, no matter what the topic, in case a connection can later be made between a book and Hannah's murder and the attempts against Ms.

Vermeer."

"Julia," said Detective Garza, "if you do see him reading any literature, then please locate it on the shelf and make a copy of the title page and table of contents so we have a record of the material. If you find any reference in a book he read to poison, mezereon shrubs or any other methods to kill, then please check out the material and bring it back to the lab for possible fingerprints and to study the contents."

"In addition, Julia, please watch for any appearances by Representative Rossman, particularly at the branch near the Hill, and make similar notes of any material she reads," Detective Thomas further instructed.

"I'll let you both know what I discover," said Julia.

"Frankly, Quinn, if Julia doesn't see Mr. Hawkins or the representative on the library tapes, then I have no idea how we can try to connect them to the murders, if they're even the culprits. As we just discussed, it's looking less and less likely they're to blame," admitted Detective Garza.

Later that day, just as Detective Garza was preparing to leave, Julia called.

"Cat, I had no idea just how long it would take to view the tapes from January to March of the various public doors into the library and the botany aisle, and I'm watching them on fast forward. I'm going to have to come back Monday morning to finish, and I'm going to ask Greg to join me so he can watch some of the tapes while I watch others. I'm also going to request that Jared and another technician go to the branch near Capitol Hill to watch the tapes there," said Julia with extreme frustration in her voice.

"That's fine, Julia. The library is open plenty of hours each week, so I'm not surprised that it's taking you so long. Better to take your time and not miss one of them appearing, so ask for even more help if you find you all need it," said Detective Garza supportively.

Julia felt greatly relieved as they ended their conversation. There was no relief, however, for Detective Garza, who left the office for the weekend feeling more baffled than she had felt the previous day.

# *Chapter Twenty-Five*

JUST BEFORE 8:30 ON MONDAY morning, the medical examiner called Detective Thomas to report her autopsy findings.

"Quinn, I just finished writing up the autopsy report and confirmed the hospital's conclusion that there were shards of sharpened bark embedded in the linings of Ms. Garian's mouth, esophagus, stomach and intestines," said Dr. Stephanie Bloomingdale, a physician renowned for her brilliance and skilled thoroughness in her medical exams. "Dr. Fanelli was correct that gastric lavage would not have removed all, if any, of these poisonous leeches. Your killer acted with precision and total malice for the person who imbibed this potion."

"Were all the bark shards you found poisonous?" asked Detective Thomas.

"No, some of the shards were from the mezereon shrub, which are, of course, poisonous, and other shards were from the forsythia shrub, which are perfectly harmless to humans. However, the shards that were embedded in her linings were from the mezereon shrub because those are the only shards that were sharpened on each end. They were even coated with a clear base fingernail polish to add strength. We found the forsythia bark shards loosely mixed in with other fluids in her stomach and intestines, as well as in the vomited fluids that coated her face," explained Dr. Bloomingdale.

"Were there any drugs or alcohol in her system besides the poison?" asked Detective Thomas.

"Traces of aspirin were in the fluids on her face and in her stomach, but no prescription or illegal drugs. She had not ingested any alcohol either. She was clean, except for the daphnetoxin," said Dr. Bloomingdale.

"Daphnetoxin? What are you talking about, Stephanie? I thought it was mezereon bark that poisoned Hannah," said Detective Thomas with confusion in her voice.

"The mezereon bark she ingested was poisonous, but the poison, or toxin, in the bark that was fatal to her is called daphnetoxin. In fact, the shrub goes by several names that I'm aware of—mezereon, mezereum, *Daphne mezereum* and *February daphne*. If I were a botanist instead of a medical doctor, then I would probably know even more names for the shrub. Despite the particular name of the shrub used, the poisonous substance is the same—daphnetoxin," explained Dr. Bloomingdale.

"Interesting. The other physicians involved with the poisonings didn't refer to the poison as 'daphnetoxin,' so this is a new term for me," said Detective Thomas.

"Is there any significance in your case to the specific name of the poison?" asked Dr. Bloomingdale.

Detective Thomas did not immediately respond, as her focus was drawn away from Dr. Bloomingdale's question.

"Quinn, are you there?" asked Dr. Bloomingdale.

"Yes, Stephanie, I am. I'm sorry, I was just thinking about the poison in the shrub. To answer your question, I'm not sure yet whether the name of the poison is meaningful, but it's given me pause and is possibly a clue that will lead me in a new direction," explained Detective Thomas.

"I'm glad it may be helpful to you because Ms. Garian suffered a torturous death and I would like to see you apprehend the killer before he or she makes Ms. Vermeer endure the same agony," said Dr. Bloomingdale.

"I intend to do my best to apprehend the murderer. Is there any other information you want to give me now or should I just read your report when it hits my desk?" inquired Detective Thomas.

"Summing it all up," said Dr. Bloomingdale, "the daphnetoxin initially caused a burning sensation in Hannah's mouth and then in the linings of her esophagus and stomach, followed by stomach pain, nausea and vomiting. As the poison entered her intestines, diarrhea commenced and she became dehydrated and weak, causing her to become disoriented, which is probably why she never called 911 or a friend or family member for assistance. Eventually, she became comatose and there was an imbalance in her electrolytes, which caused damage to her heart and resulted in her death. You can read the specifics in my report."

"Thanks, Stephanie. I'll let you know if I have any further questions." The two hung up and Detective Thomas went straight to Detective Garza's office. Detective Garza was just finishing up a call.

"Cat," said Detective Thomas after Detective Garza hung up, "I have a hunch on this Garian/Vermeer case I'd like to discuss with you."

"Sure, Quinn, what are you thinking?" asked Detective Garza.

"Stephanie just called me with a synopsis of her autopsy report on Hannah Garian. She used some terms the doctors who treated Annalisa and Hannah at the hospital never used. Stephanie told me the toxin in the mezereum shrub is called 'daphnetoxin' and that two other names for the shrub are *Daphne mezereum* and *February daphne*."

"OK, Quinn, what's the significance of those terms?"

"I'm not certain if they're significant, but when I heard 'Daphne' it reminded me of a comment Annalisa made when I called to tell her David Hawkins had been arrested. She told me she had just gotten off the phone with Daphne Wagner, a member of ASSIST. I remember the name and I believe she was one of the people sitting at Ms. Vermeer's table at the Annual Honoree Dinner. Could it be that Daphne Wagner is the one trying to murder Ms. Vermeer and she's using a poison with the same name as her to do it?"

"I'd say we have no evidence to support that hunch, but it's worth looking into," said Detective Garza. "Let's start with learning a bit about the shrub." She turned to her keyboard and started a computer search for *Daphne mezereum*.

"It says the shrub is a species of *Daphne* in the flowering plant family Thymelaeaceae," said Detective Garza. "Its common name is Mezereon, which is probably why we've heard that term used by the doctors. It's a deciduous shrub, but it flowers early, even before the leaves appear and sometimes as early as February, which I guess explains the name '*February Daphne*.' The scented flowers are pink or purple and the shrub produces bright red berries that draw a multitude of birds. *Daphne mezereum* is extremely toxic because of the daphnetoxin found especially in the berries and bark, but despite this it's commonly planted in gardens because of the beautiful flowers. The seeds can be dried and stored for future planting."

"Is there a photograph of the shrub with that article, Cat?" asked Detective Thomas.

"Yes, take a look." Detective Garza stood and offered her chair to Detective Thomas. As Detective Thomas sat looking at the computer monitor, Detective Garza continued, "Quinn, I'll print out a color copy of the photograph. If we can obtain a search warrant for the Wagner residence, we can use the photo to see if there's such a shrub there."

"That would be helpful, Cat, because I have no botanical expertise and would be unable to spot the shrub based solely on its written description," said Detective Thomas. "However, before we consider requesting a search warrant, we need to determine if we have probable cause, so we should examine the evidence we already have. Let's see if Daphne Wagner was at the journalists' fundraiser ball where Ms. Vermeer was poisoned. If my recollection is correct, then Ms. Wagner sat at the same table as Ms. Vermeer at the Annual Honoree Dinner."

"Quinn, if we find Ms. Wagner was at the fundraiser, then I'll read her interview intake to learn all she told the officer," said Detective Garza.

"Let's also do a background check on her," said Detective Thomas. "She's the wife of a senator, so she has motive to murder Ms. Vermeer if she felt her husband was threatened. In fact, we should also be looking into Senator Wagner because he would have similar access to Ms. Vermeer and may be equally drawn to use a toxin with the name 'Daphne' in it. For all we know, the Wagners may have worked in tandem."

"Quinn, I'm going to take it one step further. I'm going to search for the first name 'Daphne' in all our evidence irrespective of the last name given, just in case she used an alias at some point for her surname."

"Good idea, Cat. Also, see if you can find a photograph of her so we can determine what color her hair is. I'm going to call Ms. Vermeer to ask if Daphne Wagner has acted suspiciously around her at any point. I suspect she'll say 'no,' as she was just speaking with her on the phone the other night and raised no concerns with me."

Detective Thomas returned to her desk and dialed Annalisa's home number. It went to voicemail. When she called Annalisa's cell phone and also received no answer, she decided to leave a message to call her.

Detective Thomas went to the lab to request the tapes of the journalists' ball. She also checked the guest list, finding that the Wagners were indeed present at the event. Detective Garza walked up to Detective Thomas and handed her a photograph of Senator Wagner and his wife at the ball.

"Many who attended the ball elected to have their photo taken as if they were Hollywood stars," said Detective Garza. "As you can see, both the senator and his wife have dark brown hair, just like Representative Rossman. Senator Wagner's hair is definitely too short to match our strand, but Daphne Wagner's hair is much longer."

"Thank you, Cat. Now Jared and I can view the surveillance tapes from the ball, searching for any suspicious activity on the Wagners' part, although I suspect that the Wagner most likely to be responsible is Daphne. Since there aren't any cameras at the Literary Club, this is all we have for observing questionable activity."

"Good luck with that, Quinn. I'm off to do my own research."

Detective Garza sped off, anxious to check all their records for the presence of the name "Daphne." As she was perusing the records, Julia called and informed the detective that she and her partner had arrived at the library at seven that morning and had completed their review of the tapes. Neither David Hawkins nor Representative Rossman had visited the library. She further explained that a team of four had gained access to the library branch near Capitol Hill, also at seven that morning, and had reached the same conclusion—the two primary suspects did not set foot in the library.

Detective Garza found that Daphne Wagner attended not only the ball and the Annual Honoree Dinner, but also one of Annalisa's speeches with her name disguised as "Daphne Caldwell." In performing a background check, Detective Garza had learned Daphne Wagner's maiden name was Caldwell.

The speech was given in St. Louis and the address Daphne Wagner gave on her registration form was an address in Prairie du Rocher, Illinois—the home of her sister. Detective Garza found it suspicious that Ms. Wagner used an alias and elected to hear the speech approximately fifty miles from her sister's home when she could have attended a similar speech numerous times only a few miles from her home in DC.

Detective Garza then contacted the St. Louis hotel where the speech was given and asked security personnel to e-mail her a copy of the recording from the surveillance camera aimed at the registration table. In examining the recording, Detective Garza thought she recognized Ms. Wagner, although she was physically disguised beneath sunglasses, a powder-blue scarf and a beige raincoat. *If Ms. Wagner wasn't intent on sinister activity, then why was she surreptitiously attending the speech?* thought Detective Garza.

As Detective Garza mulled over Daphne Wagner's actions, Detective Thomas approached.

"Cat, Jared and I saw Ms. Wagner and her husband numerous times in view of the cameras at the ball, but their behavior was perfectly normal. However, it was problematic because, as we discovered during the first viewing of these tapes, the room was simply too crowded to see what transpired at Ms. Vermeer's table at every moment. Either of the Wagners could have poisoned the cherries on Ms. Vermeer's cheesecake and we wouldn't see it through the mass of people milling about. Just to be certain though, I asked Jared to finish reviewing the rest of the tapes we didn't yet watch. He'll let me know if he sees any noteworthy behavior on the part of Senator or Ms. Wagner."

"I had better luck in catching Ms. Wagner acting deceptively," said Detective Garza. "Using her maiden name, she registered for Ms. Vermeer's April 24 speech in St. Louis and used her sister's address about fifty miles away. Take a look at the view on this surveillance tape. Although disguised, it appears to be Ms. Wagner trying her best not to be identified. Why use another name and address and travel fifty miles to see Ms. Vermeer speak when she could have attended here in DC without hiding? It looks pretty suspicious to me."

"I agree. We'll definitely have to ask her why she went to such great lengths to hide her appearance at a speech. In fact, why wait? I suggest we go to her home right now and ask her. Have you finished watching the surveillance tape at the St. Louis hotel?" asked Detective Thomas.

"Yes, I have. No cameras were inside the auditorium, so all I had was the tape of her at the registration table. I'm ready to go with you to the Wagner house," said Detective Garza.

While the two detectives drove to the Wagner residence, they discussed the background check Detective Garza had performed on Daphne Wagner.

"She has no criminal record," said Detective Garza. "Her father was a US senator from Illinois and so she's lived here in DC most of her life. While her father was still serving his state in Congress, she met Senator Wagner and they married here. Her family is extremely wealthy, and the tradition is continuing with the family she's created with Senator Wagner. She has two children, both of whom are now teenagers, and she employs a staff to assist her in running her household, which is a huge estate in Sheridan-Kalorama adjoining Rock Creek Park. She's active in a number of local organizations, including ASSIST and the DC Women's Literary Club."

"It seems she has plenty to lose if her husband loses his position and power, and thereby potentially his wealth. Yet could she seriously believe Ms. Vermeer's advocacy, despite the support that Ms. Vermeer has garnered, is actually going to cause such monumental change within the next twenty years? It's unreasonable to think that congressional life and power as we know it is likely to undergo substantial change while Senator Wagner is in power," asserted Detective Thomas.

"I agree. The Wagners have no reason to personally fear Ms. Vermeer and her message. If Ms. Wagner is the one who tried to kill Ms. Vermeer, then she's under some very serious psychological delusions," maintained Detective Garza. They pulled into the Wagners' driveway and surveyed the massive grounds, imagining it would take quite a long time to search them for *February daphne* shrubs.

Meanwhile, across town Annalisa and Michael walked through the door of the Junction Tavern and glanced around for Daphne Wagner. While waiting for the hostess, Annalisa heard a voice calling, "Annalisa, Annalisa." As she looked toward the sound, she spotted Daphne waving as she leaned out of a dark wooden booth. As

Michael continued to wait for the hostess to escort him to the kitchen, Annalisa moved toward Daphne, who rose from her seat and gave Annalisa a polite hug.

"Are you fine with a booth? I chose it so we could have some privacy when we're talking about the scholarship fund," said Ms. Wagner.

"Yes, it's fine. I've never eaten here before. Do you eat here often?" asked Annalisa.

"Not often, but I've dined here several times. I particularly like it when I want privacy because the booths are like their own little rooms with the high wooden dividers and deep cushions. They block sound and sight, keeping the other patrons very separated. I like that," explained Ms. Wagner.

A waitress approached and asked them if they wanted something to drink. They each ordered iced white tea and opened their menus. After ordering, Ms. Wagner asked Annalisa how the fundraising efforts were going at her events. Annalisa happily stated that ticket sales were increasing, and with increased sales came increased donations to the scholarship fund.

"So, attendance at your speeches is improving. The Midwest passion for you must be spreading throughout the country. Congratulations on that, Annalisa."

"Thank you. I believe I'm making headway in opening the minds of people throughout this country. More and more listeners understand change can be effected in our legislative system by working within so that the basic framework isn't destroyed," explained Annalisa.

"Do you really believe that? That political parties and lobbyists can be abolished and the legislative powers of Congress watered down without destroying the basic framework of our legislative system here in DC and across this country?" asked Ms. Wagner with a tone of sincere doubt.

"Yes, I do, Daphne. Without lobbyists and party ideologies influencing our lawmakers' thinking, our legislators can review, analyze and evaluate an issue and the options for addressing that issue with clearer heads and open minds. The legislators may even determine that revoking certain laws is appropriate. I think the legislators would actually feel freer in using their own thinking to make decisions without outside pushing and prodding in any particular direction," asserted Annalisa.

"I understand your intent, but I still have difficulty believing that in practice it can work. It feels that the power of Congress would be liquidated under your plan, rather than becoming stronger," Ms. Wagner advocated.

At that moment, the waitress arrived with their meals and they tabled their conversation, talking instead about light matters—family, friends and fond memories of past vacations. As they finished eating, they shifted the conversation to Ms. Wagner's goals for the committee and how she would define the best standards to use in selecting scholarship recipients. They both ordered coffee and dessert as they brainstormed to develop the appropriate standards.

# *Chapter Twenty-Six*

Back at the Wagner residence, the detectives walked up the curving front walkway to the door and rang the bell. A smiling young woman dressed in a uniform opened the massive door.

"Hello. May I help you?" she asked.

"Yes, thank you. We're here to see Senator and Ms. Wagner. We're from the Metro Police," explained Detective Garza.

"One moment, please," said the young woman as she turned and walked into the house. As the detectives stood on the front porch and looked around, they noticed the beautifully detailed dentil molding under numerous cornices on the red brick façade of the huge home. Large expanses of glass windows covered the front of the home, allowing natural light to stream in. The detectives turned from admiring the exterior of the home when Senator Wagner came to the door with a puzzled look on his face.

"I'm Senator Wagner. How may I help you?"

"I'm Detective Thomas and this is Detective Garza. We're investigating the attempted murder of Annalisa Vermeer and the murder of Hannah Garian and we'd like to ask you and your wife some questions."

"I don't know how I can help you, but please come in. My wife isn't home, but feel free to ask me your questions," stated the ever-diplomatic Senator Wagner.

"Thank you," said Detective Thomas as they followed the senator into the library. The library's walls and ceiling were covered with darkly stained cherry wood and contained a multitude of bookcases that appeared to hold a small public library's collection of books.

"Please sit down, Detectives," invited Senator Wagner as he pointed to two high-back red leather chairs. The detectives took their seats as Senator Wagner sat across from them in a matching loveseat.

"Senator, were you aware your wife attended Ms. Vermeer's speech in St. Louis on April 24?" asked Detective Thomas.

"No, she never mentioned it. She must have gone during one of her trips to visit her sister because her sister lives relatively close by in a small town in Illinois," offered Senator Wagner.

"Do you have any reason to believe she'd want to keep her attendance a secret from you and everyone else?" asked Detective Thomas.

"No, why would she, and what does this have to do with the attempts on Ms. Vermeer's life?" asked Senator Wagner.

"We have a tape from a St. Louis hotel camera aimed on the registration desk that shows your wife registering while hidden beneath sunglasses and a scarf fully covering her head and part of her face. She also registered using her maiden name and her sister's address as her own," explained Detective Thomas.

"Given the controversial nature of Ms. Vermeer's presentations, maybe my wife didn't want anyone to know that a senator's wife would pay good money to hear such a talk. Following that line of thinking, it would make sense to attend in a town where nobody knows her. Here, the chances are far greater she'd encounter someone who recognizes her, even behind shades and a scarf," asserted Senator Wagner.

"Senator, it appears you have extensive grounds here at your home, is that correct?" asked Detective Garza.

"Yes, we have a few acres composed of grass, flowers, trees, shrubs, a pool, a pool house, verandas, porches, a greenhouse, walkways and fountains. I'm sure I missed mentioning a few other features, especially some of the hardscapes, but you get the idea. Daphne is a master gardener and loves to spend countless hours dabbling in the greenhouse, pruning this and propagating that. This house is always brimming with colorful bouquets of flowers from our grounds," explained Senator Wagner.

"It is impressive, Senator," remarked Detective Garza.

"Yes, it is, but how is it relevant to your interest in Ms. Vermeer and the other woman whom you mentioned?" asked Senator Wagner.

"Ms. Garian and Ms. Vermeer were poisoned by a toxin found in a shrub commonly known as mezereon. We'd like to know if you have any of these shrubs on your grounds," said Detective Garza.

"I really wouldn't know, but our gardener would certainly know not only if we had such a shrub, but where it is," said Senator Wagner. He stood and walked over to a nearby desk where he picked up a telephone receiver, dialed three numbers and waited for an answer.

"Ellie, would you please locate Wayne on the grounds and ask him to come to the library?" After she responded affirmatively, he hung up and returned to his seat.

"Once Wayne arrives, I'll ask him to take you on a tour of the grounds to point out the shrub you're looking for, assuming we have it planted here. While you haven't stated it directly, it's clear you believe my wife and/or I am responsible for the murder and attempted murder. I won't waste any of my energy being offended or angry at such an accusation, despite you not appearing to possess any evidence to support it. Instead, I offer you my complete cooperation, as we have no reason to hide from your investigation," explained Senator Wagner.

"We appreciate that, Senator. We will be the least intrusive that we can. Given you've offered your complete cooperation, would you be willing to give us a strand of your hair for testing?" asked Detective Thomas.

Without asking why, the senator grabbed a strand between his thumb and first finger and vigorously pulled, plucking it from his scalp. As he did so, Detective Garza removed a clear evidence bag from her pocket and opened it for the senator to put the hair inside.

"I imagine you'd also like a sample of Daphne's hair as well?" asked the senator.

"Yes, we plan to ask her for a strand," answered Detective Garza.

"There's no need to wait for her. I can get you numerous strands from her hairbrush." He again called Ellie and asked her to bring him Ms. Wagner's hairbrush, which she immediately did. Senator Wagner removed all the hair from among the bristles and placed it in a second open bag held by Detective Garza.

"While we're waiting for your gardener, Senator, I'd like to ask what contact you and your wife have had with Ms. Vermeer over the last few months," said Detective Garza. Senator Wagner stared off into space with a pensive look, apparently trying to reminisce to accurately answer the question. He turned and looked directly into Detective Garza's eyes.

"The first time I saw Ms. Vermeer was when I attended one of her local speeches at the Omni Shoreham Hotel back in late winter. I met her shortly after that when we both attended a journalist-sponsored fundraiser, also here in DC. My wife and I sat at the same table as her and her husband, and that was the first time Daphne met Ms. Vermeer because I was the one who introduced them. I didn't see her again until the recent ASSIST Annual Honoree Dinner when my wife, who's a member of the organization, and I again sat at her table. I haven't seen her since. She's a nice person, but her ideology is unrealistic," added Senator Wagner.

There was a knock at the open door. A middle-aged man with graying temples looked toward Senator Wagner. He was wearing jeans and a casual long-sleeve shirt.

"Oh, Wayne, thank you for dropping whatever you were doing

to get here so quickly. These ladies are Detectives Garza and Thomas and they're interested in looking for a particular shrub on our grounds. Please show them around, including where the shrub is, if we have one, and answer any other questions they may have," instructed Senator Wagner.

"Certainly, sir," responded Wayne with great deference and respect.

"Thank you, Senator. We'll see you when we return from the grounds," said Detective Thomas.

"I'll be here, as I'm working from home today," said Senator Wagner. The detectives followed Wayne out of the room, through the two-story foyer and into the front yard. When they reached the side of the house, Wayne stopped and turned to the detectives.

"What shrub are you looking for, Detectives?" asked Wayne.

"We're looking for a shrub commonly known as mezereon. Are you familiar with it?" asked Detective Thomas.

"Definitely. It's Ms. Wagner's favorite shrub. She told me she was named after it because her mother loved the fragrant feminine-colored flowers that bloom in February, and she was born in February. Did you know the mezereon is also called *February daphne*?" asked Wayne.

"Yes, we're aware of that. I assume since it's her favorite shrub you have one or more growing on the grounds?" inquired Detective Thomas.

"Yes, we have many, but they're clustered in one area that's in direct view of the great room and the adjacent sitting room because Ms. Wagner loves to watch them bloom each February as winter ends. She says the flowers chase away the dreariness of winter and welcome in the beauty of spring. Would you like to see them?" asked Wayne.

"Yes, we would," said Detective Thomas. They followed Wayne to the back of the house, just to the side of the pool where at least a dozen of the shrubs were planted on a berm.

"Does Ms. Wagner merely look at these shrubs or does she use her gardening skills on them?" asked Detective Thomas.

"Ms. Wagner is an excellent gardener and she does much with these shrubs. She collects some of the berries for a special feeder in the front for birds and the remainder she leaves on the shrubs for birds back here to eat. She cuts branches to propagate new shrubs and she dries and stores the seeds for future plantings. She may do more, but you'll have to ask her, as I'm generally off doing my own work while she's gardening," explained Wayne.

"Would she do all this work here in this area?" inquired Detective Thomas.

"Certainly part of it, but she also works in the greenhouse, particularly when she's sprouting new growth and working with the seeds. Follow me and I'll show you the greenhouse," said Wayne.

"Before we go to the greenhouse, we'd like to take some photographs of the shrubs and inspect them to see if any bark or branches have been cut," explained Detective Thomas.

Detective Garza pulled a small camera out of her pants pocket and began snapping shots from various angles. Meanwhile, Detective Thomas examined each shrub for signs of bark removal. As she found wounds from cut-off branches and pieces of bark sliced off from the trunks, Detective Garza took a close-up shot of the damage. While the absence of bark in certain places suggested Ms. Wagner's involvement in creating the bark shards, the detectives knew it was no more than suggestive on its own merits. It would take more than that to prove Ms. Wagner's handiwork caused Hannah's death.

"We're ready to see the greenhouse now," said Detective Thomas to Wayne.

The detectives followed Wayne deep into the backyard until the greenhouse became visible. It was not possible to see the house from the greenhouse because a large growth of tall and foliage-filled trees separated the two. Wayne unlocked the door and walked toward a long table covered with empty pots and vases, as well as bags of potting soil and fertilizer.

"This is the primary area where Ms. Wagner does her work," Wayne said. "She's particularly proficient at propagating plants. You'll be amazed to hear that probably one-quarter of the plants, shrubs and small trees on the grounds weren't purchased, but were grown from the twigs and branches she rooted and the seeds she planted." Wayne clearly had great pride in and respect for Ms. Wagner.

"Would it be fine with you if we looked around a bit in this greenhouse?" asked Detective Thomas.

"Yes, please do. I have to water a group of plantings down at the other end of the greenhouse anyway, so you look around while I do that. Just yell if you have any questions," Wayne politely offered.

"Thank you, Wayne," said Detective Thomas.

As he walked away, the detectives put on gloves and began looking on the tabletops and on each shelf, hoping to find similarly carved shards of bark that would connect Ms. Wagner to the shards found in Hannah. While no shards were found, either because there were none or because they were too small to see, as Detective Thomas pushed aside some empty pots on a shelf, she discovered a cardboard box half-filled with empty glass vials. The vials appeared identical to the two vials found in Hannah's apartment. The cardboard box appeared to be the same size and shape as the box found addressed to Hannah. A few feet away from the box was a similarly sized box containing the same vials, only they were filled with seeds, likely stored there until it was time to plant them. The vials were sealed with rubber caps that looked the same as the rubber caps on Hannah's two vials.

"Cat, I've found a concrete connection between Ms. Wagner and Hannah's murder," Detective Thomas said as she held up the box of empty vials in one hand and the box of seed-filled vials in the other.

"Wayne," Detective Thomas called. He turned and looked up

from directing a hose at various potted plants.

"Yes?" he yelled back. Detective Thomas walked toward Wayne with both boxes still in her hands. She asked him if he had ever seen Ms. Wagner use the vials in her gardening.

"Oh, yes. Ms. Wagner uses the containers to hold the seeds she gathers until she plants them in the spring or the fall," he explained.

"May we take these boxes of vials for some testing?" asked Detective Thomas.

"It's fine with me," said Wayne, "but you'd have to ask Ms. Wagner because I don't have the authority to release her seeds and supplies to anyone."

As Detective Thomas and Wayne discussed the vials, Detective Garza continued searching shelves and cabinets. In a cabinet not far from where Detective Thomas found the boxes of vials, she found a bottle of clear base fingernail polish. She approached Wayne and Detective Thomas, looked at Wayne and spoke.

"In addition to the boxes of vials, we'd also like to take this bottle of fingernail polish," said Detective Garza. "I presume it's also used by Ms. Wagner?" Wayne looked puzzled as he gazed at the bottle.

"I've never seen that before, so I'm not sure. Only Ms. Wagner and I work in this greenhouse and I have no reason to use fingernail polish," he stated with a grin. "Though I can't think of any reason why she'd need it either. It's not a substance used in gardening. You'll have to ask her, Detectives."

"We will, Wayne. Does Senator Wagner have any interest in gardening on these grounds?" asked Detective Thomas.

"No, never. I highly regard Senator Wagner, but I don't believe he knows the difference between a daffodil and a tulip," declared Wayne as he chuckled.

"I think we're done here, at least for now," said Detective Garza. "Would you please lead us back to the house?"

"Yes," said Wayne. He and the detectives left the greenhouse with the fingernail polish and two boxes of vials. When Wayne escorted them into the front foyer, Senator Wagner stepped out of the library to join them.

"Detectives, was Wayne helpful to you?"

"Yes, Senator, he was, as he showed us the shrubs we were looking for and he toured us through the greenhouse," said Detective Thomas.

Looking at the boxes in Detective Thomas' arms, Senator Wagner asked her what she was holding.

"These are two boxes of glass vials, some empty and unused and some filled with seeds for future planting. We also found a bottle of fingernail polish, although Wayne could not explain its presence in the greenhouse. We'd like to take these items back to our lab for analysis, if you'll give your consent," Detective Thomas said.

"Sure, take them, as long as you return them because I'm sure Daphne will need them. Why do you want to analyze them? How can glass vials and fingernail polish be pertinent to that woman's murder when she was poisoned? Was the poison from the shrub mixed with fingernail polish?" asked Senator Wagner, sounding quite intrigued.

"For now, Senator, we're not at liberty to discuss the details of the crimes, but these vials and the polish may have played a role. Examining them in the lab will tell us if they're relevant or not," explained Detective Garza.

"I told you I'd cooperate and that Daphne and I have absolutely no reason for harming Ms. Vermeer or the other woman, whom I don't think we even know," declared Senator Wagner.

"The other woman was your server at the Literary Club on the night of the ASSIST Annual Honoree Dinner. Do you remember her?" asked Detective Garza.

"No, I really don't. I'm sure I probably spoke with her about whether I wanted coffee or tea, or which dressing I preferred, but I can't say I focused on her. I only focused on her questions enough to answer them," explained Senator Wagner.

"It's possible your wife knows her," said Detective Thomas. "Ms. Garian had been a server at the Literary Club for a while, and I suspect your wife has been there for many lunch and dinner functions where Ms. Garian may have served her."

"That's very possible, Detective. We'll have to ask her. I expect her to arrive home any time now," said Senator Wagner.

"May I ask where she is, Senator?" asked Detective Thomas.

"Yes, she's at a luncheon meeting with Ms. Vermeer. They're working on the scholarship fund matter in which they're both involved," said Senator Wagner matter of factly.

"Where are they dining, Senator?" asked Detective Thomas with a sense of urgency in her voice.

"They're at the Junction Tavern, or at least they were. Daphne has been gone a long time, so she may have already left the restaurant and is headed home," said Senator Wagner.

"Senator, thank you for permitting us to take these items for analysis. We need to leave now, but we'll contact you if we need any further cooperation on your part," Detective Thomas said as she started to walk briskly down the front walkway with Detective Garza following close behind.

# *Chapter Twenty-Seven*

Annalisa and Daphne Wagner were finishing up their discussion about high school GPA being a standard for the scholarship program when their dessert and coffee were placed before them. Annalisa looked down at her slice of lemon meringue pie. "This looks delicious," she said. "Before I indulge, I need to use the ladies' room. I'll be right back."

"Take your time, Annalisa," encouraged Ms. Wagner, as Annalisa rose from her side of the booth and slid out. After she was out of sight, Ms. Wagner opened the clasp of her purse. She was about to put one hand inside when she heard her name being called.

"Ms. Wagner," said Detective Thomas, as she and Detective Garza stood at the edge of the booth looking down at her. Ms. Wagner closed her purse and looked up, surprised to see two women standing before her whom she did not know.

"May I help you, ladies?" asked Ms. Wagner.

"Yes, I'm Detective Thomas and this is Detective Garza, and we're from the Metro Police. Where is Annalisa Vermeer?"

"She's in the ladies' room, but I'm certain she'll be back momentarily. Is there anything wrong?" asked Ms. Wagner.

"We're not quite sure yet," said Detective Thomas. "We'll know better when we talk to Ms. Vermeer. While we're waiting for her, may we look inside your purse?"

Ms. Wagner looked at Detective Thomas in disbelief and slightly shifted her body away from the detectives.

"No, you may not look in my purse. Why would you even ask me such a question?" demanded Ms. Wagner.

At that moment, Annalisa approached the group and noticed the detectives standing next to the booth.

"Detectives, what are you doing here?" she asked.

"Hello, Ms. Vermeer," said Detective Thomas. "As you know, Detective Garza and I have been working on your case together. We recently made substantial progress in determining who it is who wants you dead. We're here to protect you and to arrest Ms. Wagner."

"What?" both Annalisa and Ms. Wagner asked simultaneously in shocked voices.

"We have evidence that will prove, once it has been analyzed in our lab, that Ms. Wagner packaged the poison—which, by the way, is named 'daphnetoxin'—that killed Hannah Garian," said Detective Thomas as she turned toward Annalisa. Detective Garza kept her eyes firmly planted on Ms. Wagner's face.

"Further, we have proof the poison ingested by Ms. Garian was intended for you, Ms. Vermeer, meaning Ms. Wagner is the person who has tried to kill you twice," revealed Detective Thomas.

"That is preposterous, Detectives," said Ms. Wagner in an angry and defiant tone.

"We'll know soon enough. Ms. Wagner, please stand up and put your hands behind your back," demanded Detective Thomas. She began giving Ms. Wagner her rights. Ms. Wagner yelled out as she rose from her seat.

"You have no right to do this to me! Do you have any idea who my husband is? He's a very powerful man and he'll ensure you are both fired for your illegal conduct against me." By this time, the restaurant patrons were staring at Ms. Wagner and Detective Thomas in disbelief.

"Ms. Wagner, Detective Garza is going to inspect the contents of your purse for weapons before we leave for the police station," explained Detective Thomas. Ms. Wagner's face fell ashen, yet her body remained firmly erect.

"How dare you invade my privacy and rummage through my purse! You do not have my permission to open it!" asserted Ms. Wagner.

"We don't need your permission, Ms. Wagner. We have arrested you, and to ensure the safety of others we must determine what you're carrying," explained Detective Garza.

"That's a lie! I'm in handcuffs, for heaven's sake. I can't even get to any alleged weapon with my hands behind my back. You don't need to open my purse!" insisted Ms. Wagner vehemently. Disregarding her persistence, Detective Garza lifted the purse from the seat, opened it and grasped hold of a glass vial filled with liquid and floating dark shards. It was a familiar sight to the detective and she held it in the air for Detective Thomas to see.

"Let's get her out of here," said Detective Thomas as Detective Garza guided Ms. Wagner toward the door. Turning her head toward Annalisa, Detective Thomas continued, "Ms. Vermeer, it looks like you'll no longer need to be concerned for your life. We have some tests to do to confirm it, but we're convinced Ms. Wagner attempted to kill you with poison twice, and was just about to attempt again as we arrived here. I'll call you to provide more details after we're certain."

Annalisa, who had been standing next to the table since she returned from the ladies' room, noticeably trembled and, after placing her hands on the table, slumped onto the seat. Detective Thomas looked down at Annalisa's pale face as she blankly stared at the wall opposite her. Her eyes were moist. She was silent.

"Annalisa, will you be all right getting home or would you like me to call Brad or someone else to pick you up?"

"Frankly, I don't really know. I've tried to remain strong

throughout this ordeal, to not allow the killer to destroy my life and work, but realizing I was just having lunch with the killer and was only moments away from being poisoned has somehow destroyed my strength. I have nothing left in me. I'm completely drained. I know Michael is here because we drove together, but would you please call Brad and ask him to come here to get me? Also, would you please have the waitress get Michael from the kitchen so he can sit with me until Brad arrives?"

"Of course." Detective Thomas immediately called Brad as she kept an eye on Annalisa. She explained to him what had just happened, as well as the emotional state in which it had put Annalisa. He was shocked to learn Daphne Wagner was the murderer, and he did not delay in driving to the restaurant where he found Michael and Annalisa still sitting in the booth. Annalisa had tears streaming down her cheeks. When Brad arrived, Michael rose and, without a word, left the restaurant. Brad sat down next to Annalisa and held her in his arms. She laid her head on his shoulder and started to quietly sob. After a couple of minutes and without saying anything, Brad walked Annalisa to his car and took her home.

When the detectives arrived at the station, Detective Thomas put Ms. Wagner in an interview room while Detective Garza took the hair samples, boxes of glass vials, fingernail polish and the glass vial from Ms. Wagner's purse to the lab. Ms. Wagner demanded to call her husband so he and their attorney could get her released. Detective Thomas permitted her to use her cell phone to call him.

"Scott, the Metro Police are absolutely reprehensible!" Ms. Wagner shouted into the phone. "I've actually just been arrested, so you need to call Carter, get over here with him and get me out!"

"Calm down, Daphne. Does this have to do with the Vermeer matter and that other woman who died?" asked Senator Wagner with extreme calmness in his voice.

"Yes, but their accusations are ludicrous! Just hurry and get down here," demanded Ms. Wagner.

"I'll call Carter right now and we'll be there shortly. Try to remain calm, as we both know this is clearly a big mistake on the part of the police. I know you're incapable of hurting anyone, so try to relax," encouraged Senator Wagner. The two hung up and Detective Thomas took the phone from Ms. Wagner.

"Ms. Wagner," began Detective Thomas, "I know your attorney is coming to represent you. Do you want to wait for him to arrive or may I ask you some questions before he gets here?"

"I'm anxious to get out of here, so go ahead and get your questions over with so when Carter and Scott get here I'll be ready to be released," said Ms. Wagner.

"Fine. I know you didn't intend to kill Ms. Garian, but you did intentionally attempt to kill Ms. Vermeer on three occasions, the most recent being today. Why do you want to see her dead?"

"I don't want to see her dead. We just had a very pleasant lunch and we were working on a joint venture when you so rudely interrupted us. My husband is an extremely powerful man and he is on his way here now with our attorney. You'll be sorry you arrested me once they get here," insisted Ms. Wagner.

"Are you threatening me, Ms. Wagner?" demanded Detective Thomas.

"Only legally with the wrath and influence my husband carries," volleyed Ms. Wagner.

"Actually, your husband has been very cooperative and I've seen no signs of his wrath," said Detective Thomas, knowing this comment would pique Ms. Wagner's curiosity.

"What are you talking about? Have you had contact with my husband?" demanded Ms. Wagner.

"Yes, Detective Garza and I were at your home today to talk to you and your husband. While you weren't home, your husband was and he answered our questions and released certain items to us to aid in our investigation. He was quite willing to provide us with exactly what we needed because he believes neither one of you had any involvement in murdering Ms. Garian and attempting to murder Ms. Vermeer. He has complete faith in you, but you and I know better, don't we?" prodded Detective Thomas.

"I'm not talking to you any longer until my attorney arrives. Then, I won't have to talk to you at all because Scott and Carter will speak to your superiors and you and I will both be leaving here," said Ms. Wagner with a snippy tone in her voice.

"You truly don't understand the gravity of your situation, Ms. Wagner. For now, we'll wait for your attorney to arrive before we speak further. I have to talk with our lab technicians to determine if any of the test results have been concluded," explained Detective Thomas. With that, she left the room, leaving Ms. Wagner alone to reflect on her predicament.

Detective Thomas entered the lab to find Julia and Greg hunched over tables working. They looked up when they heard her moving toward them.

"Quinn, you're just in time," said Greg. "I ran the liquid and shards samples from the vial in Ms. Wagner's purse and they match the mezereon bark in the vial from Ms. Garian's apartment. In both cases the bark has been similarly sharpened and all the ends have been dipped in the base fingernail polish. The polish on the shards matches both the polish from the Wagner greenhouse and the polish on the shards Ms. Garian ingested. In addition, all the vials are the same."

"That's good to hear, Greg. This is all the evidence we need to convict her," said Detective Thomas.

"I have more, Quinn," said Julia. "I compared the hair sample from the tape on the box in Ms. Garian's apartment building against the samples that Senator Wagner gave you this morning. Senator Wagner isn't a match, but both strands are from Ms. Wagner. She had contact with the box that contained the poisonous faux aphrodisiac."

"More good news. Thanks, Greg and Julia. Do you have anything else to report?" asked Detective Thomas.

"One more piece of the puzzle, Quinn," said Greg. "The twig you took off one of the shrubs at the Wagner residence—the one the gardener told you was a mezereon shrub—is definitely from a mezereon shrub. It's a good thing you were wearing gloves because contact with the bark can cause a skin rash."

"I believe we have an airtight case against Ms. Wagner. I'll report these findings to the district attorney now before Senator Wagner and his attorney arrive," said Detective Thomas.

Thirty minutes later, Senator Wagner and his attorney, Carter La Rouge, arrived at the police station. Detective Thomas was notified and met them in the lobby.

"Hello, Detective. Why do you have my wife here? She says you've arrested her. Is that true?" asked Senator Wagner.

"Yes, Senator, I'm afraid it's true. We've arrested your wife for Ms. Garian's death and the multiple attempts on Ms. Vermeer's life. Today when I arrested her during her luncheon with Ms. Vermeer, we found the same poison in her purse that caused Ms. Garian's death. It was also identically packaged," explained Detective Thomas.

Senator Wagner slightly stumbled toward a chair and sat down while his attorney looked on. Detective Thomas and the attorney said nothing, diplomatically giving the senator some time to digest the shocking revelation. After a minute, the senator spoke.

"There simply has to be some misunderstanding. Daphne is a kind and generous person who has no motive to harm either of those women. I gave you all the items you requested because I felt they would vindicate Daphne, not cause her arrest," said Senator Wagner with guilt in his voice.

"Senator, you are not responsible for your wife's arrest. She provided us with the most conclusive evidence when we found the poisonous potion in her purse. That vial of poison would have given us probable cause for a search warrant of your home, which means all the items you voluntarily relinquished to us earlier today would have been removed by force of the warrant this afternoon. All your assistance did was speed up our analysis. Do not feel guilty, as this was all your wife's doing, not yours," encouraged Detective Thomas.

"You would never have arrested her and looked in her purse had I not been so cooperative, Detective," said Senator Wagner.

"Senator, I wouldn't have shown up on your doorstep today if I didn't have reason to believe your wife murdered Ms. Garian," assured Detective Thomas, hoping she could shift the senator's focus from his own guilty feelings to his wife's present situation. Apparently, Mr. La Rouge felt the same way, as he spoke before the senator had an opportunity to continue the conversation with Detective Thomas.

"May I please see my client now, Detective?" Mr. La Rouge asked. "After I see her alone, I request you join us and explain exactly what evidence you believe you have against Ms. Wagner."

"Yes, I'll take you to her now and you can let me know when you're ready for me. Senator, please stay seated here and I'll return to get you when you can see your wife," instructed Detective Thomas.

Detective Thomas escorted Mr. La Rouge to the interview room and left him alone with Ms. Wagner. Ten minutes later, an officer appeared at Detective Thomas' office door to inform her Mr. La Rouge had asked for her to join him in the interview room. When Detective Thomas walked into the room, Ms. Wagner looked up. Her eyes were moist and tears were on her cheeks.

"Detective, Ms. Wagner insists there was no poison in her purse and you have concocted an elaborate scheme to frame her for the attacks on these women. She also doesn't want to speak with you unless her husband is in the room because she believes he can resolve this matter forthwith," said Mr. La Rouge.

"Normally we don't bring family members in during interrogations, but I believe in this case it will be more efficient in bringing this matter to a close," said Detective Thomas. "I'll find your husband in the lobby and bring him here." When Senator Wagner walked into the room, he immediately went to his wife and they embraced. Ms. Wagner looked up at her husband.

"Scott, you have to call her boss and take care of this for me. They're framing me, and you have to use your power and influence to get this woman fired and me released," demanded Ms. Wagner with a combination of indignation and fear in her voice.

"Daphne, dear, please calm down. I'm certain this matter can be amicably resolved if we just listen to what Detective Thomas has to say, and then you can explain your side of the situation," coaxed Senator Wagner.

Detective Thomas methodically explained to the three what she and her team had found: the hair on the tape matched Ms. Wagner's and the substance in the vial in her purse was most definitely poisonous and identical to the toxin Ms. Garian and Annalisa ingested, although in Annalisa's case it was delivered via berries. She further explained that fingernail polish and glass vials were found in Ms. Wagner's greenhouse, that the greenhouse polish matched the polish on the bark shards and that the vials in the greenhouse were identical to the vials in Ms. Garian's apartment. While she explained the facts, Greg entered the room and handed her the lab reports, which verified what she said. She handed the reports to Mr. La Rouge.

"These are lies, Scott," said Ms. Wagner. "I never gave her my hair and I never consented to her rummaging around in my greenhouse. Either she's lying about having those items or she illegally obtained them," she insisted, sounding as if she were the attorney in the room.

"Daphne, she's telling the truth. "I gave her your hair and admitted her into our home and your greenhouse. I consented to her taking the fingernail polish and the vials. I did all this in order to prove you had no involvement in any murder or attempts at murder," explained Senator Wagner.

Ms. Wagner looked at her husband in utter disbelief. She glanced at Detective Thomas. She looked back at her husband.

"Scott, how could you do this to me—to us? I'm the love of your life, the mother of your children, the trophy on your shelf. We're a team—a powerful team, a beautiful team and one not to be reckoned with, particularly by the likes of this detective or Annalisa Vermeer," asserted Ms. Wagner.

Mr. La Rouge quickly sensed the negative direction in which Ms. Wagner's statements were heading and attempted to disarm her immediately.

"Ms. Wagner, I believe it's in your best interest to say no more on this matter. Let us simply have an immediate arraignment and I'll seek bail so you can be released today. We can debate the merits of the police's case against you in trial, and you and your husband can discuss this matter more thoroughly in private," suggested Mr. La Rouge firmly.

"No, Carter, I'm sick and tired of Ms. Vermeer and I want to talk about her right now. She is a terrorist in that she is devoted to destroying not only my life and my husband's life, but also the lives of all legislators and their families here and throughout the country. She may not physically possess a bomb, so she doesn't blow up buildings, but her book and her speeches are just as incendiary. Detective, you need to go arrest her for terrorism, and I should be given an award for trying to save this country from her," declared Ms. Wagner defiantly.

"Daphne," said Senator Wagner, "there is no power behind Ms. Vermeer's words. You give her far too much credit. Not only is she no terrorist, she also lacks credibility, influence and power. She can speak day and night for the next forty years and it won't make an iota of difference in this country."

"No, Scott, you don't understand. The people in Illinois, Missouri and Kansas aren't only hearing her fiery words, but they're listening to them and advocating that her words be put into action. I've read a multitude of newspaper articles during visits to my sister's home that support this, and I've been afraid, as I fear for your livelihood, power and position. So, I decided to take matters into my own hands because the police haven't done so. Yes, I tried to kill her to save our lives. We are important and powerful people, Scott, and Ms. Vermeer can't threaten us as she's been doing. Her words are spreading like a wildfire, and if she's not stopped, her words will continue to spread until this country is destroyed," exclaimed Ms. Wagner.

"Daphne, my dear Daphne, you truly don't understand. This country is controlled by us legislators, and no person outside of our domain has any chance to control how this country operates at its highest levels. The United States Congress controls Ms. Vermeer and everyone else with its power to make laws, rules, regulations, policies and on and on. Ms. Vermeer is free to speak because she never will be free to do more than speak. Should she ever be deemed a threat, those of us in power can squash her and her ideas in an instant within the legal parameters afforded us. The members of Congress are supreme, and our power, influence and position will at no time ever be diminished by any of the powerless people beneath us," an aroused and imperious Senator Wagner proclaimed in a loud and contemptuous voice.